CC

THE COLLECTED
SHORT STORIES
OF JACK LONDON

THE COLLECTED SHORT STORIES OF JACK LONDON

Jack London

HarperLargePrint Classics
An Imprint of HarperCollins*Publishers*

HarperCollins books may be purchased for educational, business, or sales promotional use. For information please write: Special Markets Department, HarperCollins Publishers, Inc., 10 East 53rd Street, New York, NY 10022.

First HarperLargePrint Classics edition published 2000.

HarperLargePrint Classics are published by HarperLargePrint, an imprint of HarperCollins Publishers.

ISBN 0-06-095573-2

09 10 11 12 ❖/RRD 10 9 8 7 6 5 4

This Large Print Book carries the
Seal of Approval of N.A.V.H.

CONTENTS

TO BUILD A FIRE

Day had broken cold and gray, exceedingly cold and gray, when the man turned aside from the main Yukon trail and climbed the high earth-bank, where a dim and little-traveled trail led eastward through the fat spruce timberland. It was a steep bank, and he paused for breath at the top, excusing the act to himself by looking at his watch. It was nine o'clock. There was no sun nor hint of sun, though there was not a cloud in the sky. It was a clear day, and yet there seemed an intangible pall over the face of things, a subtle gloom that made the day dark, and that was due to the absence of sun. This fact did not worry the man. He was used to the lack of sun. It had been days since he had seen the sun, and he knew that a few more days must pass before that cheerful orb, due south, would just peep above the sky line and dip immediately from view.

The man flung a look back along the way he had come. The Yukon lay a mile wide and hidden under three feet of ice. On top of this ice were as many feet of snow. It was all pure white, rolling in gentle undulations where the ice jams of the freeze-up had formed. North and south, as far as his eye could see, it was unbroken white, save for a dark hairline that curved and twisted from around the spruce-covered island to the south, and that curved and twisted away into the north, where it disappeared behind another spruce-covered island. This dark hairline was the trail—the main trail—that led south five hundred miles to the Chilcoot Pass, Dyea, and salt water; and that led north seventy miles to Dawson, and still on to the north a thousand miles to Nulato, and finally to St. Michael on Bering Sea, a thousand miles and half a thousand more.

But all this—the mysterious, far-reaching hairline trail, the absence of sun from the sky, the tremendous cold, and the strangeness and weirdness of it all—made no impression on the man. It was not because he was long used to it. He was a newcomer in the land, a *chechaquo,* and this was his first winter. The trouble with him was that he was without imagination. He was quick and alert in the things of life, but only in the things, and not in the significances. Fifty degrees below zero meant eighty-odd degrees of frost. Such fact impressed him as being cold and uncomfortable, and that was all. It did not lead him to meditate upon his frailty as a creature of temperature, and upon man's frailty in general, able only to live within certain narrow limits of heat and cold; and from there on it did not lead him to the conjectural field of immortality and man's place in the universe. Fifty degrees below zero stood for a bite of frost that hurt and that must be guarded against by the use of mittens, ear flaps, warm moccasins, and thick socks. Fifty degrees below zero was to him just precisely fifty degrees below zero. That there should be anything more to it than that was a thought that never entered his head.

As he turned to go on, he spat speculatively. There was a sharp, explosive crackle that startled him. He spat again. And again, in the air, before it could fall to the snow, the spittle crackled. He knew that at fifty below spittle crackled on the snow, but this spittle had crackled in the air. Undoubtedly it was colder than fifty below—how much colder he did not know. But the temperature did not matter. He was bound for the old claim on the left fork of Henderson Creek, where the boys were already. They had come over across the divide from the Indian Creek country, while he had come the roundabout way to take a look at the possibilities of getting out logs in the spring from the islands in the Yukon. He would be in to camp by six o'clock; a bit after dark, it was true, but the boys would be there, a fire would be going, and a hot supper would be ready. As for lunch, he pressed his hand against the protruding bundle under his jacket. It was also under his shirt, wrapped up in a handkerchief and lying against the naked skin. It was the only way to keep the biscuits from freezing. He smiled agreeably to himself as he thought of those biscuits, each cut open and sopped in bacon grease, and each enclosing a generous slice of fried bacon.

He plunged in among the big spruce trees. The trail was faint. A foot of snow had fallen since the last sled had passed over, and he was glad he was without a sled, travelling light. In fact, he carried nothing but

the lunch wrapped in the handkerchief. He was surprised, however, at the cold. It certainly was cold, he
concluded, as he rubbed his numb nose and cheekbones with his mittened hand. He was a warm-
whiskered man, but the hair on his face did not
protect the high cheekbones and the eager nose that
thrust itself aggressively into the frosty air.

At the man's heels trotted a dog, a big native
husky, the proper wolf dog, gray-coated and without
any visible or temperamental difference from its
brother, the wild wolf. The animal was depressed by
the tremendous cold. It knew that it was no time for
travelling. Its instinct told it a truer tale than was
told to the man by the man's judgment. In reality, it
was not merely colder than fifty below zero; it was
colder than sixty below, than seventy below. It was
seventy-five below zero. Since the freezing point is
thirty-two above zero, it meant that one hundred and
seven degrees of frost obtained. The dog did not
know anything about thermometers. Possibly in its
brain there was no sharp consciousness of a condition
of very cold such as was in the man's brain. But the
brute had its instinct. It experienced a vague but
menacing apprehension that subdued it and made it
slink along at the man's heels, and that made it question eagerly every unwonted movement of the man as
if expecting him to go into camp or to seek shelter
somewhere and build a fire. The dog had learned fire,
and it wanted fire, or else to burrow under the snow
and cuddle its warmth away from the air.

The frozen moisture of its breathing had settled on its fur in a fine powder of frost, and especially were its jowls, muzzle, and eyelashes whitened by its crystalled breath. The man's red beard and mustache were likewise frosted, but more solidly, the deposit taking the form of ice and increasing with every warm, moist breath he exhaled. Also, the man was chewing tobacco, and the muzzle of ice held his lips so rigidly that he was unable to clear his chin when he expelled the juice. The result was that a crystal beard of the color and solidity of amber was increasing its length on his chin. If he fell down it would shatter itself, like glass, into brittle fragments. But he did not mind the appendage. It was the penalty all tobacco chewers paid in that country, and he had been out before in two cold snaps. They had not been so cold as this, he knew, but by the spirit thermometer at Sixty Mile he knew they had been registered at fifty below and at fifty-five.

He held on through the level stretch of woods for several miles, crossed a wide flat of nigger heads, and dropped down a bank to the frozen bed of a small stream. This was Henderson Creek, and he knew he was ten miles from the forks. He looked at his watch. It was ten o'clock. He was making four miles an hour, and he calculated that he would arrive at the forks at half-past twelve. He decided to celebrate that event by eating his lunch there.

The dog dropped in again at his heels, with a tail drooping discouragement, as the man swung along the creek bed. The furrow of the old sled trail was plainly visible, but a dozen inches of snow covered the marks of the last runners. In a month no man had come up or down that silent creek. The man held steadily on. He was not much given to thinking, and just then particularly he had nothing to think about save that he would eat lunch at the forks and that at six o'clock he would be in camp with the boys. There was nobody to talk to; and, had there been, speech would have been impossible because of the ice muzzle on his mouth. So he continued monotonously to chew tobacco and to increase the length of his amber beard.

Once in a while the thought reiterated itself that it was very cold and that he had never experienced such cold. As he walked along he rubbed his cheekbones and nose with the back of his mittened hand. He did this automatically, now and again changing hands. But rub as he would, the instant he stopped his cheekbones went numb, and the following instant the end of his nose went numb. He was sure to frost his cheeks; he knew that, and experienced a pang of regret that he had not devised a nose-strap of the sort Bud wore in cold snaps. Such a strap passed across the cheeks, as well, and saved them. But it didn't matter much, after all. What were frosted cheeks? A bit painful, that was all; they were never serious.

Empty as the man's mind was of thoughts, he was keenly observant, and he noticed the changes in the creek, the curves and bends and timber jams, and always he sharply noted where he placed his feet. Once, coming around a bend, he shied abruptly, like a startled horse, curved away from the place where he had been walking, and retreated several paces back along the trail. The creek he knew was frozen clear to the bottom—no creek could contain water in that arctic winter—but he knew also that there were springs that bubbled out from the hillsides and ran along under the snow and on top the ice of the creek. He knew that the coldest snaps never froze these springs, and he knew likewise their danger. They were traps. They hid pools of water under the snow that might be three inches deep, or three feet. Sometimes a skin of ice half an inch thick covered them, and in turn was covered by the snow. Sometimes there were alternate layers of water and ice skin, so that when one broke through he kept on breaking through for a while, sometimes wetting himself to the waist.

That was why he had shied in such panic. He had felt the give under his feet and heard the crackle of a snow-hidden ice skin. And to get his feet wet in such a temperature meant trouble and danger. At the very least it meant delay, for he would be forced to stop and build a fire, and under its protection to bare his feet while he dried his socks and moccasins. He stood and studied the creek bed and its banks, and decided that the flow of water came from the right. He reflected awhile, rubbing his nose and cheeks, then skirted to the left, stepping gingerly and testing the footing for each step. Once clear of the danger, he took a fresh chew of tobacco and swung along at his four-mile gait.

In the course of the next two hours he came upon several similar traps. Usually the snow above the hidden pools had a sunken, candied appearance that advertised the danger. Once again, however, he had a close call; and once, suspecting danger, he compelled the dog to go on in front. The dog did not want to go. It hung back until the man shoved it forward, and then it went quickly across the white, unbroken surface. Suddenly it broke through, floundered to one side, and got away to firmer footing. It had wet its forefeet and legs, and almost immediately the water that clung to it turned to ice. It made quick efforts to lick the ice off its legs, then dropped down in the snow and began to bite out the ice that had formed between the toes. This was a matter of instinct. To permit the ice to remain would mean sore feet. It did not know this. It merely obeyed the mysterious prompting that arose from the deep crypts of its being. But the man knew, having achieved a judgment on the subject, and he removed the mitten from his right hand and helped tear out the ice-particles. He did not expose his fingers more than a minute, and was astonished at the swift numbness that smote them. It certainly was cold. He pulled on the mitten hastily, and beat the hand savagely across his chest.

At twelve o'clock the day was at its brightest. Yet the sun was too far south on its winter journey to clear the horizon. The bulge of the earth intervened between it and Henderson Creek, where the man walked under a clear sky at noon and cast no shadow. At half-past twelve, to the minute, he arrived at the forks of the creek. He was pleased at the speed he had made. If he kept it up, he would certainly be with the boys by six. He unbuttoned his jacket and shirt and drew forth his lunch. The action consumed no more than a quarter of a minute, yet in that brief moment the numbness laid hold of the exposed fingers. He did not put the mitten on, but, instead, struck the fingers a dozen sharp smashes against his leg. Then he sat down on a snow-covered log to eat. The sting that followed upon the striking of his fingers against his leg ceased so quickly that he was startled. He had had no chance to take a bite of biscuit. He struck the fingers repeatedly and returned them to the mitten, baring the other hand for the purpose of eating. He tried to take a mouthful, but the ice muzzle prevented. He had forgotten to build a fire and thaw out. He chuckled at his foolishness, and as he chuckled he noted the numbness creeping into the exposed fingers. Also, he noted that the stinging which had first come to his toes when he sat down was already passing away. He wondered whether the toes were warm or numb. He moved them inside the moccasins and decided that they were numb.

He pulled the mitten on hurriedly and stood up. He was a bit frightened. He stamped up and down until the stinging returned into the feet. It certainly was cold, was his thought. That man from Sulphur

Creek had spoken the truth when telling how cold it sometimes got in the country. And he had laughed at him at the time! That showed one must not be too sure of things. There was no mistake about it, it was cold. He strode up and down, stamping his feet and threshing his arms, until reassured by the returning warmth. Then he got out matches and proceeded to make a fire. From the undergrowth, where high water of the previous spring had lodged a supply of seasoned twigs, he got his firewood. Working carefully from a small beginning, he soon had a roaring fire, over which he thawed the ice from his face and in the protection of which he ate his biscuits. For the moment the cold of space was outwitted. The dog took satisfaction in the fire, stretching out close enough for warmth and far enough away to escape being singed.

When the man had finished, he filled his pipe and took his comfortable time over a smoke. Then he pulled on his mittens, settled the ear flaps of his cap firmly about his ears, and took the creek trail up the left fork. The dog was disappointed and yearned back toward the fire. This man did not know cold. Possibly all the generations of his ancestry had been ignorant of cold, of real cold, of cold one hundred and seven degrees below freezing point. But the dog knew; all its ancestry knew, and it had inherited the knowledge. And it knew that it was not good to walk abroad in such fearful cold. It was the time to lie snug in a hole in the snow and wait for a curtain of cloud to be drawn across the face of outer space whence this cold came. On the other hand, there was no keen intimacy between the dog and the man. The one was the toil slave of the other, and the only caresses it had ever received were the caresses of the whip lash and of harsh and menacing throat sounds that threatened the whip lash. So the dog made no effort to communicate its apprehension to the man. It was not concerned in the welfare of the man; it was for its own sake that it yearned back toward the fire. But the man whistled, and spoke to it with the sound of whip lashes, and the dog swung in at the man's heels and followed after.

The man took a chew of tobacco and proceeded to start a new amber beard. Also, his moist breath quickly powdered with white his mustache, eyebrows, and lashes. There did not seem to be so many springs on the left fork of the Henderson, and for half an hour the man saw no signs of any. And then it happened. At a place where there were no signs, where the soft, unbroken snow seemed to advertise solidity beneath, the man broke through. It was not deep. He wet himself halfway to the knees before he floundered out to the firm crust.

He was angry, and cursed his luck aloud. He had hoped to get into camp with the boys at six o'clock, and this would delay him an hour, for he would have to build a fire and dry out his footgear. This was imperative at that low temperature—he knew that much; and he turned aside to the bank, which he climbed. On top, tangled in the underbrush about the trunks of several small spruce trees, was a high-water deposit of dry firewood—sticks and twigs, principally, but also larger portions of seasoned branches and fine, dry, last year's grasses. He threw down several large pieces on top of the snow. This served for a foundation and prevented the young flame from drowning itself in the snow it otherwise would melt. The flame he got by touching a match to a small shred of birch bark that he took from his pocket. This burned even more readily than paper. Placing it on the foundation, he fed the young flame with wisps of dry grass and with the tiniest dry twigs.

He worked slowly and carefully, keenly aware of his danger. Gradually, as the flame grew stronger, he increased the size of the twigs with which he fed it. He squatted in the snow, pulling the twigs out from their entanglement in the brush and feeding directly to the flame. He knew there must be no failure. When it is seventy-five below zero, a man must not fail in his first attempt to build a fire—that is, if his feet are wet. If his feet are dry, and he fails, he can run along the trail for half a mile and restore his circulation. But the circulation of wet and freezing feet cannot be restored by running when it is seventy-five below. No matter how fast he runs, the wet feet will freeze the harder.

All this the man knew. The old-timer on Sulphur Creek had told him about it the previous fall, and now he was appreciating the advice. Already all sensation had gone out of his feet. To build the fire he had been forced to remove his mittens, and the fingers had quickly gone numb. His pace of four miles an hour had kept his heart pumping blood to the surface of his body and to all the extremities. But the instant he stopped, the action of the pump eased down. The cold of space smote the unprotected tip of the planet, and he, being on that unprotected tip, received the full force of the blow. The blood of his body recoiled before it. The blood was alive, like the dog, and like the dog it wanted to hide away and cover itself up from the fearful cold. So long as he walked four miles an hour, he pumped that blood, willy-nilly, to the surface; but now it ebbed away and sank down into the recesses of his body. The extremities were the first to feel its absence. His wet feet froze the faster, and his exposed fingers numbed the faster, though they had not yet begun to freeze. Nose and cheeks were already freezing, while the skin of all his body chilled as it lost its blood.

But he was safe. Toes and nose and cheeks would be only touched by the frost, for the fire was beginning to burn with strength. He was feeding it with twigs the size of his finger. In another minute he would be able to feed it with branches the size of his wrist, and then he could remove his wet footgear, and, while it dried, he could keep his naked feet warm by the fire, rubbing them at first, of course, with snow. The fire was a success. He was safe. He remembered the advice of the old-timer on Sulphur Creek, and smiled. The old-timer had been very serious in laying down the law that no man must travel alone in the Klondike after fifty below. Well, here he was; he had had the accident; he was alone; and he had saved himself. Those old-timers were rather womanish, some of them, he thought. All a man had to do was to keep his head, and he was all right. Any man who was a man could travel alone. But it was surprising, the rapidity with which his cheeks and nose were freezing. And he had not thought his fingers could go lifeless in so short a time. Lifeless they were, for he could scarcely make them move together to grip a twig, and they seemed remote from his body and from him. When he touched a twig, he had to look and see whether or not he had hold of it. The wires were pretty well down between him and his finger ends.

All of which counted for little. There was the fire, snapping and crackling and promising life with every dancing flame. He started to untie his moccasins. They were coated with ice; the thick German socks were like sheaths of iron halfway to the knees; and the moccasin strings were like rods of steel all twisted and knotted as by some conflagration. For a moment he tugged with his numb fingers, then, realizing the folly of it, he drew his sheath knife.

But before he could cut the strings, it happened. It was his own fault or, rather, his mistake. He should not have built the fire under the spruce tree. He should have built it in the open. But it had been easier to pull the twigs from the brush and drop them directly on the fire. Now the tree under which he had done this carried a weight of snow on its boughs. No wind had blown for weeks, and each bough was fully freighted. Each time he had pulled a twig he had communicated a slight agitation to the tree—an imperceptible agitation, so far as he was concerned, but an agitation sufficient to bring about the disaster. High up in the tree one bough capsized its load of snow. This fell on the boughs beneath, capsizing them. This process continued, spreading out and involving the whole tree. It grew like an avalanche, and it descended without warning upon the man and the fire, and the fire was blotted out! Where it had burned was a mantle of fresh and disordered snow.

The man was shocked. It was as though he had just heard his own sentence of death. For a moment he sat and stared at the spot where the fire had been. Then he grew very calm. Perhaps the old-timer on Sulphur Creek was right. If he had only had a trail-mate he would have been in no danger now. The trail-mate could have built the fire. Well, it was up to him to build the fire over again, and this second time there must be no failure. Even if he succeeded, he would most likely lose some toes. His feet must be badly frozen by now, and there would be some time before the second fire was ready.

Such were his thoughts, but he did not sit and think them. He was busy all the time they were pass-

ing through his mind. He made a new foundation for
a fire, this time in the open, where no treacherous tree
could blot it out. Next, he gathered dry grasses and
tiny twigs from the high-water flotsam. He could not
bring his fingers together to pull them out, but he
was able to gather them by the handful. In this way
he got many rotten twigs and bits of green moss that
were undesirable, but it was the best he could do. He
worked methodically, even collecting an armful of the
larger branches to be used later when the fire gathered strength. And all the while the dog sat and
watched him, a certain yearning wistfulness in its
eyes, for it looked upon him as the fire provider, and
the fire was slow in coming.

When all was ready, the man reached in his pocket
for a second piece of birch bark. He knew the bark
was there, and, though he could not feel it with his
fingers, he could hear its crisp rustling as he fumbled
for it. Try as he would, he could not clutch hold of it.
And all the time, in his consciousness, was the
knowledge that each instant his feet were freezing.
This thought tended to put him in a panic, but he
fought against it and kept calm. He pulled on his
mittens with his teeth, and threshed his arms back
and forth, beating his hands with all his might
against his sides. He did this sitting down, and he
stood up to do it; and all the while the dog sat in the
snow, its wolf brush of a tail curled around warmly
over its forefeet, its sharp wolf ears pricked forward
intently as it watched the man. And the man, as he

beat and threshed with his arms and hands, felt a great surge of envy as he regarded the creature that was warm and secure in its natural covering.

After a time he was aware of the first faraway signals of sensation in his beaten fingers. The faint tingling grew stronger till it evolved into a stinging ache that was excruciating, but which the man hailed with satisfaction. He stripped the mitten from his right hand and fetched forth the birch bark. The exposed fingers were quickly going numb again. Next he brought out his bunch of sulphur matches. But the tremendous cold had already driven the life out of his fingers. In his effort to separate one match from the others, the whole bunch fell in the snow. He tried to pick it out of the snow, but failed. The dead fingers could neither touch nor clutch. He was very careful. He drove the thought of his freezing feet, and nose, and cheeks, out of his mind, devoting his whole soul to the matches. He watched, using the sense of vision in place of that of touch, and when he saw his fingers on each side the bunch, he closed them—that is, he willed to close them, for the wires were down, and the fingers did not obey. He pulled the mitten on the right hand, and beat it fiercely against his knee. Then, with both mittened hands, he scooped the bunch of matches, along with much snow, into his lap. Yet he was no better off.

After some manipulation he managed to get the bunch between the heels of his mittened hands. In this fashion he carried it to his mouth. The ice crackled and snapped when by a violent effort he opened his mouth. He drew the lower jaw in, curled the upper lip out of the way, and scraped the bunch with his upper teeth in order to separate a match. He succeeded in getting one, which he dropped on his lap. He was no better off. He could not pick it up. Then he devised a way. He picked it up in his teeth and scratched it on his leg. Twenty times he scratched before he succeeded in lighting it. As it flamed he held it with his teeth to the birch bark. But the burning brimstone went up his nostrils and into his lungs, causing him to cough spasmodically. The match fell into the snow and went out.

The old-timer on Sulphur Creek was right, he thought in the moment of controlled despair that ensued: after fifty below, a man should travel with a partner. He beat his hands, but failed in exciting any sensation. Suddenly he bared both hands, removing the mittens with his teeth. He caught the whole bunch between the heels of his hands. His arm muscles not being frozen enabled him to press the hand-heels tightly against the matches. Then he scratched the bunch along his leg. It flared into flame, seventy sulphur matches at once! There was no wind to blow them out. He kept his head to one side to escape the strangling fumes, and held the blazing bunch to the birch bark. As he so held it, he became aware of sensation in his hand. His flesh was burning. He could smell it. Deep down below the surface he could feel it. The sensation developed into pain that grew acute.

And still he endured it, holding the flame of the matches clumsily to the bark that would not light readily because his own burning hands were in the way, absorbing most of the flame.

At last, when he could endure no more, he jerked his hands apart. The blazing matches fell sizzling into the snow, but the birch bark was alight. He began laying dry grasses and the tiniest twigs on the flame. He could not pick and choose, for he had to lift the fuel between the heels of his hands. Small pieces of rotten wood and green moss clung to the twigs, and he bit them off as well as he could with his teeth. He cherished the flame carefully and awkwardly. It meant life, and it must not perish. The withdrawal of blood from the surface of his body now made him begin to shiver, and he grew more awkward. A large piece of green moss fell squarely on the little fire. He tried to poke it out with his fingers, but his shivering frame made him poke too far, and he disrupted the nucleus of the little fire, the burning grasses and tiny twigs separating and scattering. He tried to poke them together again, but in spite of the tenseness of the effort, his shivering got away with him, and the twigs were hopelessly scattered. Each twig gushed a puff of smoke and went out. The fire provider had failed. As he looked apathetically about him, his eyes chanced on the dog, sitting across the ruins of the fire from him, in the snow, making restless, hunching movements, slightly lifting one forefoot and then the other, shifting its weight back and forth on them with wistful eagerness.

The sight of the dog put a wild idea into his head. He remembered the tale of the man, caught in a blizzard, who killed a steer and crawled inside the carcass, and so was saved. He would kill the dog and bury his hands in the warm body until the numbness went out of them. Then he could build another fire. He spoke to the dog, calling it to him; but in his voice was a strange note of fear that frightened the animal, who had never known the man to speak in such way before. Something was the matter, and its suspicious nature sensed danger—it knew not what danger, but somewhere, somehow, in its brain arose an apprehension of the man. It flattened its ears down at the sound of the man's voice, and its restless, hunching movements and the liftings and shiftings of its forefeet became more pronounced; but it would not come to the man. He got on his hands and knees and crawled toward the dog. This unusual posture again excited suspicion, and the animal sidled mincingly away.

The man sat up in the snow for a moment and struggled for calmness. Then he pulled on his mittens, by means of his teeth, and got upon his feet. He glanced down at first in order to assure himself that he was really standing up, for the absence of sensation in his feet left him unrelated to the earth. His erect position in itself started to drive the webs of suspicion from the dog's mind; and when he spoke peremptorily, with the sound of whip lashes in his voice, the dog rendered its customary allegiance and came to him. As it came within reaching distance, the man lost his control. His arms flashed out to the dog, and he experienced genuine surprise when he discovered that his hands could not clutch, that there was neither bend nor feeling in the fingers. He had forgotten for the moment that they were frozen and that they were freezing more and more. All this happened quickly, and before the animal could get away, he encircled its body with his arms. He sat down in the snow, and in this fashion held the dog, while it snarled and whined and struggled.

But it was all he could do, hold its body encircled in his arms and sit there. He realized that he could not kill the dog. There was no way to do it. With his helpess hands he could neither draw nor hold his sheath knife nor throttle the animal. He released it, and it plunged wildly away, with tail between its legs, and still snarling. It halted forty feet away and surveyed him curiously, with ears sharply pricked forward.

The man looked down at his hands in order to locate them, and found them hanging on the ends of his arms. It struck him as curious that one should have to use his eyes in order to find out where his hands were. He began threshing his arms back and forth, beating the mittened hands against his sides. He did this for five minutes, violently, and his heart pumped enough blood up to the surface to put a stop to his shivering. But no sensation was aroused in the hands. He had an impression that they hung like weights on the ends of his arms, but when he tried to run the impression down, he could not find it.

A certain fear of death, dull and oppressive, came to him. This fear quickly became poignant as he realized that it was no longer a mere matter of freezing his fingers and toes, or of losing his hands and feet, but that it was a matter of life and death with the chances against him. This threw him into a panic, and he turned and ran up the creek bed along the old, dim trail. The dog joined in behind and kept up with him. He ran blindly, without intention, in fear such as he had never known in his life. Slowly, as he ploughed and floundered through the snow, he began to see things again—the banks of the creek, the old timber jams, the leafless aspens, and the sky. The running made him feel better. He did not shiver. Maybe, if he ran on, his feet would thaw out; and, anyway, if he ran far enough, he would reach camp and the boys. Without doubt he would lose some fingers and toes and some of his face; but the boys would take care of him, and save the rest of him when he got there. And at the same time there was another thought in his mind that said he would never get to the camp and the boys; that it was too many miles away, that the freezing had too great a start on him, and that he would soon be stiff and dead. This thought he kept in the background and refused to consider. Sometimes it pushed itself forward and demanded to be heard, but he thrust it back and strove to think of other things.

It struck him as curious that he could run at all on feet so frozen that he could not feel them when they struck the earth and took the weight of his body. He seemed to himself to skim along above the surface, and to have no connection with the earth. Somewhere he had once seen a winged Mercury, and he wondered if Mercury felt as he felt when skimming over the earth.

His theory of running until he reached camp and the boys had one flaw in it: he lacked the endurance. Several times he stumbled, and finally he tottered, crumpled up, and fell. When he tried to rise, he failed. He must sit and rest, he decided, and next time he would merely walk and keep on going. As he sat and regained his breath, he noted that he was feeling quite warm and comfortable. He was not shivering, and it even seemed that a warm glow had come to his chest and trunk. And yet, when he touched his nose or cheeks, there was no sensation. Running would not thaw them out. Nor would it thaw out his hands and feet. Then the thought came to him that the frozen portions of his body must be extending. He tried to keep this thought down, to forget it, to think of something else; he was aware of the panicky feeling that it caused, and he was afraid of the panic. But the thought asserted itself, and persisted, until it produced a vision of his body totally frozen. This was too much, and he made another wild run along the trail. Once he slowed down to a walk, but the thought of the freezing extending itself made him run again.

And all the time the dog ran with him, at his heels. When he fell down a second time, it curled its tail over its forefeet and sat in front of him, facing him, curiously eager and intent. The warmth and security of the animal angered him, and he cursed it till it flattened down its ears appeasingly. This time the shivering came more quickly upon the man. He was losing in his battle with the frost. It was creeping into his body from all sides. The thought of it drove him on, but he ran no more than a hundred feet, when he staggered and pitched headlong. It was his last panic. When he had recovered his breath and control, he sat up and entertained in his mind the conception of meeting death with dignity. However, the conception did not come to him in such terms. His idea of it was that he had been making a fool of himself, running around like a chicken with its head cut off—such was the simile that occurred to him. Well, he was bound to freeze anyway, and he might as well take it decently. With this new-found peace of mind came the first glimmerings of drowsiness. A good idea, he thought, to sleep off to death. It was like taking an anaesthetic. Freezing was not so bad as people thought. There were lots worse ways to die.

He pictured the boys finding his body next day. Suddenly he found himself with them, coming along the trail and looking for himself. And, still with them, he came around a turn in the trail and found himself lying in the snow. He did not belong with himself any more, for even then he was out of himself, standing with the boys and looking at himself in the snow. It certainly was cold, was his thought.

When he got back to the States he could tell the folks what real cold was. He drifted on from this to a vision of the old-timer on Sulphur Creek. He could see him quite clearly, warm and comfortable, and smoking a pipe.

"You were right, old hoss; you were right," the man mumbled to the old-timer of Sulphur Creek.

Then the man drowsed off into what seemed to him the most comfortable and satisfying sleep he had ever known. The dog sat facing him and waiting. The brief day drew to a close in a long, slow twilight. There were no signs of a fire to be made, and, besides, never in the dog's experience had it known a man to sit like that in the snow and make no fire. As the twilight drew on, its eager yearning for the fire mastered it, and with a great lifting and shifting of forefeet, it whined softly, then flattened its ears down in anticipation of being chidden by the man. But the man remained silent. Later, the dog whined loudly. And still later it crept close to the man and caught the scent of death. This made the animal bristle and back away. A little longer it delayed, howling under the stars that leaped and danced and shone brightly in the cold sky. Then it turned and trotted up the trail in the direction of the camp it knew, where were the other food providers and fire providers.

AN ODYSSEY OF THE NORTH

The sleds were singing their eternal lament to the creaking of the harness and the tinkling bells of the leaders; but the men and dogs were tired and made no sound. The trail was heavy with new-fallen snow, and they had come far, and the runners, burdened with flintlike quarters of frozen moose, clung tenaciously to the unpacked surface and held back with a stubbornness almost human. Darkness was coming on, but there was no camp to pitch that night. The snow fell gently through the pulseless air, not in flakes, but in tiny frost crystals of delicate design. It was very warm—barely ten below zero—and the men did not mind. Meyers and Bettles had raised their ear flaps, while Malemute Kid had even taken off his mittens.

The dogs had been fagged out early in the afternoon, but they now began to show new vigor. Among the more astute there was a certain restlessness—an impatience at the restraint of the traces, an indecisive quickness of movement, a sniffing of snouts and pricking of ears. These became incensed at their more phlegmatic brothers, urging them on with numerous sly nips on their hinder quarters. Those, thus chidden, also contracted and helped spread the contagion. At last the leader of the foremost sled uttered a sharp whine of satisfaction, crouching lower in the snow and throwing himself against the collar. The rest followed suit. There was an ingathering of back hands, a tightening of traces; the sleds leaped forward, and the men clung to the gee poles, violently accelerating the uplift of their feet that they might escape going under the runners. The weariness of the day fell from them, and they whooped encouragement to the dogs. The animals responded with joyous yelps. They were swinging through the gathering darkness at a rattling gallop.

"Gee! Gee!" the men cried, each in turn, as their sleds abruptly left the main trail, heeling over on single runners like luggers on the wind.

Then came a hundred yards' dash to the lighted parchment window, which told its own story of the home cabin, the roaring Yukon stove, and the steaming pots of tea. But the home cabin had been invaded. Threescore huskies chorused defiance, and as many furry forms precipitated themselves upon the dogs which drew the first sled. The door was flung open, and a man, clad in the scarlet tunic of the Northwest Police, waded knee-deep among the furious brutes, calmly and impartially dispensing soothing justice with the butt end of a dog whip. After that the men shook hands; and in this wise was Malemute Kid welcomed to his own cabin by a stranger.

Stanley Prince, who should have welcomed him, and who was responsible for the Yukon stove and hot tea aforementioned, was busy with his guests. There were a dozen or so of them, as nondescript a crowd as

ever served the Queen in the enforcement of her laws
or the delivery of her mails. They were of many breeds,
but their common life had formed of them a certain
type—a lean and wiry type, with trail-hardened muscles, and sun-browned faces, and untroubled souls
which gazed frankly forth, clear-eyed and steady. They
drove the dogs of the Queen, wrought fear in the
hearts of her enemies, ate of her meager fare, and were
happy. They had seen life, and done deeds, and lived
romances; but they did not know it.

And they were very much at home. Two of them
were sprawled upon Malemute Kid's bunk, singing
chansons which their French forebears sang in the
days when first they entered the Northwest land and
mated with its Indian women. Bettles' bunk had suffered a similar invasion, and three or four lusty
voyageurs worked their toes among its blankets as they
listened to the tale of one who had served on the boat
brigade with Wolseley when he fought his way to
Khartoum. And when he tired, a cowboy told of
courts and kings and lords and ladies he had seen
when Buffalo Bill toured the capitals of Europe. In a
corner two half-breeds, ancient comrades in a lost
campaign, mended harnesses and talked of the days
when the Northwest flamed with insurrection and
Louis Riel was king.

Rough jests and rougher jokes went up and down,
and great hazards by trail and river were spoken of in
the light of commonplaces, only to be recalled by
virtue of some grain of humor or ludicrous happen-

ing. Prince was led away by these uncrowned heroes who had seen history made, who regarded the great and the romantic as but the ordinary and the incidental in the routine of life. He passed his precious tobacco among them with lavish disregard, and rusty chains of reminiscence were loosened, and forgotten odysseys resurrected for his especial benefit.

When conversation dropped and the travelers filled the last pipes and lashed their tight-rolled sleeping furs, Prince fell back upon his comrade for further information.

"Well, you know what the cowboy is," Malemute Kid answered, beginning to unlace his moccasins; "and it's not hard to guess the British blood in his bed partner. As for the rest, they're all children of the *coureurs du bois*, mingled with God knows how many other bloods. The two turning in by the door are the regulation 'breeds' or *Boisbrûles*. That lad with the worsted breech scarf—notice his eyebrows and the turn of his jaw—shows a Scotchman wept in his mother's smoky tepee. And that handsome-looking fellow putting the capote under his head is a French half-breed—you heard him talking; he doesn't like the two Indians turning in next to him. You see, when the 'breeds' rose under Riel the full-bloods kept the peace, and they've not lost much love for one another since."

"But I say, what's that glum-looking fellow by the stove? I'll swear he can't talk English. He hasn't opened his mouth all night."

"You're wrong. He knows English well enough. Did you follow his eyes when he listened? I did. But he's neither kith nor kin to the others. When they talked their own patois you could see he didn't understand. I've been wondering myself what he is. Let's find out."

"Fire a couple of sticks into the stove!" Malemute Kid commanded, raising his voice and looking squarely at the man in question.

He obeyed at once.

"Had discipline knocked into him somewhere." Prince commented in a low tone.

Malemute Kid nodded, took off his socks, and picked his way among recumbent men to the stove. There he hung his damp footgear among a score or so of mates.

"When do you expect to get to Dawson?" he asked tentatively.

The man studied him a moment before replying. "They say seventy-five mile. So? Maybe two days."

The very slightest accent was perceptible, while there was no awkward hesitancy or groping for words.

"Been in the country before?"

"No."

"Northwest Territory?"

"Yes."

"Born there?"

"No."

"Well, where the devil were you born? You're none

of these." Malemute Kid swept his hand over the dog drivers, even including the two policemen who had turned into Prince's bunk. "Where did you come from? I've seen faces like yours before, though I can't remember just where."

"I know you," he irrelevantly replied, at once turning the drift of Malemute Kid's questions.

"Where? Ever see me?"

"No; your partner, him priest, Pastilik, long time ago. Him ask me if I see you, Malemute Kid. Him give me grub. I no stop long. You hear him speak 'bout me?"

"Oh! you're the fellow that traded the otter skins for the dogs?"

The man nodded, knocked out his pipe, and signified his disinclination for conversation by rolling up in his furs. Malemute Kid blew out the slush lamp and crawled under the blankets with Prince.

"Well, what is he?"

"Don't know—turned me off, somehow, and then shut up like a clam. But he's a fellow to whet your curiosity. I've heard of him. All the coast wondered about him eight years ago. Sort of mysterious, you know. He came down out of the North in the dead of winter, many a thousand miles from here, skirting Bering Sea and traveling as though the devil were after him. No one ever learned where he came from, but he must have come far. He was badly travel-worn when he got food from the Swedish missionary on Golovin Bay and asked the way south. We heard of all this afterward. Then he abandoned the shore line, heading right across Norton Sound. Terrible weather, snowstorms and high winds, but he pulled through where a thousand other men would have died, missing St. Michaels and making the land at Pastilik. He'd lost all but two dogs, and was nearly gone with starvation.

"He was so anxious to go on that Father Roubeau fitted him out with grub; but he couldn't let him have any dogs, for he was only waiting my arrival to go on a trip himself. Mr. Ulysses knew too much to start on without animals, and fretted around for several days. He had on his sled a bunch of beautifully cured otter skins, sea otters, you know, worth their weight in gold. There was also at Pastilik an old Shylock of a Russian trader, who had dogs to kill. Well, they didn't dicker very long, but when the Strange One headed south again, it was in the rear of a spanking dog team. Mr. Shylock, by the way, had the otter skins. I saw them, and they were magnificent. We figured it up and found the dogs brought him at least five hundred apiece. And it wasn't as if the Strange One didn't know the value of sea otter; he was an Indian of some sort, and what little he talked showed he'd been among white men.

"After the ice passed out of the sea, word came up from Nunivak Island that he'd gone in there for grub. Then he dropped from sight, and this is the first heard of him in eight years. Now where did he come from? and what was he doing there? and why did he come from there? He's Indian, he's been nobody knows where, and he's had discipline, which is unusual for an Indian. Another mystery of the North for you to solve, Prince."

"Thanks awfully, but I've got too many on hand as it is," he replied.

Malemute Kid was already breathing heavily; but the young mining engineer gazed straight up through the thick darkness, waiting for the strange orgasm which stirred his blood to die away. And when he did sleep, his brain worked on, and for the nonce he, too, wandered through the white unknown, struggled with the dogs on endless trails, and saw men live, and toil, and die like men.

*   *   *

The next morning, hours before daylight, the dog drivers and policemen pulled out for Dawson. But the powers that saw to Her Majesty's interests and ruled the destinies of her lesser creatures gave the mailmen little rest, for a week later they appeared at Stuart River, heavily burdened with letters for Salt Water. However, their dogs had been replaced by fresh ones; but, then, they were dogs.

The men had expected some sort of a layover in which to rest up; besides, this Klondike was a new section of the Northland, and they had wished to see a little something of the Golden City where dust flowed like water and dance halls rang with never-ending revelry. But they dried their socks and smoked their evening pipes with much the same gusto as on their former visit, though one or two bold spirits speculated on desertion and the possibility of crossing the unexplored Rockies to the east, and thence, by the Mackenzie Valley, of gaining their old stamping grounds in the Chippewyan country. Two or three even decided to return to their homes by that route when their terms of service had expired, and they began to lay plans forthwith, looking forward to the hazardous undertaking in much the same way a city-bred man would to a day's holiday in the woods.

He of the Otter Skins seemed very restless, though he took little interest in the discussion, and at last he drew Malemute Kid to one side and talked for some time in low tones. Prince cast curious eyes in their direction, and the mystery deepened when they put on caps and mittens and went outside. When they returned, Malemute Kid placed his gold scales on the table, weighed out the matter of sixty ounces, and transferred them to the Strange One's sack. Then the chief of the dog drivers joined the conclave, and certain business was transacted with him. The next day the gang went on upriver, but He of the Otter Skins took several pounds of grub and turned his steps back toward Dawson.

"Didn't know what to make of it," said Malemute Kid in response to Prince's queries; "but the poor beggar wanted to be quit of the service for some reason or other—at least it seemed a most important one to him, though he wouldn't let on what. You see, it's just like the army: he signed for two years, and the only way to get free was to buy himself out. He couldn't desert and then stay here, and he was just wild to remain in the country. Made up his mind when he got to Dawson, he said; but no one knew him, hadn't a cent, and I was the only one he'd spoken two words with. So he talked it over with the lieutenant-governor, and made arrangements in case he could get the money from me—loan, you know. Said he'd pay back in the year, and, if I wanted, would put me onto something rich. Never'd seen it, but he knew it was rich.

"And talk! why, when he got me outside he was ready to weep. Begged and pleaded; got down in the snow to me till I hauled him out of it. Palavered around like a crazy man. Swore he's worked to this very end for years and years, and couldn't bear to be disappointed now. Asked him what end, but he wouldn't say. Said they might keep him on the other half of the trail and he wouldn't get to Dawson in two years, and then it would be too late. Never saw a man take on so in my life. And when I said I'd let him have it, had to yank him out of the snow again. Told him to consider it in the light of a grubstake. Think he'd have it? No sir! Swore he'd give me all he found, make me rich beyond the dreams of avarice, and all such stuff. Now a man who puts his life and time against a grubstake ordinarily finds it hard enough to turn over half of what he finds. Something behind all this, Prince; just you make a note of it. We'll hear of him if he stays in the country——"

"And if he doesn't?"

"Then my good nature gets a shock, and I'm sixty some odd ounces out."

*   *   *

The cold weather had come on with the long nights, and the sun had begun to play his ancient game of peekaboo along the southern snow line ere aught was heard of Malemute Kid's grubstake. And then, one bleak morning in early January, a heavily laden dog train pulled into his cabin below Stuart River. He of the Otter Skins was there, and with him walked a man such as the gods have almost forgotten how to fashion. Men never talked of luck and pluck and five-hundred-dollar dirt without bringing in the name of Axel Gunderson; nor could tales of nerve or strength or daring pass up and down the campfire without the summoning of his presence. And when the conversation flagged, it blazed anew at mention of the woman who shared his fortunes.

As has been noted, in the making of Axel Gunderson the gods had remembered their old-time cunning and cast him after the manner of men who were born when the world was young. Full seven feet he towered in his picturesque costume which marked a king of Eldorado. His chest, neck, and limbs were those of a giant. To bear his three hundred pounds of bone and muscle, his snowshoes were greater by a generous yard than those of other men. Rough-hewn, with rugged brow and massive jaw and unflinching eyes of palest blue, his face told the tale of one who knew but the law of might. Of the yellow of ripe corn silk, his frost-incrusted hair swept like day across the night and fell far down his coat of bearskin. A vague tradition of the sea seemed to cling about him as he swung down the narrow trail in advance of the dogs; and he brought the butt of his dog whip against Malemute Kid's door as a Norse sea rover, on southern foray, might thunder for admittance at the castle gate.

Prince bared his womanly arms and kneaded sourdough bread, casting, as he did so, many a glance at the three guests—three guests the like of which might never come under a man's roof in a lifetime. The Strange One, whom Malemute Kid had surnamed Ulysses, still fascinated him; but his interest chiefly gravitated between Axel Gunderson and Axel Gunderson's wife. She felt the day's journey, for she had softened in comfortable cabins during the many days since her husband mastered the wealth of frozen pay streaks, and she was tired. She rested against his great breast like a slender flower against a wall, replying lazily to Malemute Kid's good-natured banter, and stirring Prince's blood strangely with an occasional sweep of her deep, dark eyes. For Prince was a man, and healthy, and had seen few women in many months. And she was older than he, and an Indian besides. But she was different from all native wives he had met: she had traveled—had been in his country among others, he gathered from the conversation; and she knew most of the things the women of his own race knew, and much more that it was not in the nature of things for them to know. She could make a meal of sun-dried fish or a bed in the snow; yet she teased them with tantalizing details of many-course dinners, and caused strange internal dissensions to arise at the mention of various quondam dishes which they had well-nigh forgotten. She knew the ways of the moose, the bear, and the little blue fox, and of the wild amphibians of the Northern seas; she was skilled in the lore of the woods, and the streams, and the tale writ by man and bird and beast upon the delicate snow crust was to her an open book; yet Prince caught the appreciative twinkle in her eye as she read the Rules of the Camp. These rules had been fathered by the Unquenchable Bettles at a time when his blood ran high, and were remarkable for the terse simplicity of their humor. Prince always turned them to the wall before the arrival of ladies; but who could suspect that this native wife—— Well, it was too late now.

This, then, was the wife of Axel Gunderson, a woman whose name and fame had traveled with her husband's, hand in hand, through all the Northland. At table, Malemute Kid baited her with the assurance of an old friend, and Prince shook off the shyness of first acquaintance and joined in. But she held her own in the unequal contest, while her husband, slower in wit, ventured naught but applause. And he was very proud of her; his every look and action revealed the magnitude of the place she occupied in his life. He of the Otter Skins ate in silence, forgotten in the merry battle; and long ere the others were done he pushed back from the table and went out among the dogs. Yet all too soon his fellow travelers drew on their mittens and parkas and followed him.

There had been no snow for many days, and the sleds slipped along the hard-packed Yukon trail as easily as if it had been glare ice. Ulysses led the first sled; with the second came Prince and Axel Gunderson's wife; while Malemute Kid and the yellow-haired giant brought up the third.

"It's only a hunch, Kid," he said, "but I think it's straight. He's never been there, but he tells a good story, and shows a map I heard of when I was in the Kootenay country years ago. I'd like to have you go along; but he's a strange one, and swore point-blank to throw it up if anyone was brought in. But when I come back you'll get first tip, and I'll stake you next to me, and give you a half share in the town site besides."

"No! no!" he cried, as the other strove to interrupt. "I'm running this, and before I'm done it'll need two heads. If it's all right, why, it'll be a second Cripple Creek, man; do you hear?—a second Cripple Creek! It's quartz, you know, not placer; and if we work it right we'll corral the whole thing—millions upon millions. I've heard of the place before, and so have you. We'll build a town—thousands of workmen—good waterways—steamship lines—big carrying trade—light-draught steamers for head reaches—survey a railroad, perhaps—sawmills—electric-light plant—do our own banking—commercial company—syndicate—— Say! Just you hold your hush till I get back!"

The sleds came to a halt where the trail crossed the mouth of Stuart River. An unbroken sea of frost, its wide expanse stretched away into the unknown east. The snowshoes were withdrawn from the lashings of the sleds. Axel Gunderson shook hands and stepped to the fore, his great webbed shoes sinking a fair half yard into the feathery surface and packing the snow so the dogs should not wallow. His wife fell in behind the last sled, betraying long practice in the art of handling the awkward footgear. The stillness was broken with cheery farewells; the dogs whined; and He of the Otter Skins talked with his whip to a recalcitrant wheeler.

An hour later the train had taken on the likeness of a black pencil crawling in a long, straight line across a mighty sheet of foolscap.

II

One night, many weeks later, Malemute Kid and Prince fell to solving chess problems from the torn page of an ancient magazine. The Kid had just returned from his Bonanza properties and was resting up preparatory to a long moose hunt. Prince, too, had been on creek and trail nearly all winter, and had grown hungry for a blissful week of cabin life.

"Interpose the black knight, and force the king. No, that won't do. See, the next move——"

"Why advance the pawn two squares? Bound to take it in transit, and with the bishop out of the way——"

"But hold on! That leaves a hole, and——"

"No; it's protected. Go ahead! You'll see it works."

It was very interesting. Somebody knocked at the door a second time before Malemute Kid said, "Come in." The door swung open. Something staggered in. Prince caught one square look and sprang to his feet. The horror in his eyes caused Malemute Kid to whirl about; and he, too, was startled, though he had seen bad things before. The thing tottered blindly toward them. Prince edged away till he reached the nail from which hung his Smith & Wesson.

"My God! what is it?" he whispered to Malemute Kid.

"Don't know. Looks like a case of freezing and no grub," replied the Kid, sliding away in the opposite direction. "Watch out! It may be mad," he warned, coming back from closing the door.

The thing advanced to the table. The bright flame of the slush lamp caught its eye. It was amused, and gave voice to eldritch cackles which betokened mirth. Then, suddenly, he—for it was a man—swayed back, with a hitch to his skin trousers, and began to sing a chantey, such as men lift when they swing around the capstan circle and the sea snorts in their ears:

> "YAN-KEE SHIP COME DOWN DE RI-IB-ER,
>   PULL! MY BULLY BOYS! PULL!
> D'YEH WANT——TO KNOW DE CAPTAIN RU-UNS HER?
>   PULL! MY BULLY BOYS! PULL!
> JON-A-THAN JONES OB SOUTH CAHO-LI-IN-A,
>   PULL! MY BULLY——"

He broke off abruptly, tottered with a wolfish snarl to the meat shelf, and before they could intercept was tearing with his teeth at a chunk of raw bacon. The struggle was fierce between him and Malemute Kid; but his mad strength left him as suddenly as it had come, and he weakly surrendered the spoil. Between them they got him upon a stool, where he sprawled with half his body across the table. A small dose of whiskey strengthened him, so that he could dip a spoon into the sugar caddy which Malemute Kid placed before him. After his appetite had been somewhat cloyed, Prince, shuddering as he did so, passed him a mug of weak beef tea.

The creature's eyes were alight with a somber frenzy, which blazed and waned with every mouthful. There was very little skin to the face. The face, for that matter, sunken and emaciated, bore little likeness to human countenance. Frost after frost had bitten deeply, each depositing its stratum of scab upon the half-healed scar that went before. This dry, hard surface was of a bloody-black color, serrated by grievous cracks wherein the raw red flesh peeped forth. His skin garments were dirty and in tatters, and the fur of one side was singed and burned away, showing where he had lain upon his fire.

Malemute Kid pointed to where the sun-tanned hide had been cut away, strip by strip—the grim signature of famine.

"Who—are—you?" slowly and distinctly enunciated the Kid.

The man paid no heed.

"Where do you come from?"

"Yan-kee ship come down de ri-ib-er," was the quavering response.

"Don't doubt the beggar came down the river," the Kid said, shaking him in an endeavor to start a more lucid flow of talk.

But the man shrieked at the contact, clapping a hand to his side in evident pain. He rose slowly to his feet, half leaning on the table.

"She laughed at me—so—with the hate in her eye; and she—would—not—come."

His voice died away, and he was sinking back when Malemute Kid gripped him by the wrist and shouted, "Who? Who would not come?"

"She, Unga. She laughed, and struck at me, so, and so. And then——"

"Yes?"

"And then——"

"And then what?"

"And then he lay very still in the snow a long time. He is—still in—the—snow."

The two men looked at each other helplessly.

"Who is in the snow?"

"She, Unga. She looked at me with the hate in her eye, and then——"

"Yes, yes."

"And then she took the knife, so; and once, twice—she was weak. I traveled very slow. And there is much gold in that place, very much gold."

"Where is Unga?" For all Malemute Kid knew, she might be dying a mile away. He shook the man savagely, repeating again and again, "Where is Unga? Who is Unga?"

"She—is—in—the—snow."

"Go on!" The Kid was pressing his wrist cruelly.

"So—I—would—be—in—the snow—but—I—had—a—debt—to—pay. It—was—heavy—I—had—a—debt—to—pay—a—debt—to—pay I—had——" The faltering monosyllables ceased as he fumbled in his pouch and drew forth a buckskin sack. "A—debt—to—pay—five—pounds—of—gold—grub—stake—Mal—e—mute—Kid—I——" The exhausted head dropped upon the table; nor could Malemute Kid rouse it again.

"It's Ulysses," he said quietly, tossing the bag of dust on the table. "Guess it's all day with Axel Gunderson and the woman. Come on, let's get him between the blankets. He's Indian; he'll pull through and tell a tale besides."

As they cut his garments from him, near his right breast could be seen two unhealed, hard-lipped knife thrusts.

III

"I will talk of the things which were in my own way; but you will understand. I will begin at the beginning, and tell of myself and the woman, and, after that, of the man."

He of the Otter Skins drew over to the stove as do men who have been deprived of fire and are afraid the Promethean gift may vanish at any moment. Malemute Kid picked up the slush lamp and placed it so its light might fall upon the face of the narrator. Prince slid his body over the edge of the bunk and joined them.

"I am Naass, a chief, and the son of a chief, born between a sunset and a rising, on the dark seas, in my father's oomiak. All of a night the men toiled at the paddles, and the women cast out the waves which threw in upon us, and we fought with the storm. The salt spray froze upon my mother's breast till her breath passed with the passing of the tide. But I—I raised my voice with the wind and the storm, and lived.

"We dwelt in Akatan——"

"Where?" asked Malemute Kid.

"Akatan, which is in the Aleutians; Akatan, beyond Chignik, beyond Kardalak, beyond Unimak. As I say, we dwelt in Akatan, which lies in the midst of the sea on the edge of the world. We farmed the salt seas for the fish, the seal, and the otter; and our homes shouldered about one another on the rocky strip between the rim of the forest and the yellow beach where our kayaks lay. We were not many, and the world was very small. There were strange lands to the east—islands like Akatan; so we thought all the world was islands and did not mind.

"I was different from my people. In the sands of the beach were the crooked timbers and wave-warped planks of a boat such as my people never built; and I remember on the point of the island which overlooked the ocean three ways there stood a pine tree which never grew there, smooth and straight and tall. It is said the two men came to that spot, turn about, through many days, and watched with the passing of the light. These two men came from out of the sea in the boat which lay in pieces on the beach. And they were white like you, and weak as the little children when the seal have gone away and the hunters come home empty. I know of these things from the old men and the old women, who got them from their fathers and mothers before them. These strange white men did not take kindly to our ways at first, but they grew strong, what of the fish and the oil, and fierce. And they built them each his own house, and took the pick of our women, and in time children came. Thus he was born who was to become the father of my father's father.

"As I said, I was different from my people, for I carried the strong, strange blood of this white man who came out of the sea. It is said we had other laws in the days before these men; but they were fierce and quarrelsome, and fought with our men till there were no more left who dared to fight. Then they made themselves chiefs, and took away our old laws, and gave us new ones, insomuch that the man was the son of his father, and not his mother, as our way had been. They also ruled that the son, first-born, should have all things which were his father's before him, and that the brothers and sisters should shift for themselves. And they gave us other laws. They showed us new ways in the catching of fish and the killing of bear which were thick in the woods; and they taught us to lay by bigger stores for the time of famine. And these things were good.

"But when they had become chiefs, and there were no more men to face their anger, they fought, these strange white men, each with the other. And the one whose blood I carry drove his seal spear the length of an arm through the other's body. Their children took up the fight, and their children's children; and there was great hatred between them, and black doings, even to my time, so that in each family but one lived to pass down the blood of them that went before. Of my blood I was alone; of the other man's there was but a girl. Unga, who lived with her mother. Her father and my father did not come back from the fishing one night; but afterward they washed up to the beach on the big tides, and they held very close to each other.

"The people wondered, because of the hatred between the houses, and the old men shook their heads and said the fight would go on when children were born to her and children to me. They told me this as a boy, till I came to believe, and to look upon Unga as a foe, who was to be the mother of children which were to fight with mine. I thought of these things day by day, and when I grew to a stripling I came to ask why this should be so. And they answered, 'We do not know, but that in such way your fathers did.' And I marveled that those which were to come should fight the battles of those that were gone, and in it I could see no right. But the people said it must be, and I was only a stripling.

"And they said I must hurry, that my blood might be the older and grow strong before hers. This was easy, for I was head man, and the people looked up to me because of the deeds and the laws of my fathers, and the wealth which was mine. Any maiden would come to me, but I found none to my liking. And the old men and the mothers of maidens told me to hurry, for even then were the hunters bidding high to the mother of Unga; and should her children grow strong before mine, mine would surely die.

"Nor did I find a maiden till one night coming back from the fishing. The sunlight was lying, so, low and full in the eyes, the wind free, and the kay-acks racing with the white seas. Of a sudden the kayak of Unga came driving past me, and she looked upon me, so, with her black hair flying like a cloud of night and the spray wet on her cheek. As I say, the sunlight was full in the eyes, and I was a stripling; but somehow it was all clear, and I knew it to be the call of kind to kind. As she whipped ahead she looked back within the space of two strokes—looked as only the woman Unga could look—and again I knew it as the call of kind. The people shouted as we ripped past the lazy oomiaks and left them far behind. But she was quick at the paddle, and my heart was like the belly of a sail, and I did not gain. The wind freshened, the sea whitened, and, leaping like the seals on the windward breech, we roared down the golden pathway of the sun."

Naass was crouched half out of his stool, in the attitude of one driving a paddle, as he ran the race anew. Somewhere across the stove he beheld the tossing kayak and the flying hair of Unga. The voice of the wind was in his ears, and its salt beat fresh upon his nostrils.

"But she made the shore, and ran up the sand, laughing, to the house of her mother. And a great thought came to me that night—a thought worthy of him that was chief over all the people of Akatan. So, when the moon was up, I went down to the house of her mother, and looked upon the goods of Yash-Noosh, which were piled by the door—the goods of Yash-Noosh, a strong hunter who had it in mind to be the father of the children of Unga. Other young men had piled their goods there and taken them away again; and each young man had made a pile greater than the one before.

"And I laughed to the moon and the stars, and went to my own house where my wealth was stored. And many trips I made, till my pile was greater by the fingers of one hand than the pile of Yash-Noosh. There were fish, dried in the sun and smoked; and forty hides of the hair seal, and half as many of the fur, and each hide was tied at the mouth and big bellied with oil; and ten skins of bear which I killed in the woods when they came out in the spring. And there were beads and blankets and scarlet cloths, such as I got in trade from the people who lived to the east, and who got them in trade from the people who lived still beyond in the east. And I looked upon the pile of Yash-Noosh and laughed, for I was head man in Akatan, and my wealth was greater than the wealth of all my young men, and my fathers had done deeds, and given laws, and put their names for all time in the mouths of the people.

"So, when the morning came, I went down to the beach, casting out of the corner of my eye at the house of the mother of Unga. My offer yet stood untouched. And the women smiled, and said sly things one to the other. I wondered, for never had such a price been offered; and that night I added more to the pile, and put beside it a kayak of well-tanned skins which never yet had swam in the sea. But in the day it was yet there, open to the laughter of all men. The mother of Unga was crafty, and I grew angry at the shame in which I stood before my people. So that night I added till it became a great pile, and I hauled up my oomiak, which was of the value of twenty kayaks. And in the morning there was no pile.

"Then made I preparation for the wedding, and the people that lived even to the east came for the food of the feast and the potlatch token. Unga was older than I by the age of four suns in the way we reckoned the years. I was only a stripling; but then I was a chief, and the son of a chief, and it did not matter.

"But a ship shoved her sails above the floor of the ocean, and grew larger with the breath of the wind.

From her scuppers she ran clear water, and the men were in haste and worked hard at the pumps. On the bow stood a mighty man, watching the depth of the water and giving commands with a voice of thunder. His eyes were of the pale blue of the deep waters, and his head was maned like that of a sea lion. And his hair was yellow, like the straw of a southern harvest or the manila rope yarns which sailormen plait.

"Of late years we had seen ships from afar, but this was the first to come to the beach of Akatan. The feast was broken, and the women and children fled to the houses, while we men strung our bows and waited with spears in hand. But when the ship's fore-foot smelled the beach the strange men took no notice of us, being busy with their own work. With the falling of the tide they careened the schooner and patched a great hole in her bottom. So the women crept back, and the feast went on.

"When the tide rose, the sea wanderers kedged the schooner to deep water and then came among us. They bore presents and were friendly; so I made room for them, and out of the largeness of my heart gave them tokens such as I gave all the guests, for it was my wedding day, and I was head man in Akatan. And he with the mane of the sea lion was there, so tall and strong that one looked to see the earth shake with the fall of his feet. He looked much and straight at Unga, with his arms folded, so, and stayed till the sun went away and the stars came out. Then he went down to his ship. After that I took Unga by the hand and led her to my own house. And there was singing and great laughter, and the women said sly things, after the manner of women at such times. But we did not care. Then the people left us alone and went home.

"The last noise had not died away when the chief of the sea wanderers came in by the door. And he had with him black bottles, from which we drank and made merry. You see, I was only a stripling, and had lived all my days on the edge of the world. So my blood became as fire, and my heart as light as the froth that flies from the surf to the cliff. Unga sat silent among the skins in the corner, her eyes wide, for she seemed to fear. And he with the mane of the sea lion looked upon her straight and long. Then his men came in with bundles of goods, and he piled before me wealth such as was not in all Akatan. There were guns, both large and small, and powder and shot and shell, and bright axes and knives of steel, and cunning tools, and strange things the like of which I had never seen. When he showed me by sign that it was all mine, I thought him a great man to be so free; but he showed me also that Unga was to go away with him in his ship. Do you understand?—that Unga was to go away with him in his ship. The blood of my fathers flamed hot on the sudden, and I made to drive him through with my spear. But the spirit of the bottles had stolen the life from my arm, and he took me by the neck, so, and knocked my head against the wall of the house. And I was made weak like a newborn child, and my legs would no more stand under me. Unga screamed, and she laid hold of the things of the house with her hands, till they fell all about us as he dragged her to the door. Then he took her in his great arms, and when she tore at his yellow hair laughed with a sound like that of the big bull seal in the rut.

"I crawled to the beach and called upon my people, but they were afraid. Only Yash-Noosh was a man, and they struck him on the head with an oar, till he lay with his face in the sand and did not move. And they raised the sails to the sound of their songs, and the ship went away on the wind.

"The people said it was good, for there would be no more war of the bloods in Akatan; but I said never a word, waiting till the time of the full moon, when I put fish and oil in my kayak and went away to the east. I saw many islands and many people, and I, who had lived on the edge, saw that the world was very large. I talked by signs; but they had not seen a schooner nor a man with the mane of a sea lion, and they pointed always to the east. And I slept in queer places, and ate odd things, and met strange faces. Many laughed, for they thought me light of head; but sometimes old men turned my face to the light and blessed me, and the eyes of the young women grew soft as they asked me of the strange ship, and Unga, and the men of the sea.

"And in this manner, through rough seas and great storms, I came to Unalaska. There were two schooners there, but neither was the one I sought. So

I passed on to the east, with the world growing ever larger, and in the island of Unamok there was no word of the ship, nor in Kadiak, nor in Atognak. And so I came one day to a rocky land, where men dug great holes in the mountain. And there was a schooner, but not my schooner, and men loaded upon it the rocks which they dug. This I thought childish, for all the world was made of rocks; but they gave me food and set me to work. When the schooner was deep in the water, the captain gave me money and told me to go; but I asked which way he went, and he pointed south. I made signs that I would go with him, and he laughed at first, but then, being short of men, took me to help work the ship. So I came to talk after their manner, and to heave on ropes, and to reef the stiff sails in sudden squalls, and to take my turn at the wheel. But it was not strange, for the blood of my fathers was the blood of the men of the sea.

"I had thought it an easy task to find him I sought, once I got among his own people; and when we raised the land one day, and passed between a gateway of the sea to a port, I looked for perhaps as many schooners as there were fingers to my hands. But the ships lay against the wharves for miles, packed like so many little fish; and when I went among them to ask for a man with the mane of a sea lion, they laughed, and answered me in the tongues of many peoples. And I found that they hailed from the uttermost parts of the earth.

"And I went into the city to look upon the face of

every man. But they were like the cod when they run thick on the banks, and I could not count them. And the noise smote upon me till I could not hear, and my head was dizzy with much movement. So I went on and on, through the lands which sang in the warm sunshine; where the harvests lay rich on the plains; and where great cities were fat with men that lived like women, with false words in their mouths and their hearts black with the lust of gold. And all the while my people of Akatan hunted and fished, and were happy in the thought that the world was small.

"But the look in the eyes of Unga coming home from the fishing was with me always, and I knew I would find her when the time was met. She walked down quiet lanes in the dusk of the evening, or led me chases across the thick fields wet with the morning dew, and there was a promise in her eyes such as only the woman Unga could give.

"So I wandered through a thousand cities. Some were gentle and gave me food, and others laughed, and still others cursed; but I kept my tongue between my teeth, and went strange ways and saw strange sights. Sometimes I, who was a chief and the son of a chief, toiled for men—men rough of speech and hard as iron, who wrung gold from the sweat and sorrow of their fellow men. Yet no word did I get of my quest till I came back to the sea like a homing seal to the rookeries. But this was at another port, in another country which lay to the north. And there I heard dim tales of the yellow-haired sea wanderer, and I learned that he was a hunter of seals, and that even then he was abroad on the ocean.

"So I shipped on a seal schooner with the lazy Siwashes, and followed his trackless trail to the north where the hunt was then warm. And we were away weary months, and spoke many of the fleet, and heard much of the wild doings of him I sought; but never once did we raise him above the sea. We went north, even to the Pribilofs, and killed the seals in herds on the beach, and brought their warm bodies aboard till our scuppers ran grease and blood and no man could stand upon the deck. Then were we chased by a ship of slow steam, which fired upon us with great guns. But we put sail till the sea was over our decks and washed them clean, and lost ourselves in a fog.

"It is said, at this time, while we fled with fear at our hearts, that the yellow-haired sea wanderer put in to the Pribilofs, right to the factory, and while the part of his men held the servants of the company, the rest loaded ten thousand green skins from the salt houses. I say it is said, but I believe; for in the voyages I made on the coast with never a meeting the northern seas rang with his wildness and daring, till the three nations which have lands there sought him with their ships. And I heard of Unga, for the captains sang loud in her praise, and she was always with him. She had learned the ways of his people, they said, and was happy. But I knew better—knew that her heart harked back to her own people by the yellow beach of Akatan.

"So, after a long time, I went back to the port which is by a gateway of the sea, and there I learned that he had gone across the girth of the great ocean to hunt for the seal to the east of the warm land which runs south from the Russian seas. And I, who was become a sailorman, shipped with men of his own race, and went after him in the hunt of the seal. And there were few ships off that new land; but we hung on the flank of the seal pack and harried it north through all the spring of the year. And when the cows were heavy with pup and crossed the Russian line, our men grumbled and were afraid. For there was much fog, and every day men were lost in the boats. They would not work, so the captain turned the ship back toward the way it came. But I knew the yellow-haired sea wanderer was unafraid, and would hang by the pack, even to the Russian Isles, where few men go. So I took a boat, in the black of night, when the lookout dozed on the fo'c'slehead, and went alone to the warm, long land. And I journeyed south to meet the men by Yeddo Bay, who are wild and unafraid. And the Yoshiwara girls were small, and bright like steel, and good to look upon; but I could not stop, for I knew that Unga rolled on the tossing floor by the rookeries of the north.

"The men by Yeddo Bay had met from the ends of the earth, and had neither gods nor homes, sailing under the flag of the Japanese. And with them I went to the rich beaches of Copper Island, where our salt piles became high with skins. And in that silent sea we saw no man till we were ready to come away. Then one day the fog lifted on the edge of a heavy wind, and there jammed down upon us a schooner, with close in her wake the cloudy funnels of a Russian man-of-war. We fled away on the beam of the wind, with the schooner jamming still closer and plunging ahead three feet to our two. And upon her poop was the man with the mane of the sea lion, pressing the rails under with the canvas and laughing in his strength of life. And Unga was there—I knew her on the moment—but he sent her below when the cannons began to talk across the sea. As I say, with three feet to our two, till we saw the rudder lift green at every jump—and I swinging on to the wheel and cursing, with my back to the Russian shot. For we knew he had it in mind to run before us, that he might get away while we were caught. And they knocked our masts out of us till we dragged into the wind like a wounded gull; but he went on over the edge of the sky line—he and Unga.

"What could we? The fresh hides spoke for themselves. So they took us to a Russian port, and after that to a lone country, where they set us to work in the mines to dig salt. And some died, and—and some did not die."

Naass swept the blanket from his shoulders, disclosing the gnarled and twisted flesh, marked with the unmistakable striations of the knout. Prince hastily covered him, for it was not nice to look upon.

"We were there a weary time and sometimes men

got away to the south, but they always came back.
So, when we who hailed from Yeddo Bay rose in the
night and took the guns from the guards, we went to
the north. And the land was very large, with plains,
soggy with water, and great forests. And the cold
came, with much snow on the ground, and no man
knew the way. Weary months we journeyed through
the endless forest—I do not remember, now, for
there was little food and often we lay down to die.
But at last we came to the cold sea, and but three
were left to look upon it. One had shipped from
Yeddo as captain, and he knew in his head the lay of
the great lands, and of the place where men may
cross from one to the other on the ice. And he led
us—I do not know, it was so long—till there were
but two. When we came to that place we found five
of the strange people which live in that country, and
they had dogs and skins, and we were very poor. We
fought in the snow till they died, and the captain
died, and the dogs and skins were mine. Then I
crossed on the ice, which was broken, and once I
drifted till a gale from the west put me upon the
shore. And after that, Golovin Bay, Pastilik, and the
priest. Then south, south, to the warm sunlands
where first I wandered.

"But the sea was no longer fruitful, and those who
went upon it after the seal went to little profit and
great risk. The fleets scattered, and the captains and
the men had no word of those I sought. So I turned
away from the ocean which never rests, and went

among the lands, where the trees, the houses, and the mountains sit always in one place and do not move. I journeyed far, and came to learn many things, even to the way of reading and writing from books. It was well I should do this, for it came upon me that Unga must know these things, and that someday, when the time was met—we—you understand, when the time was met.

"So I drifted, like those little fish which raise a sail to the wind but cannot steer. But my eyes and my ears were open always, and I went among men who traveled much, for I knew they had but to see those I sought to remember. At last there came a man, fresh from the mountains, with pieces of rock in which the free gold stood to the size of peas, and he had heard, he had met, he knew them. They were rich, he said, and lived in the place where they drew the gold from the ground.

"It was in a wild country, and very far away; but in time I came to the camp, hidden between the mountains, where men worked night and day, out of the sight of the sun. Yet the time was not come. I listened to the talk of the people. He had gone away—they had gone away—to England, it was said, in the matter of bringing men with much money together to form companies. I saw the house they had lived in; more like a palace, such as one sees in the old countries. In the nighttime I crept in through a window that I might see in what manner he treated her. I went from room to room, and in such way thought kings and queens must live, it was all so very good. And they all said he treated her like a queen, and many marveled as to what breed of woman she was for there was other blood in her veins, and she was different from the women of Akatan, and no one knew her for what she was. Aye, she was a queen; but I was a chief, and the son of a chief, and I had paid for her an untold price of skin and boat and bead.

"But why so many words? I was a sailorman, and knew the way of the ships on the seas. I followed to England, and then to other countries. Sometimes I heard of them by word of mouth, sometimes I read of them in the papers; yet never once could I come by them, for they had much money, and traveled fast, while I was a poor man. Then came trouble upon them, and their wealth slipped away one day like a curl of smoke. The papers were full of it at the time; but after that nothing was said, and I knew they had gone back where more gold could be got from the ground.

"They had dropped out of the world, being now poor, and so I wandered from camp to camp, even north to the Kootenay country, where I picked up the cold scent. They had come and gone, some said this way, and some that, and still others that they had gone to the country of the Yukon. And I went this way, and I went that, ever journeying from place to place, till it seemed I must grow weary of the world which was so large. But in the Kootenay I traveled a bad trail, and a long trail, with a breed of the North-

west, who saw fit to die when the famine pinched. He
had been to the Yukon by an unknown way over the
mountains, and when he knew his time was near gave
me the map and the secret of a place where he swore
by his gods there was much gold.

"After that all the world began to flock into the
north. I was a poor man; I sold myself to be a driver
of dogs. The rest you know. I met him and her in
Dawson. She did not know me, for I was only a
stripling, and her life had been large, so she had no
time to remember the one who had paid for her an
untold price.

"So? You bought me from my term of service. I
went back to bring things about in my own way, for
I had waited long, and now that I had my hand upon
him was in no hurry. As I say, I had it in mind to do
my own way, for I read back in my life, through all I
had seen and suffered, and remembered the cold and
hunger of the endless forest by the Russian seas. As
you know, I led him into the east—him and Unga—
into the east where many have gone and few returned.
I led them to the spot where the bones and the curses
of men lie with the gold which they may not have.

"The way was long and the trail unpacked. Our
dogs were many and ate much; nor could our sleds
carry till the break of spring. We must come back before the river ran free. So here and there we cached
grub, that our sleds might be lightened and there be
no chance of famine on the back trip. At the Mc-
Question there were three men, and near them we

built a cache, as also did we at the Mayo, where was a hunting camp of a dozen Pellys which had crossed the divide from the south. After that, as we went on into the east, we saw no men; only the sleeping river, the moveless forest, and the White Silence of the North. As I say, the way was long and the trail un-packed. Sometimes, in a day's toil, we made no more than eight miles, or ten, and at night we slept like dead men. And never once did they dream that I was Naass, head man of Akatan, the righter of wrongs.

"We now made smaller caches, and in the night-time it was a small matter to go back on the trail we had broken and change them in such way that one might deem the wolverines the thieves. Again there be places where there is a fall to the river, and the water is unruly, and the ice makes above and is eaten away beneath. In such a spot the sled I drove broke through, and the dogs; and to him and Unga it was ill luck, but no more. And there was much grub on that sled, and the dogs the strongest. But he laughed, for he was strong of life, and gave the dogs that were left little grub till we cut them from the harnesses one by one and fed them to their mates. We would go home light, he said, traveling and eating from cache to cache, with neither dogs nor sleds; which was true, for our grub was very short, and the last dog died in the traces the night we came to the gold and the bones and the curses of men.

"To reach that place—and the map spoke true—in the heart of the great mountains, we cut ice steps against the wall of a divide. One looked for a valley beyond, but there was no valley; the snow spread away, level as the great harvest plains, and here and there about us mighty mountains shoved their white heads among the stars. And midway on that strange plain which should have been a valley the earth and the snow fell away, straight down toward the heart of the world. Had we not been sailormen our heads would have swung round with the sight, but we stood on the dizzy edge that we might see a way to get down. And on one side, and one side only, the wall had fallen away till it was like the slope of the decks in a topsail breeze. I do not know why this thing should be so, but it was so. 'It is the mouth of hell,' he said; 'let us go down.' And we went down.

"And on the bottom there was a cabin, built by some man, of logs which he had cast down from above. It was a very old cabin, for men had died there alone at different times, and on pieces of birch bark which were there we read their last words and their curses. One had died of scurvy; another's partner had robbed him of his last grub and powder and stolen away; a third had been mauled by a baldface grizzly; a fourth had hunted for game and starved—and so it went, and they had been loath to leave the gold, and had died by the side of it in one way or another. And the worthless gold they had gathered yellowed the floor of the cabin like in a dream.

"But his soul was steady, and his head clear, this man I had led thus far. 'We have nothing to eat,' he said, 'and we will only look upon this gold, and see whence it comes and how much there be. Then we will go away quick, before it gets into our eyes and steals away our judgment. And in this way we may return in the end, with more grub, and possess it all.' So we looked upon the great vein, which cut the wall of the pit as a true vein should, and we measured it, and traced it from above and below, and drove the stakes of the claims and blazed the trees in token of our rights. Then, our knees shaking with lack of food, and a sickness in our bellies, and our hearts chugging close to our mouths, we climbed the mighty wall for the last time and turned our faces to the back trip.

"The last stretch we dragged Unga between us, and we fell often, but in the end we made the cache. And lo, there was no grub. It was well done, for he thought it the wolverines, and damned them and his gods in one breath. But Unga was brave, and smiled, and put her hand in his, till I turned away that I might hold myself. "We will rest by the fire," she said, "till morning, and we will gather strength from our moccasins." So we cut the tops of our moccasins in strips, and boiled them half of the night, that we might chew them and swallow them. And in the morning we talked of our chance. The next cache was five days' journey; we could not make it. We must find game.

"'We will go forth and hunt,' he said.

"'Yes,' said I, 'we will go forth and hunt.'

"And he ruled that Unga stay by the fire and save

her strength. And we went forth, he in quest of the moose and I to the cache I had changed. But I ate little, so they might not see in me much strength. And in the night he fell many times as he drew into camp. And I, too, made to suffer great weakness, stumbling over my snowshoes as though each step might be my last. And we gathered strength from our moccasins.

"He was a great man. His soul lifted his body to the last; nor did he cry aloud, save for the sake of Unga. On the second day I followed him, that I might not miss the end. And he lay down to rest often. That night he was near gone; but in the morning he swore weakly and went forth again. He was like a drunken man, and I looked many times for him to give up, but his was the strength of the strong, and his soul the soul of a giant, for he lifted his body through all the weary day. And he shot two ptarmigan, but would not eat them. He needed no fire; they meant life; but his thought was for Unga, and he turned toward camp. He no longer walked, but crawled on hand and knee through the snow. I came to him, and read death in his eyes. Even then it was not too late to eat of the ptarmigan. He cast away his rifle and carried the birds in his mouth like a dog. I walked by his side, upright. And he looked at me during the moments he rested, and wondered that I was so strong. I could see it, though he no longer spoke; and when his lips moved, they moved without sound. As I say, he was a great man, and my heart spoke for softness; but I read back in my life, and remembered the cold and hunger of the endless forest by the Russian seas. Besides, Unga was mine, and I had paid for her an untold price of skin and boat and bead.

"And in this manner we came through the white forest, with the silence heavy upon us like a damp sea mist. And the ghosts of the past were in the air and all about us; and I saw the yellow beach of Akatan, and the kayaks racing home from the fishing, and the houses on the rim of the forest. And the men who had made themselves chiefs were there, the lawgivers whose blood I bore and whose blood I had wedded in Unga. Aye, and Yash-Noosh walked with me, the wet sand in his hair, and his war spear, broken as he fell upon it, still in his hand. And I knew the time was meet, and saw in the eyes of Unga the promise.

"As I say, we came thus through the forest, till the smell of the camp smoke was in our nostrils. And I bent above him, and tore the ptarmigan from his teeth. He turned on his side and rested, the wonder mounting in his eyes, and the hand which was under slipping slow toward the knife at his hip. But I took it from him, smiling close in his face. Even then he did not understand. So I made to drink from black bottles, and to build high upon the snow a pile—of goods, and to live again the things which had happened on the night of my marriage. I spoke no word, but he understood. Yet was he unafraid. There was a sneer to his lips, and cold anger, and he gathered new strength with the knowledge. It was not far, but the snow was deep, and he dragged himself very slow.

Once he lay so long I turned him over and gazed into his eyes. And sometimes he looked forth, and sometimes death. And when I loosed him he struggled on again. In this way we came to the fire. Unga was at his side on the instant. His lips moved without sound; then he pointed at me, that Unga might understand. And after that he lay in the snow, very still, for a long while. Even now is he there in the snow.

"I said no word till I had cooked the ptarmigan. Then I spoke to her, in her own tongue, which she had not heard in many years. She straightened herself so, and her eyes were wonder-wide, and she asked who I was, and where I had learned that speech.

"'I am Naass,' I said.

"'You?' she said. 'You?' And she crept close that she might look upon me.

"'Yes,' I answered; 'I am Naass, head man of Akatan, the last of the blood, as you are the last of the blood.'

"And she laughed. By all the things I have seen and the deeds I have done may I never hear such a laugh again. It put the chill to my soul, sitting there in the White Silence, alone with death and this woman who laughed.

"'Come!' I said, for I thought she wandered. 'Eat of the food and let us be gone. It is a far fetch from here to Akatan.'

"But she shoved her face in his yellow mane, and laughed till it seemed the heavens must fall about our ears. I had thought she would be overjoyed at the sight of me, and eager to go back to the memory of old times, but this seemed a strange form to take.

"'Come!' I cried, taking her strong by the hand. 'The way is long and dark. Let us hurry!'

"'Where?' she asked, sitting up, and ceasing from her strange mirth.

"'To Akatan,' I answered, intent on the light to grow on her face at the thought. But it became like his, with a sneer to the lips, and cold anger.

"'Yes,' she said; 'we will go, hand in hand, to Akatan, you and I. And we will live in the dirty huts, and eat of the fish and oil, and bring forth a spawn— a spawn to be proud of all the days of our life. We will forget the world and be happy, very happy. It is good, most good. Come! Let us hurry. Let us go back to Akatan.'

"And she ran her hand through his yellow hair, and smiled in a way which was not good. And there was no promise in her eyes.

"I sat silent, and marveled at the strangeness of woman. I went back to the night when he dragged her from me and she screamed and tore at his hair— at his hair which now she played with and would not leave. Then I remembered the price and the long years of waiting; and I gripped her close, and dragged her away as he had done. And she held back, even as on that night, and fought like a she-cat for its whelp. And when the fire was between us and the man, I loosed her, and she sat and listened. And I told her of all that lay between, of all that had happened to me on strange seas, of all that I had done in strange lands; of my weary quest, and the hungry years, and the promise which had been mine from the first. Aye, I told all, even to what had passed that day between the man and me, and in the days yet young. And as I spoke I saw the promise grow in her eyes, full and large like the break of dawn. And I read pity there, the tenderness of woman, the love, the heart and the soul of Unga. And I was a stripling again, for the look was the look of Unga as she ran up the beach, laughing, to the home of her mother. The stern unrest was gone, and the hunger, and the weary waiting. The time was met. I felt the call of her breast, and it seemed there I must pillow my head and forget. She opened her arms to me, and I came against her. Then, sudden, the hate flamed in her eye, her hand was at my hip. And once, twice, she passed the knife.

"'Dog!' she sneered, as she flung me into the snow. 'Swine!' And then she laughed till the silence cracked, and went back to her dead.

"As I say, once she passed the knife, and twice; but she was weak with hunger, and it was not meant that I should die. Yet was I minded to stay in that place, and to close my eyes in the last long sleep with those whose lives had crossed with mine and led my feet on unknown trails. But there lay a debt upon me which would not let me rest.

"And the way was long, the cold bitter, and there was little grub. The Pellys had found no moose, and had robbed my cache. And so had the three white men, but they lay thin and dead in their cabins as I passed. After that I do not remember, till I came here, and found food and fire—much fire."

As he finished, he crouched closely, even jealously, over the stove. For a long while the slush-lamp shadows played tragedies upon the wall.

"But Unga!" cried Prince, the vision still strong upon him.

"Unga? She would not eat of the ptarmigan. She lay with her arms about his neck, her face deep in his yellow hair. I drew the fire close, that she might not feel the frost, but she crept to the other side. And I built a fire there; yet it was little good, for she would not eat. And in this manner they still lie up there in the snow."

"And you?" asked Malemute Kid.

"I do not know; but Akatan is small, and I have little wish to go back and live on the edge of the world. Yet is there small use in life. I can go to Constantine, and he will put irons upon me, and one day they will tie a piece of rope, so, and I will sleep good. Yet—no; I do not know."

"But, Kid," protested Prince, "this is murder!"

"Hush!" commanded Malemute Kid. "There be things greater than our wisdom, beyond our justice. The right and the wrong of this we cannot say, and it is not for us to judge."

Naass drew yet closer to the fire. There was a great silence, and in each man's eyes many pictures came and went.

THE HEATHEN

I met him first in a hurricane. And though we had been through the hurricane on the same schooner, it was not until the schooner had gone to pieces under us that I first laid eyes on him. Without doubt I had seen him with the rest of the Kanaka crew on board, but I had not consciously been aware of his existence, for the *Petite Jeanne* was rather overcrowded. In addition to her eight or ten Kanaka sea men, her white captain, mate, and supercargo, and her six cabin passengers, she sailed from Rangiroa with something like eighty-five deck passengers—Paumotuans and Tahitians, men, women, and children, each with a trade box, to say nothing of sleeping mats, blankets, and clothes bundles.

The pearling season in the Paumotus was over, and all hands were returning to Tahiti. The six of us cabin passengers were pearl buyers. Two were Americans, one was Ah Choon, the whitest Chinese I have ever known, one was a German, one was a Polish Jew, and I completed the half dozen.

It had been a prosperous season. Not one of us had cause for complaint, nor one of the eighty-five deck passengers either. All had done well, and all were looking forward to a rest-off and a good time in Papeete.

Of course the *Petite Jeanne* was overloaded. She was

only seventy tons, and she had no right to carry a tithe of the mob she had on board. Beneath her hatches she was crammed and jammed with pearl shell and copra. Even the trade room was packed full of shell. It was a miracle that the sailors could work her. There was no moving about the decks. They simply climbed back and forth along the rails.

In the nighttime they walked upon the sleepers, who carpeted the deck, two deep, I'll swear. Oh, and there were pigs and chickens on deck, and sacks of yams, while every conceivable place was festooned with strings of drinking coconuts and bunches of bananas. On both sides, between the fore and main shrouds, guys had been stretched, just low enough for the foreboom to swing clear; and from each of these guys at least fifty bunches of bananas were suspended.

It promised to be a messy passage, even if we did make it in the two or three days that would have been required if the southeast trades had been blowing fresh. But they weren't blowing fresh. After the first five hours, the trade died away in a dozen gasping fans. The calm continued all that night and the next day—one of those glaring, glossy calms when the very thought of opening one's eyes to look at it is sufficient to cause a headache.

The second day a man died—an Easter Islander, one of the best divers that season in the lagoon. Smallpox, that is what it was; though how smallpox could come on board when there had been no known cases ashore when we left Rangiroa is beyond me.

There it was, though—smallpox, a man dead, and three others down on their backs.

There was nothing to be done. We could not segregate the sick, nor could we care for them. We were packed like sardines. There was nothing to do but die—that is, there was nothing to do after the night that followed the first death. On that night, the mate, the supercargo, the Polish Jew, and four native divers sneaked away in the large whaleboat. They were never heard of again. In the morning the captain promptly scuttled the remaining boats, and there we were.

That day there were two deaths; the following day three; then it jumped to eight. It was curious to see how we took it. The natives, for instance, fell into a condition of dumb, stolid fear. The captain— Oudouse, his name was, a Frenchman—became very nervous and voluble.

The German, the two Americans, and myself bought up all the Scotch whisky and proceeded to drink. The theory was beautiful—namely, if we kept ourselves soaked in alcohol, every smallpox germ that came into contact with us would immediately be scorched to a cinder. And the theory worked, though I must confess that neither Captain Oudouse nor Ah Choon was attacked by the disease either. The Frenchman did not drink at all, while Ah Choon restricted himself to one drink daily.

It was a pretty time. The sun, going into northern declination, was straight overhead. There was no wind, except for frequent squalls, which blew fiercely for from five minutes to half an hour, and wound up by deluging us with rain. After each squall the awful sun would come out, drawing clouds of steam from the soaked decks.

The steam was not nice. It was the vapor of death, freighted with millions and millions of germs. We always took another drink when we saw it going up from the dead and dying, and usually we took two or three more drinks, mixing them exceptionally stiff. Also we made it a rule to take an additional several each time they hove the dead over to the sharks that swarmed about us.

We had a week of it, and then the whisky gave out. It was just as well, or I shouldn't be alive now. It took a sober man to pull through what followed, as you will agree when I mention the little fact that only two men did pull through. The other man was the Heathen—at least that was what I heard Captain Oudouse call him at the moment I first became aware of the Heathen's existence. But to come back.

It was at the end of the week that I happened to glance at the barometer that hung in the cabin companion-way. Its normal register in the Paumotus was 29.90, and it was quite customary to see it vacillate between 29.85 and 30.00, or even 30.05; but to see it, as I saw it, down to 29.62, was sufficient to chill the blood of any pearl buyer in Oceania.

I called Captain Oudouse's attention to it, only to be informed that he had watched it going down for several hours. There was little to do, but that little he did very well, considering the circumstances. He took off the light sails, shortened right down to storm canvas, spread life lines, and waited for the wind. His mistake lay in what he did after the wind came. He hove to on the port tack, which was the right thing to do south of the Equator, if—and there was the rub—*if* one were *not* in the direct path of the hurricane.

We were in the direct path. I could see that by the steady increase of the wind and the equally steady fall of the barometer. I wanted him to turn and run with the wind on the port quarter until the barometer ceased falling, and then to heave to. We argued till he was reduced to hysteria, but budge he would not. The worst of it was that I could not get the rest of the pearl-buyers to back me up. Who was I, anyway, to know more about the sea and its ways than a properly qualified captain?

Of course, the sea rose with the wind, frightfully, and I shall never forget the first three seas the *Petite Jeanne* shipped. She had fallen off, as vessels do when hove to, and the first sea made a clean breach. The lifelines were only for the strong and well, and little good were they even for them when the women and children, the bananas and coconuts, the pigs and trade boxes, the sick and the dying, were swept along in a solid, screeching, groaning mass.

The second sea filled the *Petite Jeanne's* decks flush with the rails; and as her stern sank down and her bow tossed skyward, all the miserable dunnage of life and luggage poured aft. It was a human torrent. They came head first, feet first, sidewise, rolling over and over, twisting, squirming, writhing, and crumpling up. Now and again one or another caught a grip on a stanchion or a rope, but the weight of the bodies behind tore such grips loose.

One man I noticed fetch up, head on and square on, with the starboard bitt. His head cracked like an egg. I saw what was coming, sprang on top the cabin, and from there into the mainsail itself. Ah Choon and one of the Americans tried to follow me, but I was one jump ahead of them. The American was swept away and over the stern like a piece of chaff. Ah Choon caught a spoke of the wheel and swung in behind it. But a strapping Rarotonga *wahine* (woman)—she must have weighed two hundred and fifty—brought up against him and got an arm around his neck. He clutched the Kanaka steersman with his other hand. And just at that moment the schooner flung down to starboard.

The rush of bodies and sea that was coming along the port runway between the cabin and the rail turned abruptly and poured to starboard. Away they went—*wahine*, Ah Choon, and steersman; and I swear I saw Ah Choon grin at me with philosophic resignation as he cleared the rail and went under.

The third sea—the biggest of the three—did not do so much damage. By the time it arrived, nearly everybody was in the rigging. On deck perhaps a dozen gasping, half-drowned, and half-stunned wretches were rolling about or attempting to crawl into safety. They went by the board, as did the wreckage of the two remaining boats. The other pearl buyers and myself, between seas, managed to get about fifteen women and children into the cabin and battened down. Little good it did the poor creatures in the end.

Wind? Out of all my experiences I could not have believed it possible for the wind to blow as it did. There is no describing it. How can one describe a nightmare? It was the same way with that wind. It tore the clothes off our bodies. I say *tore them off,* and I mean it. I am not asking you to believe it. I am merely telling something that I saw and felt. There are times when I do not believe it myself. I went through it, and that is enough. One could not face that wind and live. It was a monstrous thing, and the most monstrous thing about it was that it increased and continued to increase.

Imagine countless millions and billions of tons of sand. Imagine this sand tearing along at ninety, a hundred, a hundred and twenty, or any other number of miles per hour. Imagine, further, this sand to be invisible, impalpable, yet to retain all the weight and density of sand. Do all this, and you may get a vague inkling of what that wind was like.

Perhaps sand is not the right comparison. Consider it mud, invisible, impalpable, but heavy as mud. Nay, it goes beyond that. Consider every molecule of air to be a mudbank in itself. Then try to

imagine the multitudinous impact of mudbanks—
no, it is beyond me. Language may be adequate to express the ordinary conditions of life, but it cannot possibly express any of the conditions of so enormous a blast of wind. It would have been better had I stuck by my original intention of not attempting a description.

I will say this much: The sea, which had risen at first, was beaten down by that wind. More, it seemed as if the whole ocean had been sucked up in the maw of the hurricane and hurled on through that portion of space which previously had been occupied by the air. Of course, our canvas had gone long before. But Captain Oudouse had on the *Petite Jeanne* something I had never before seen on a South Sea schooner————a sea anchor. It was a conical canvas bag, the mouth of which was kept open by a huge hoop of iron. The sea anchor was bridled something like a kite, so that it bit into the water as a kite bites into the air, but with a difference. The sea anchor remained just under the surface of the ocean, in a perpendicular position. A long line, in turn, connected it with the schooner. As a result, the *Petite Jeanne* rode bow on to the wind and to what little sea there was.

The situation really would have been favorable, had we not been in the path of the storm. True, the wind itself tore our canvas out of the gaskets, jerked out our topmasts, and made a raffle of our running gear, but still we would have come through nicely had we not been square in front of the advancing storm center. That was what fixed us. I was in a state of stunned, numbed, paralyzed collapse from enduring the impact of the wind, and I think I was just about ready to give up and die when the center smote us. The blow we received was an absolute lull. There was not a breath of air. The effect on one was sickening.

Remember that for hours we had been at terrific muscular tension, withstanding the awful pressure of that wind. And then, suddenly, the pressure was removed. I know that I felt as though I were about to expand, to fly apart in all directions. It seemed as if every atom composing my body was repelling every other atom, and was on the verge of rushing off irresistibly into space. But that lasted only for a moment. Destruction was upon us.

In the absence of the wind and its pressure, the sea rose. It jumped, it leaped, it soared straight toward the clouds. Remember, from every point of the compass that inconceivable wind was blowing in toward the center of calm. The result was that the seas sprang up from every point of the compass. There was no wind to check them. They popped up like corks released from the bottom of a pail of water. There was no system to them, no stability. They were hollow, maniacal seas. They were eighty feet high at the least. They were not seas at all. They resembled no sea a man had ever seen.

They were splashes, monstrous splashes, that is all, splashes that were eighty feet high. Eighty! They

were more than eighty. They went over our mast-
heads. They were spouts, explosions. They were
drunken. They fell anywhere, anyhow. They jostled
one another, they collided. They rushed together and
collapsed upon one another, or fell apart like a thousand waterfalls all at once. It was no ocean any man
ever dreamed of, that hurricane-center. It was confusion thrice confounded. It was anarchy. It was a hell-
pit of sea water gone mad.

The *Petite Jeanne*? I don't know. The Heathen told
me afterward that he did not know. She was literally
torn apart, ripped wide open, beaten into a pulp,
smashed into kindling wood, annihilated. When I
came to, I was in the water, swimming automatically,
though I was about two-thirds drowned. How I got
there I had no recollection. I remembered seeing the
Petite Jeanne fly to pieces at what must have been the
instant that my own consciousness was buffeted out
of me. But there I was, with nothing to do but make
the best of it, and in that best there was little
promise. The wind was blowing again, the sea was
much smaller and more regular, and I knew that I
had passed through the center. Fortunately, there
were no sharks about. The hurricane had dissipated
the ravenous horde that had surrounded the death
ship and fed off the dead.

It was about midday when the *Petite Jeanne* went to
pieces, and it must have been two hours afterward
when I picked up with one of her hatch covers. Thick
rain was driving at the time, and it was the merest

chance that flung me and the hatch cover together. A short length of line was trailing from the rope handle, and I knew that I was good for a day at least, if the sharks did not return. Three hours later, possibly a little longer, sticking close to the cover and, with closed eyes, concentrating my whole soul upon the task of breathing in enough air to keep me going and, at the same time, to avoid breathing in enough water to drown me, it seemed to me that I heard voices. The rain had ceased, and wind and sea were easing marvelously. Not twenty feet away from me, on another hatch cover, were Captain Oudouse and the Heathen. They were fighting over the possession of the cover— at least the Frenchman was.

"Paien noir!" I heard him scream, and at the same time I saw him kick the Kanaka.

Now, Captain Oudouse had lost all his clothes except his shoes, and they were heavy brogans. It was a cruel blow, for it caught the Heathen on the mouth and the point of the chin, half stunning him. I looked for him to retaliate, but he contented himself with swimming about forlornly, a safe ten feet away. Whenever a fling of the sea threw him closer, the Frenchman, hanging on with his hands, kicked out at him with both feet. Also, at the moment of delivering each kick, he called the Kanaka a black heathen.

"For two centimes I'd come over there and drown you, you white beast!" I yelled.

The only reason I did not go was that I felt too tired. The very thought of the effort to swim over was nauseating. So I called to the Kanaka to come to me, and proceeded to share the hatch cover with him. Otoo, he told me his name was (pronounced ō-tō-ō); also he told me that he was a native of Bora Bora, the most westerly of the Society Group. As I learned afterward, he had got the hatch-cover first, and, after some time, encountering Captain Oudouse, had offered to share it with him, and had been kicked off for his pains.

And that was how Otoo and I first came together. He was no fighter. He was all sweetness and gentleness, a love creature though he stood nearly six feet tall and was muscled like a gladiator. He was no fighter, but he was also no coward. He had the heart of a lion, and in the years that followed I have seen him run risks that I would never dream of taking. What I mean is that, while he was no fighter, and while he always avoided precipitating a row, he never ran away from trouble when it started. And it was "'Ware shoal!" when once Otoo went into action. I shall never forget what he did to Bill King. It occurred in German Samoa. Bill King was hailed the champion heavyweight of the American navy. He was a big brute of a man, a veritable gorilla, one of those hard-hitting, rough-housing chaps, and clever with his fists as well. He picked the quarrel, and he kicked Otoo twice and struck him once before Otoo felt it to be necessary to fight. I don't think it lasted four minutes, at the end of which time Bill King was the unhappy possessor of four broken ribs, a broken forearm, and a dislocated shoulder blade. Otoo knew nothing of scientific boxing. He was merely a manhandler, and Bill King was something like three months in recovering from the bit of manhandling he received that afternoon on Apia beach.

But I am running ahead of my yarn. We shared the hatch cover between us. We took turn and turn about, one lying flat on the cover and resting, while the other, submerged to the neck, merely held on with his hands. For three days and nights, spell and spell, on the cover and in the water, we drifted over the ocean. Toward the last I was delirious most of the time, and there were times, too, when I heard Otoo babbling and raving in his native tongue. Our continuous immersion prevented us from dying of thirst, though the sea water and the sunshine gave us the prettiest imaginable combination of salt pickle and sunburn.

In the end, Otoo saved my life; for I came to, lying on the beach twenty feet from the water, sheltered from the sun by a couple of coconut leaves. No one but Otoo could have dragged me there and stuck up the leaves for shade. He was lying beside me. I went off again, and the next time I came around it was cool and starry night and Otoo was pressing a drinking coconut to my lips.

We were the sole survivors of the *Petite Jeanne*. Captain Oudouse must have succumbed to exhaustion, for several days later his hatch cover drifted ashore without him. Otoo and I lived with the natives of the atoll for a week, when we were rescued by a French cruiser and taken to Tahiti. In the meantime, however, we had performed the ceremony of exchanging names. In the South Seas such a ceremony binds two men closer together than blood brothership. The initiative had been mine, and Otoo was rapturously delighted when I suggested it.

"It is well," he said, in Tahitian. "For we have been mates together for three days on the lips of Death."

"But Death stuttered," I smiled.

"It was a brave deed you did, master," he replied, "and Death was not vile enough to speak."

"Why do you 'master' me?" I demanded, with a show of hurt feelings. "We have exchanged names. To you I am Otoo. To me you are Charley. And between you and me, forever and forever, you shall be Charley and I shall be Otoo. It is the way of the custom. And when we die, if it does happen that we live again, somewhere beyond the stars and the sky, still shall you be Charley to me and I Otoo to you."

"Yes, master," he answered, his eyes luminous and soft with joy.

"There you go!" I cried indignantly.

"What does it matter what my lips utter?" he argued. "They are only my lips. But I shall think Otoo always. Whenever I think of myself I shall think of you. Whenever men call me by name I shall think of you. And beyond the sky and beyond the stars always and forever you shall be Otoo to me. Is it well, master?"

I hid my smile and answered that it was well.

We parted at Papeete. I remained ashore to recuperate, and he went on in a cutter to his own island, Bora Bora. Six weeks later he was back. I was surprised, for he had told me of his wife and said that he was returning to her and would give over sailing on far voyages.

"Where do you go, master?" he asked, after our first greetings.

I shrugged my shoulders. It was a hard question.

"All the world," was my answer, "all the world, all the sea, and all the islands that are in the sea."

"I will go with you," he said simply. "My wife is dead."

I never had a brother, but from what I have seen of other men's brothers, I doubt if any man ever had one who was to him what Otoo was to me. He was brother and father and mother as well. And this I know: I lived a straighter and a better man because of Otoo. I had to live straight in Otoo's eyes. Because of him I dared not tarnish myself. He made me his ideal, compounding me, I fear, chiefly out of his own love and worship; and there were times when I stood close to the steep pitch of hell and would have taken the plunge had not the thought of Otoo restrained me. His pride in me entered into me until it became one of the major rules in my personal code to do nothing that would diminish that pride of his.

Naturally, I did not learn right away what his feelings were toward me. He never criticized, never censured, and slowly the exalted place I held in his eyes dawned upon me, and slowly I grew to comprehend the hurt I could inflict upon him by being anything less than my best.

For seventeen years we were together. For seventeen years he was at my shoulder, watching while I slept, nursing me through fever and wounds—aye, and receiving wounds in fighting for me. He signed on the same ships with me, and together we ranged the Pacific from Hawaii to Sydney Head and from Torres Strait to the Galápagos. We blackbirded from the New Hebrides and the Line Islands over to the westward, clear through the Louisiades, New Britain, New Ireland, and New Hanover. We were wrecked three times—in the Gilberts, in the Santa Cruz group, and in the Fijis. And we traded and salved wherever a dollar promised in the way of pearl and pearl shell, copra, bêche-de-mer, hawkbill turtle shell, and stranded wrecks.

It began in Papeete, immediately after his announcement that he was going with me over all the sea and the islands in the midst thereof. There was a club in those days in Papeete, where the pearlers, traders, captains, and South Sea adventurers foregathered. The play ran high and the drink ran high, and I am very much afraid that I kept later hours than were becoming or proper. No matter what the hour was when I left the club, there was Otoo waiting to see me safely home.

At first I smiled; next I chided him. Then I told

him flatly I stood in need of no wet-nursing. After that I did not see him when I came out of the club. Quite by accident, a week or so later, I discovered that he still saw me home, lurking across the street among the shadows of the mango trees. What could I do? I know what I did do.

Insensibly I began to keep better hours. On wet and stormy nights, in the thick of the folly and the fun, the thought would persist in coming to me of Otoo keeping his dreary vigil under the dripping mangoes. Truly, he made a better man of me. Yet he was not strait-laced. And he knew nothing of common Christian morality. All the people on Bora Bora were Christians. But he was a heathen, the only unbeliever on the island, a gross materialist who believed that when he died he was dead. He believed merely in fair play and square dealing. Petty meanness, in his code, was almost as serious as wanton homicide, and I am sure that he respected a murderer more than a man given to small practices.

Concerning me, personally, he objected to my doing anything that was hurtful to me. Gambling was all right. He was an ardent gambler himself. But late hours, he explained, were bad for one's health. He had seen men who did not take care of themselves die of fever. He was no teetotaler, and welcomed a stiff nip any time when it was wet work in the boats. On the other hand, he believed in liquor in moderation. He had seen many men killed or disgraced by squareface or Scotch.

Otoo had my welfare always at heart. He thought ahead for me, weighed my plans and took a greater interest in them than I did myself. At first, when I was unaware of this interest of his in my affairs, he had to divine my intentions, as, for instance, at Papeete, when I contemplated going partners with a knavish fellow countryman on a guano venture. I did not know he was a knave. Nor did any white man in Papeete. Neither did Otoo know; but he saw how thick we were getting and found out for me, and that without my asking. Native sailors from the ends of the seas knock about on the beach in Tahiti, and Otoo, suspicious merely, went among them till he had gathered sufficient data to justify his suspicions. Oh, it was a nice history, that of Randolph Waters! I couldn't believe it when Otoo first narrated it, but when I sheeted it home to Waters he gave in without a murmur and got away on the first steamer to Auckland.

At first, I am free to confess, I resented Otoo's poking his nose into my business. But I knew that he was wholly unselfish, and soon I had to acknowledge his wisdom and discretion. He had his eyes open always to my main chance, and he was both keen-sighted and farsighted. In time he became my counselor, until he knew more of my business than I did myself. He really had my interest at heart more than I did. Mine was the magnificent carelessness of youth, for I preferred romance to dollars, and adventure to a comfortable billet with all night in. So it was well that I had someone to look out for me. I know that if it had not been for Otoo, I should not be here today.

Of numerous instances, let me give one. I had had some experience in blackbirding before I went pearling in the Paumotus. Otoo and I were on the beach in Samoa—we really were on the beach and hard aground—when my chance came to go as a recruiter on a blackbird brig. Otoo signed on before the mast, and for the next half-dozen years, in as many ships, we knocked about the wildest portions of Melanesia. Otoo saw to it that he always pulled stroke oar in my boat. Our custom, in recruiting labor, was to land the recruiter on the beach. The covering boat always lay on its oars several hundred feet off shore, while the recruiter's boat, also lying on its oars, kept afloat on the edge of the beach. When I landed with my trade goods, leaving my steering sweep apeak, Otoo left his stroke position and came into the stern sheets, where a Winchester lay ready to hand under a flap of canvas. The boat's crew was also armed, the Sniders concealed under canvas flaps that ran the length of the gunwales. While I was busy arguing and persuading the woolly-headed cannibals to come and labor on the Queensland plantations Otoo kept watch. And often and often his low voice warned me of suspicious actions and impending treachery. Sometimes it was the quick shot from his rifle, knocking a nigger over, that was the first warning I received. And in my rush to the boat his hand was always there to jerk me flying aboard. Once, I remember, on *Santa Anna,* the boat grounded just as the trouble began. The covering boat was dashing to our assistance, but the several score of savages would have wiped us out before it arrived. Otoo took a flying leap ashore, dug both hands into the trade goods, and scattered tobacco, beads, tomahawks, knives, and calicoes in all directions.

This was too much for the woolly-heads. While they scrambled for the treasures, the boat was shoved clear and we were aboard and forty feet away. And I got thirty recruits off that very beach in the next four hours.

The particular instance I have in mind was on Malaita, the most savage island in the easterly Solomons. The natives had been remarkably friendly; and how were we to know that the whole village had been taking up a collection for over two years with which to buy a white man's head? The beggars are all head-hunters, and they especially esteem that of a white man. The fellow who captured the head would receive the whole collection. As I say, they appeared very friendly, and this day I was fully a hundred yards down the beach from the boat. Otoo had cautioned me, and, as usual when I did not heed him, I came to grief.

The first thing I knew, a cloud of spears sailed out of the mangrove swamp at me. At least a dozen were sticking into me. I started to run, but tripped over one that was fast in my calf and went down. The woolly-heads made a run for me, each with a long-handled, fantail tomahawk with which to hack off my head. They were so eager for the prize that they got in one another's way. In the confusion I avoided several hacks by throwing myself right and left on the sand.

Then Otoo arrived—Otoo the manhandler. In some way he had got hold of a heavy war club, and at close quarters it was a far more efficient weapon than a rifle. He was right in the thick of them, so that they could not spear him, while their tomahawks seemed worse than useless. He was fighting for me, and he was in a true Berserker rage. The way he handled that club was amazing. Their skulls squashed like overripe oranges. It was not until he had driven them back, picked me up in his arms, and started to run, that he received his first wounds. He arrived in the boat with four spear thrusts, got his Winchester, and with it got a man for every shot. Then we pulled aboard the schooner and doctored up.

Seventeen years we were together. He made me. I should today be a supercargo, a recruiter, or a memory, if it had not been for him.

"You spend your money, and you go out and get more," he said one day. "It is easy to get money, now. But when you get old, your money will be spent and you will not be able to go out and get more. I know, master. I have studied the way of white men. On the beaches are many old men who were young once and who could get money just like you. Now they are old, and they have nothing, and they wait about for the young men like you to come ashore and buy drinks for them.

"The black boy is a slave on the plantations. He gets twenty dollars a year. He works hard. The overseer does not work hard. He rides a horse and watches the black boy work. He gets twelve hundred dollars a year. I am a sailor on the schooner. I get fifteen dollars a month. That is because I am a good sailor. I work hard. The captain has a double awning and drinks beer out of long bottles. I have never seen him haul a rope or pull an oar. He gets one hundred and fifty dollars a month. I am a sailor. He is a navigator. Master, I think it would be very good for you to know navigation."

Otoo spurred me on to it. He sailed with me as second mate on my first schooner, and he was far prouder of my command than was I myself. Later on it was:

"The captain is well paid, master, but the ship is in his keeping and he is never free from the burden. It is the owner who is better paid—and the owner who sits ashore with many servants and turns his money over."

"True, but a schooner costs five thousand dollars— an old schooner at that," I objected. "I should be an old man before I saved five thousand dollars."

"There be short ways for white men to make money," he went on, pointing ashore at the coconut-fringed beach.

We were in the Solomons at the time, picking up

a cargo of ivory-nuts along the east coast of Guadal-canar.

"Between this river mouth and the next it is two miles," he said. "The flat land runs far back. It is worth nothing now. Next year—who knows!—or the year after—men will pay much money for that land. The anchorage is good. Big steamers can lie close up. You can buy the land four miles deep from the old chief for ten thousand sticks of tobacco, ten bottles of squareface, and a Snider, which will cost you maybe one hundred dollars. Then you place the deed with the commissioner, and the next year, or the year after, you sell and become the owner of a ship."

I followed his lead, and his words came true, though in three years instead of two. Next came the grasslands deal on Guadalcanar—twenty thousand acres on a governmental nine hundred and ninety-nine years' lease at a nominal sum. I owned the lease for precisely ninety days, when I sold it to the Moon-light Soap crowd for half a fortune. Always it was Otoo who looked ahead and saw the opportunity. He was responsible for the salving of the *Doncaster*—bought in at auction for five hundred dollars and clearing fifteen thousand after every expense was paid. He led me into the Savaii plantation and the cocoa venture on Upolu.

We did not go seafaring so much as in the old days now. I was too well off. I married and my standard of living rose; but Otoo remained the same old-time Otoo, moving about the house or trailing through the office, his wooden pipe in his mouth, a shilling under-shirt on his back, and a four-shilling lava-lava about his loins. I could not get him to spend money. There was no way of repaying him except with love, and God knows he got that in full measure from all of us. The children worshiped him, and if he had been spoilable my wife would surely have been his undoing.

The children! He really was the one who showed them the way of their feet in the world practical. He began by teaching them to walk. He sat up with them when they were sick. One by one, when they were scarcely toddlers, he took them down to the lagoon and made them into amphibians. He taught them more than I ever knew of the habits of fish and the ways of catching them. In the bush it was the same thing. At seven, Tom knew more woodcraft than I ever dreamed existed. At six, Mary went over the Sliding Rock without a quiver, and I have seen strong men balk at that feat. And when Frank had just turned six he could bring up shillings from the bottom in three fathoms.

"My people in Bora Bora do not like heathen—they are all Christians; and I do not like Bora Bora Christians," he said one day, when I, with the idea of getting him to spend some of the money that was rightfully his, had been trying to persuade him to make a visit to his own island in one of our schooners—a special voyage that I had hoped to make a record breaker in the matter of prodigal expense.

I say one of *our* schooners, though legally, at the

time, they belonged to me. I struggled long with him to enter into partnership.

"We have been partners from the day the *Petite Jeanne* went down," he said at last. "But if your heart so wishes, then shall we become partners by the law. I have no work to do, yet are my expenses large. I drink and eat and smoke in plenty—it costs much, I know. I do not pay for the playing of billiards, for I play on your table; but still the money goes. Fishing on the reef is only a rich man's pleasure. It is shocking, the cost of hooks and cotton line. Yes; it is necessary that we be partners by the law. I need the money. I shall get it from the head clerk in the office."

So the papers were made out and recorded. A year later I was compelled to complain.

"Charley," said I, "you are a wicked old fraud, a miserly skinflint, a miserable land crab. Behold, your share for the year in all our partnership has been thousands of dollars. The head clerk has given me this paper. It says that during the year you have drawn just eighty-seven dollars and twenty cents."

"Is there any owing me?" he asked anxiously.

"I tell you thousands and thousands," I answered.

His face brightened as with an immense relief.

"It is well," he said. "See that the head clerk keeps good account of it. When I want it, I shall want it, and there must not be a cent missing."

"If there is," he added fiercely, after a pause, "it must come out of the clerk's wages."

And all the time, as I afterward learned, his will,

drawn up by Carruthers and making me sole benefi-
ciary, lay in the American consul's safe.

But the end came as the end must come to all
human associations. It occurred in the Solomons,
where our wildest work had been done in the wild
young days, and where we were once more—principally on a holiday, incidentally to look after our hold-
ings on Florida Island and to look over the pearling
possibilities of the Mboli Pass. We were lying at Savo,
having run in to trade for curios.

Now Savo is alive with sharks. The custom of the
woolly-heads of burying their dead in the sea did not
tend to discourage the sharks from making the adja-
cent waters a hang-out. It was my luck to be coming
aboard in a tiny, overloaded, native canoe, when the
thing capsized. There were four woolly-heads and myself in it, or rather, hanging to it. The schooner was a
hundred yards away. I was just hailing for a boat when
one of the woolly-heads began to scream. Holding on
to the end of the canoe, both he and that portion of the
canoe were dragged under several times. Then he
loosed his clutch and disappeared. A shark had got
him.

The three remaining woolly-heads tried to climb
out of the water upon the bottom of the canoe. I
yelled and cursed and struck at the nearest with my
fist, but it was no use. They were in a blind funk. The
canoe could barely have supported one of them.
Under the three it upended and rolled sidewise,
throwing them back into the water.

I abandoned the canoe and started to swim toward the schooner, expecting to be picked up by the boat before I got there. One of the woolly-heads elected to come with me, and we swam along silently, side by side, now and again putting our faces into the water and peering about for sharks. The screams of the men who stayed by the canoe informed us that they were taken. I was peering into the water when I saw a big shark pass directly beneath me. He was fully sixteen feet in length. I saw the whole thing. He got the woolly-head by the middle and away he went, the poor devil, head, shoulders, and arms out of water all the time, screeching in a heart-rending way. He was carried along in this fashion for several hundred feet, when he was dragged beneath the surface.

I swam doggedly on, hoping that that was the last unattached shark. But there was another. Whether it was one that had attacked the natives earlier, or whether it was one that had made a good meal elsewhere, I do not know. At any rate, he was not in such haste as the others. I could not swim so rapidly now, for a large part of my effort was devoted to keeping track of him. I was watching him when he made his first attack. By good luck I got both hands on his nose, and, though his momentum nearly shoved me under, I managed to keep him off. He veered clear and began circling about again. A second time I escaped him by the same maneuver. The third rush was a miss on both sides. He sheered at the moment my hands should have landed on his nose, but his sandpaper hide (I had on a sleeveless undershirt) scraped the skin off one arm from elbow to shoulder.

By this time I was played out and gave up hope. The schooner was still two hundred feet away. My face was in the water and I was watching him maneuver for another attempt, when I saw a brown body pass between us. It was Otoo.

"Swim for the schooner, master," he said, and he spoke gaily, as though the affair was a mere lark. "I know sharks. The shark is my brother."

I obeyed, swimming slowly on, while Otoo swam about me, keeping always between me and the shark, foiling his rushes and encouraging me.

"The davit tackle carried away, and they are rigging the falls," he explained a minute or so later, and then went under to head off another attack.

By the time the schooner was thirty feet away I was about done for. I could scarcely move. They were heaving lines at us from on board, but these continually fell short. The shark, finding that it was receiving no hurt, had become bolder. Several times it nearly got me, but each time Otoo was there just the moment before it was too late. Of course Otoo could have saved himself any time. But he stuck by me.

"Good-by, Charley, I'm finished," I just managed to gasp.

I knew that the end had come and that the next moment I should throw up my hands and go down.

But Otoo laughed in my face, saying:

"I will show you a new trick. I will make that shark damn sick."

He dropped in behind me, where the shark was preparing to come at me.

"A little more to the left!" he next called out. "There is a line there on the water. To the left, master—to the left."

I changed my course and struck out blindly. I was by that time barely conscious. As my hand closed on the line I heard an exclamation from on board. I turned and looked. There was no sign of Otoo. The next instant he broke surface. Both hands were off at the wrist, the stumps spouting blood.

"Otoo," he called softly, and I could see in his gaze the love that thrilled in his voice. Then, and then only, at the very last of all our years, he called me by that name.

"Good-by, Otoo," he called.

Then he was dragged under, and I was hauled aboard, where I fainted in the captain's arms.

And so passed Otoo, who saved me and made me a man, and who saved me in the end. We met in the maw of a hurricane and parted in the maw of a shark, with seventeen intervening years of comradeship, the like of which I dare to assert have never befallen two men, the one brown and the other white. If Jehovah be from His high place watching every sparrow fall, not least in His Kingdom shall be Otoo, the one heathen of Bora Bora.

LOVE OF LIFE

This out of all will remain—
  They have lived and have tossed:
So much of the game will be gain,
  Though the gold of the dice has been lost.

They limped painfully down the bank, and once the foremost of the two men staggered among the rough-strewn rocks. They were tired and weak, and their faces had the drawn expression of patience which comes of hardship long endured. They were heavily burdened with blanket packs which were strapped to their shoulders. Head straps, passing across the fore-head, helped support these packs. Each man carried a rifle. They walked in a stooped posture, the shoulders well forward, the head still farther forward, the eyes bent upon the ground.

"I wish we had just about two of them cartridges that's layin' in that cache of ourn," said the second man.

His voice was utterly and drearily expressionless. He spoke without enthusiasm; and the first man, limping into the milky stream that foamed over the rocks, vouchsafed no reply.

The other man followed at his heels. They did not remove their foot-gear, though the water was icy cold—so cold that their ankles ached and their feet went numb. In places the water dashed against their knees, and both men staggered for footing.

The man who followed slipped on a smooth boulder, nearly fell, but recovered himself with a violent effort, at the same time uttering a sharp exclamation of pain. He seemed faint and dizzy and put out his free hand while he reeled, as though seeking support against the air. When he had steadied himself he stepped forward, but reeled again and nearly fell. Then he stood still and looked at the other man, who had never turned his head.

The man stood still for fully a minute, as though debating with himself. Then he called out:

"I say, Bill, I've sprained my ankle."

Bill staggered on through the milky water. He did not look around. The man watched him go, and though his face was expressionless as ever, his eyes were like the eyes of a wounded deer.

The other man limped up the farther bank and continued straight on without looking back. The man in the stream watched him. His lips trembled a little, so that the rough thatch of brown hair which covered them was visibly agitated. His tongue even strayed out to moisten them.

"Bill!" he cried out.

It was the pleading cry of a strong man in distress, but Bill's head did not turn. The man watched him go, limping grotesquely and lurching forward with stammering gait up the slow slope toward the soft sky line of the low-lying hill. He watched him go till he passed over the crest and disappeared. Then he turned his gaze and slowly took in the circle of the world that remained to him now that Bill was gone.

Near the horizon the sun was smouldering dimly, almost obscured by formless mists and vapors, which gave an impression of mass and density without outline or tangibility. The man pulled out his watch, the while resting his weight on one leg. It was four o'clock, and as the season was near the last of July or first of August—he did not know the precise date within a week or two—he knew that the sun roughly marked the northwest. He looked to the south and knew that somewhere beyond those bleak hills lay the Great Bear Lake; also, he knew that in that direction the Arctic Circle cut its forbidding way across the Canadian Barrens. This stream in which he stood was a feeder to the Coppermine River, which in turn flowed north and emptied into Coronation Gulf and the Arctic Ocean. He had never been there, but he had seen it, once, on a Hudson Bay Company chart.

Again his gaze completed the circle of the world about him. It was not a heartening spectacle. Everywhere was soft sky line. The hills were all low-lying. There were no trees, no shrubs, no grasses—naught but a tremendous and terrible desolation that sent fear swiftly dawning into his eyes.

"Bill!" he whispered, once and twice; "Bill!"

He cowered in the midst of the milky water, as though the vastness were pressing in upon him with overwhelming force, brutally crushing him with its complacent awfulness. He began to shake as with an ague fit, till the gun fell from his hand with a splash. This served to rouse him. He fought with his fear and pulled himself together, groping in the water and recovering the weapon. He hitched his pack farther over on his left shoulder, so as to take a portion of its weight from off the injured ankle. Then he proceeded, slowly and carefully, wincing with pain, to the bank.

He did not stop. With a desperation that was madness, unmindful of the pain, he hurried up the slope to the crest of the hill over which his comrade had disappeared—more grotesque and comical by far than that limping, jerking comrade. But at the crest he saw a shallow valley, empty of life. He fought with his fear again, overcame it, hitched the pack still farther over on his left shoulder, and lurched on down the slope.

The bottom of the valley was soggy with water, which the thick moss held, spongelike, close to the surface. This water squirted out from under his feet at every step, and each time he lifted a foot the action culminated in a sucking sound as the wet moss reluctantly released its grip. He picked his way from muskeg to muskeg, and followed the other man's footsteps along and across the rocky ledges which thrust like islets through the sea of moss.

Though alone, he was not lost. Farther on he knew he would come to where dead spruce and fir, very small and weazened, bordered the shore of a little lake, the *titchin-nichilie,* in the tongue of the country, the "land of little sticks." And into that lake flowed a small stream, the water of which was not milky. There was rush grass on that stream—this he remembered well—but no timber, and he would follow it till its first trickle ceased at a divide. He would cross this divide to the first trickle of another stream, flowing to the west, which he would follow until it emptied into the river Dease, and here he would find a cache under an upturned canoe and piled over with many rocks. And in this cache would be ammunition for his empty gun, fishhooks and lines, a small net— all the utilities for the killing and snaring of food. Also, he would find flour—not much—a piece of bacon, and some beans.

Bill would be waiting for him there, and they would paddle away south down the Dease to the Great Bear Lake. And south across the lake they would go, ever south, till they gained the Mackenzie. And south, still south, they would go, while the winter raced vainly after them, and the ice formed in the eddies, and the days grew chill and crisp, south to some warm Hudson Bay Company post, where timber grew tall and generous and there was grub without end.

These were the thoughts of the man as he strove onward. But hard as he strove with his body, he strove equally hard with his mind, trying to think that Bill had not deserted him, that Bill would surely wait for him at the cache. He was compelled to think this thought, or else there would not be any use to strive, and he would have lain down and died. And as the dim ball of the sun sank slowly into the northwest he covered every inch—and many times—of his and Bill's flight south before the downcoming winter. And he conned the grub of the cache and the grub of the Hudson Bay Company post over and over again. He had not eaten for two days; for a far longer time he had not had all he wanted to eat. Often he stooped and picked pale muskeg berries, put them into his mouth, and chewed and swallowed them. A muskeg berry is a bit of seed enclosed in a bit of water. In the mouth the water melts away and the seed chews sharp and bitter. The man knew there was no nourishment in the berries, but he chewed them patiently with a hope greater than knowledge and defying experience.

At nine o'clock he stubbed his toe on a rocky ledge, and from sheer weariness and weakness staggered and fell. He lay for some time, without movement, on his side. Then he slipped out of the pack-straps and clumsily dragged himself into a sitting posture. It was not yet dark, and in the lingering twilight he groped about among the rocks for shreds of dry moss. When he had gathered a heap he built a fire—a smouldering, smudgy fire—and put a tin pot of water on to boil.

He unwrapped his pack and the first thing he did was to count his matches. There were sixty-seven. He counted them three times to make sure. He divided them into several portions, wrapping them in oil paper, disposing of one bunch in his empty tobacco pouch, of another bunch in the inside band of his battered hat, of a third bunch under his shirt on the chest. This accomplished, a panic came upon him, and he unwrapped them all and counted them again. There were still sixty-seven.

He dried his wet footgear by the fire. The moccasins were in soggy shreds. The blanket socks were worn through in places, and his feet were raw and bleeding. His ankle was throbbing, and he gave it an examination. It had swollen to the size of his knee. He tore a long strip from one of his two blankets and bound the ankle tightly. He tore other strips and bound them about his feet to serve for both moccasins and socks. Then he drank the pot of water, steaming hot, wound his watch, and crawled between his blankets.

He slept like a dead man. The brief darkness around midnight came and went. The sun arose in the northeast—at least the day dawned in that quarter, for the sun was hidden by gray clouds.

At six o'clock he awoke, quietly lying on his back. He gazed straight up into the gray sky and knew that he was hungry. As he rolled over on his elbow he was startled by a loud snort, and saw a bull caribou regarding him with alert curiosity. The animal was not mere than fifty feet away, and instantly into the man's mind leaped the vision and the savor of a caribou steak sizzling and frying over a fire. Mechanically he reached for the empty gun, drew a bead, and pulled the trigger. The bull snorted and leaped away, his hoofs rattling and clattering as he fled across the ledges.

The man cursed and flung the empty gun from him. He groaned aloud as he started to drag himself to his feet. It was a slow and arduous task. His joints were like rusty hinges. They worked harshly in their sockets, with much friction, and each bending or unbending was accomplished only through a sheer exertion of will. When he finally gained his feet, another minute or so was consumed in straightening up, so that he could stand erect as a man should stand.

He crawled up a small knoll and surveyed the prospect. There were no trees, no bushes, nothing but a gray sea of moss scarcely diversified by gray rocks, gray lakelets, and gray streamlets. The sky was gray. There was no sun nor hint of sun. He had no idea of north, and he had forgotten the way he had come to this spot the night before. But he was not lost. He knew that. Soon he would come to the land of the little sticks. He felt that it lay off to the left somewhere, not far—possibly just over the next low hill.

He went back to put his pack into shape for traveling. He assured himself of the existence of his three separate parcels of matches, though he did not stop to count them. But he did linger, debating, over a squat moose-hide sack. It was not large. He could hide it under his two hands. He knew that it weighed fifteen pounds—as much as all the rest of the pack—and it worried him. He finally set it to one side and pro-

ceeded to roll the pack. He paused to gaze at the
squat moose-hide sack. He picked it up hastily with
a defiant glance about him, as though the desolation
were trying to rob him of it; and when he rose to his
feet to stagger on into the day, it was included in the
pack on his back.

He bore away to the left, stopping now and again
to eat muskeg berries. His ankle had stiffened, his
limp was more pronounced, but the pain of it was as
nothing compared with the pain of his stomach. The
hunger pangs were sharp. They gnawed and gnawed
until he could not keep his mind steady on the course
he must pursue to gain the land of little sticks. The
muskeg berries did not allay this gnawing, while
they made his tongue and the roof of his mouth sore
with their irritating bite.

He came upon a valley where rock ptarmigan rose
on whirring wings from the ledges and muskegs.
"Ker—ker—ker" was the cry they made. He threw
stones at them, but could not hit them. He placed his
pack on the ground and stalked them as a cat stalks a
sparrow. The sharp rocks cut through his pants' legs
till his knees left a trail of blood; but the hurt was lost
in the hurt of his hunger. He squirmed over the wet
moss, saturating his clothes and chilling his body;
but he was not aware of it, so great was his fever for
food. And always the ptarmigan rose, whirring, before him, till their "ker—ker—ker" became a mock
to him, and he cursed them and cried aloud at them
with their own cry.

Once he crawled upon one that must have been asleep. He did not see it till it shot up in his face from its rocky nook. He made a clutch as startled as was the rise of the ptarmigan, and there remained in his hand three tailfeathers. As he watched its flight he hated it, as though it had done him some terrible wrong. Then he returned and shouldered his pack.

As the day wore along he came into valleys or swales where game was more plentiful. A band of caribou passed by, twenty and odd animals, tantalizingly within rifle range. He felt a wild desire to run after them, a certitude that he could run them down. A black fox came toward him, carrying a ptarmigan in his mouth. The man shouted. It was a fearful cry, but the fox, leaping away in fright, did not drop the ptarmigan.

Late in the afternoon he followed a stream, milky with lime, which ran through sparse patches of rush grass. Grasping these rushes firmly near the root, he pulled up what resembled a young onion sprout no larger than a shingle nail. It was tender, and his teeth sank into it with a crunch that promised deliciously of food. But its fibers were tough. It was composed of stringy filaments saturated with water, like the berries, and devoid of nourishment. He threw off his pack and went into the rush grass on hands and knees, crunching and munching, like some bovine creature.

He was very weary and often wished to rest—to lie down and sleep; but he was continually driven on, not so much by his desire to gain the land of little sticks as by his hunger. He searched little ponds for frogs and dug up the earth with his nails for worms, though he knew in spite that neither frogs nor worms existed so far north.

He looked into every pool of water vainly, until, as the long twilight came on, he discovered a solitary fish, the size of a minnow, in such a pool. He plunged his arm in up to the shoulder, but it eluded him. He reached for it with both hands and stirred up the milky mud at the bottom. In his excitement he fell in, wetting himself to the waist. Then the water was too muddy to admit of his seeing the fish, and he was compelled to wait until the sediment had settled.

The pursuit was renewed, till the water was again muddied. But he could not wait. He unstrapped the tin bucket and began to bale the pool. He baled wildly at first, splashing himself and flinging the water so short a distance that it ran back into the pool. He worked more carefully, striving to be cool, though his heart was pounding against his chest and his hands were trembling. At the end of half an hour the pool was nearly dry. Not a cupful of water remained. And there was no fish. He found a hidden crevice among the stones through which it had escaped to the adjoining and larger pool—a pool which he could not empty in a night and a day. Had he known of the crevice, he could have closed it with a rock at the beginning and the fish would have been his.

Thus he thought, and crumpled up and sank down upon the wet earth. At first he cried softly to himself, then he cried loudly to the pitiless desolation that ringed him around; and for a long time after he was shaken by great dry sobs.

He built a fire and warmed himself by drinking quarts of hot water, and made camp on a rocky ledge in the same fashion he had the night before. The last thing he did was to see that his matches were dry and to wind his watch. The blankets were wet and clammy. His ankle pulsed with pain. But he knew only that he was hungry, and through his restless sleep he dreamed of feasts and banquets and of food served and spread in all imaginable ways.

He awoke chilled and sick. There was no sun. The gray of earth and sky had become deeper, more profound. A raw wind was blowing, and the first flurries of snow were whitening the hilltops. The air about him thickened and grew white while he made a fire and boiled more water. It was wet snow, half rain, and the flakes were large and soggy. At first they melted as soon as they came in contact with the earth, but ever more fell, covering the ground, putting out the fire, spoiling his supply of moss fuel.

This was a signal for him to strap on his pack and stumble onward, he knew not where. He was not concerned with the land of little sticks, nor with Bill and the cache under the upturned canoe by the river Dease. He was mastered by the verb "to eat." He was hunger-mad. He took no heed of the course he pursued, so long as that course led him through the swale bottoms. He felt his way through the wet snow to the watery muskeg berries, and went by feel as he pulled up the rush grass by the roots. But it was tasteless stuff and did not satisfy. He found a weed that tasted sour and he ate all he could find of it, which was not much, for it was a creeping growth, easily hidden under the several inches of snow.

He had no fire that night, nor hot water, and crawled under his blanket to sleep the broken hunger sleep. The snow turned into a cold rain. He awakened many times to feel it falling on his upturned face. Day came—a gray day and no sun. It had ceased raining. The keenness of his hunger had departed. Sensibility, as far as concerned the yearning for food, had been exhausted. There was a dull, heavy ache in his stomach, but it did not bother him so much. He was more rational, and once more he was chiefly interested in the land of little sticks and the cache by the river Dease.

He ripped the remnant of one of his blankets into strips and bound his bleeding feet. Also, he recinched the injured ankle and prepared himself for a day of travel. When he came to his pack, he paused long over the squat moose-hide sack, but in the end it went with him.

The snow had melted under the rain, and only the hilltops showed white. The sun came out, and he succeeded in locating the points of the compass, though he knew now that he was lost. Perhaps, in his previous days' wanderings, he had edged away too far to the left. He now bore off to the right to counteract the possible deviation from his true course.

Though the hunger pangs were no longer so exquisite, he realized that he was weak. He was compelled to pause for frequent rests, when he attacked the muskeg berries and rush-grass patches. His tongue felt dry and large, as though covered with a fine hairy growth, and it tasted bitter in his mouth. His heart gave him a great deal of trouble. When he had traveled a few minutes it would begin a remorseless thump, thump, thump, and then leap up and away in a painful flutter of beats that choked him and made him go faint and dizzy.

In the middle of the day he found two minnows in a large pool. It was impossible to bale it, but he was calmer now and managed to catch them in his tin bucket. They were no longer than his little finger, but he was not particularly hungry. The dull ache in his stomach had been growing duller and fainter. It seemed almost that his stomach was dozing. He ate the fish raw, masticating with painstaking care, for the eating was an act of pure reason. While he had no desire to eat, he knew that he must eat to live.

In the evening he caught three more minnows, eating two and saving the third for breakfast. The sun had dried stray shreds of moss, and he was able to warm himself with hot water. He had not covered more than ten miles that day; and the next day, traveling whenever his heart permitted him, he covered no more than five miles. But his stomach did not give him the slightest uneasiness. It had gone to sleep. He was in a strange country, too, and the caribou were growing more plentiful, also the wolves. Often their yelps drifted across the desolation, and once he saw three of them slinking away before his path.

Another night; and in the morning, being more rational, he untied the leather string that fastened the squat moose-hide sack. From its open mouth poured a yellow stream of coarse gold dust and nuggets. He roughly divided the gold in halves, caching one half on a prominent ledge, wrapped in a piece of blanket, and returning the other half to the sack. He also began to use strips of the one remaining blanket for his feet. He still clung to his gun, for there were cartridges in that cache by the river Dease.

This was a day of fog, and this day hunger awoke in him again. He was very weak and was afflicted with a giddiness which at times blinded him. It was no uncommon thing now for him to stumble and fall; and stumbling once, he fell squarely into a ptarmigan nest. There were four newly hatched chicks, a day old—little specks of pulsating life no more than a mouthful; and he ate them ravenously, thrusting them alive into his mouth and crunching them like eggshells between his teeth. The mother ptarmigan beat about him with great outcry. He used his gun as a club with which to knock her over, but she dodged out of reach. He threw stones at her and with one chance shot broke a wing. Then she fluttered away, running, trailing the broken wing, with him in pursuit.

The little chicks had no more than whetted his appetite. He hopped and bobbed clumsily along on his injured ankle, throwing stones and screaming hoarsely at times; at other times hopping and bobbing silently along, picking himself up grimly and patiently when he fell, or rubbing his eyes with his hand when the giddiness threatened to overpower him.

The chase led him across swampy ground in the bottom of the valley, and he came upon footprints in the soggy moss. They were not his own—he could see that. They must be Bill's. But he could not stop, for the mother ptarmigan was running on. He would catch her first, then he would return and investigate.

He exhausted the mother ptarmigan; but he exhausted himself. She lay panting on her side. He lay panting on his side, a dozen feet away, unable to crawl to her. And as he recovered she recovered, fluttering out of reach as his hungry hand went out to her. The chase was resumed. Night settled down and she escaped. He stumbled from weakness and pitched head foremost on his face, cutting his cheek, his pack upon his back. He did not move for a long while; then he rolled over on his side, wound his watch, and lay there until morning.

Another day of fog. Half of his last blanket had gone into foot-wrappings. He failed to pick up Bill's trail. It did not matter. His hunger was driving him too compellingly—only—only he wondered if Bill, too, were lost. By midday the irk of his pack became too oppressive. Again he divided the gold, this time merely spilling half of it on the ground. In the afternoon he threw the rest of it away, there remaining to him only the half blanket, the tin bucket, and the rifle.

An hallucination began to trouble him. He felt confident that one cartridge remained to him. It was in the chamber of the rifle and he had overlooked it. On the other hand, he knew all the time that the chamber was empty. But the hallucination persisted. He fought it off for hours, then threw his rifle open and was confronted with emptiness. The disappointment was as bitter as though he had really expected to find the cartridge.

He plodded on for half an hour, when the hallucination arose again. Again he fought it, and still it persisted, till for very relief he opened his rifle to unconvince himself. At times his mind wandered farther afield, and he plodded on, a mere automaton, strange conceits and whimsicalities gnawing at his brain like worms. But these excursions out of the real were of brief duration, for ever the pangs of the hunger bite called him back. He was jerked back abruptly once from such an excursion by a sight that caused him nearly to faint. He reeled and swayed, doddering like a drunken man to keep from falling. Before him stood a horse. A horse! He could not believe his eyes. A thick mist was in them, intershot with sparkling points of light. He rubbed his eyes savagely to clear his vision, and beheld, not a horse, but a great brown bear. The animal was studying him with bellicose curiosity.

The man had brought his gun halfway to his shoulder before he realized. He lowered it and drew his hunting knife from its beaded sheath at his hip. Before him was meat and life. He ran his thumb along the edge of his knife. It was sharp. The point was sharp. He would fling himself upon the bear and kill it. But his heart began its warning thump, thump, thump. Then followed the wild upward leap and tattoo of flutters, the pressing as of an iron band about his forehead, the creeping of the dizziness into his brain.

His desperate courage was evicted by a great surge of fear. In his weakness, what if the animal attacked him? He drew himself up to his most imposing stature, gripping the knife and staring hard at the bear. The bear advanced clumsily a couple of steps, reared up, and gave vent to a tentative growl. If the man ran, he would run after him; but the man did not run. He was animated now with the courage of fear. He, too, growled, savagely, terribly, voicing the fear that is to life germane and that lies twisted about life's deepest roots.

The bear edged away to one side, growling menacingly, himself appalled by this mysterious creature that appeared upright and unafraid. But the man did not move. He stood like a statue till the danger was past, when he yielded to a fit of trembling and sank down into the wet moss.

He pulled himself together and went on, afraid now in a new way. It was not the fear that he should die passively from lack of food, but that he should be destroyed violently before starvation had exhausted the last particle of the endeavor in him that made toward surviving. There were the wolves. Back and forth across the desolation drifted their howls, weaving the very air into a fabric of menace that was so tangible that he found himself, arms in the air, pressing it back from him as it might be the walls of a wind-blown tent.

Now and again the wolves, in packs of two and three, crossed his path. But they sheered clear of him. They were not in sufficient numbers, and besides they were hunting the caribou, which did not battle, while this strange creature that walked erect might scratch and bite.

In the late afternoon he came upon scattered bones where the wolves had made a kill. The debris had been a caribou calf an hour before, squawking and running and very much alive. He contemplated the bones, clean-picked and polished, pink with the cell-life in them which had not yet died. Could it possibly be that he might be that ere the day was done! Such was life, eh? A vain and fleeting thing. It was only life that pained. There was no hurt in death. To die was to sleep. It meant cessation, rest. Then why was he not content to die?

But he did not moralize long. He was squatting in the moss, a bone in his mouth, sucking at the shreds of life that still dyed it faintly pink. The sweet meaty taste, thin and elusive almost as a memory, maddened him. He closed his jaws on the bones and crunched. Sometimes it was the bone that broke, sometimes his teeth. Then he crushed the bones between rocks, pounded them to a pulp, and swallowed them. He pounded his fingers, too, in his haste, and yet found a moment in which to feel surprise at the fact that his fingers did not hurt much when caught under the descending rock.

Came frightful days of snow and rain. He did not know when he made camp, when he broke camp. He traveled in the night as much as in the day. He rested wherever he fell, crawled on whenever the dying life in him flickered up and burned less dimly. He, as a man, no longer strove. It was the life in him, unwilling to die, that drove him on. He did not suffer. His nerves had become blunted, numb, while his mind was filled with weird visions and delicious dreams.

But ever he sucked and chewed on the crushed bones of the caribou calf, the least remnants of which he had gathered up and carried with him. He crossed no more hills or divides, but automatically followed a large stream which flowed through a wide and shallow valley. He did not see this stream nor this valley. He saw nothing save visions. Soul and body walked or crawled side by side, yet apart, so slender was the thread that bound them.

He awoke in his right mind, lying on his back on a rocky ledge. The sun was shining bright and warm. Afar off he heard the squawking of caribou calves. He was aware of vague memories of rain and wind and snow, but whether he had been beaten by the storm for two days or two weeks he did not know.

For some time he lay without movement, the genial sunshine pouring upon him and saturating his miserable body with its warmth. A fine day, he thought. Perhaps he could manage to locate himself. By a painful effort he rolled over on his side. Below him flowed a wide and sluggish river. Its unfamiliarity puzzled him. Slowly he followed it with his eyes, winding in wide sweeps among the bleak, bare hills, bleaker and barer and lower-lying than any hills he had yet encountered. Slowly, deliberately, without excitement or more than the most casual interest, he followed the course of the strange stream toward the sky-line and saw it emptying into a bright and shining sea. He was still unexcited. Most unusual, he thought, a vision or a mirage—more likely a vision, a trick of his disordered mind. He was confirmed in this by sight of a ship lying at anchor in the midst of the shining sea. He closed his eyes for a while, then opened them. Strange how the vision persisted! Yet not strange. He knew there were no seas or ships in the heart of the barren lands, just as he had known there was no cartridge in the empty rifle.

He heard a snuffle behind him—a half-choking gasp or cough. Very slowly, because of his exceeding weakness and stiffness, he rolled over on his other side. He could see nothing near at hand, but he waited patiently. Again came the snuffle and cough, and outlined between two jagged rocks not a score of feet away he made out the gray head of a wolf. The sharp ears were not pricked so sharply as he had seen them on other wolves; the eyes were bleared and bloodshot, the head seemed to droop limply and forlornly. The animal blinked continually in the sunshine. It seemed sick. As he looked it snuffled and coughed again.

This, at least, was real, he thought, and turned on the other side so that he might see the reality of the world which had been veiled from him before by the vision. But the sea still shone in the distance and the ship was plainly discernible. Was it reality, after all? He closed his eyes for a long while and thought, and then it came to him. He had been making north by east, away from the Dease Divide and into the Coppermine Valley. This wide and sluggish river was the Coppermine. That shining sea was the Arctic Ocean. That ship was a whaler, strayed east, far east, from the mouth of the Mackenzie, and it was lying at anchor in Coronation Gulf. He remembered the Hudson Bay Company chart he had seen long ago, and it was all clear and reasonable to him.

He sat up and turned his attention to immediate affairs. He had worn through the blanket wrappings, and his feet were shapeless lumps of raw meat. His last blanket was gone. Rifle and knife were both missing. He had lost his hat somewhere, with the bunch of matches in the band, but the matches against his chest were safe and dry inside the tobacco pouch and oil paper. He looked at his watch. It marked eleven o'clock and was still running. Evidently he had kept it wound.

He was calm and collected. Though extremely weak, he had no sensation of pain. He was not hungry. The thought of food was not even pleasant to him, and whatever he did was done by his reason alone. He ripped off his pants' legs to the knees and bound them about his feet. Somehow he had succeeded in retaining the tin bucket. He would have some hot water before he began what he foresaw was to be a terrible journey to the ship.

His movements were slow. He shook as with a palsy. When he started to collect dry moss, he found he could not rise to his feet. He tried again and again, then contented himself with crawling about on hands and knees. Once he crawled near to the sick wolf. The animal dragged itself reluctantly out of his way, licking its chops with a tongue which seemed hardly to have the strength to curl. The man noticed that the tongue was not the customary healthy red. It was a yellowish brown and seemed coated with a rough and half-dry mucus.

After he had drunk a quart of hot water the man found he was able to stand, and even to walk as well as a dying man might be supposed to walk. Every minute or so he was compelled to rest. His steps were feeble and uncertain, just as the wolf's that trailed him were feeble and uncertain; and that night, when the shining sea was blotted out by blackness, he knew he was nearer to it by no more than four miles.

Throughout the night he heard the cough of the sick wolf, and now and then the squawking of the caribou calves. There was life all around him, but it was strong life, very much alive and well, and he knew the sick wolf clung to the sick man's trail in the hope that the man would die first. In the morning, on opening his eyes, he beheld it regarding him with a wistful and hungry stare. It stood crouched, with tail between its legs, like a miserable and woe-begone dog. It shivered in the chill morning wind, and grinned dispiritedly when the man spoke to it in a voice that achieved no more than a hoarse whisper.

The sun rose brightly, and all morning the man tottered and fell toward the ship on the shining sea. The weather was perfect. It was the brief Indian Summer of the high latitudes. It might last a week. Tomorrow or next day it might be gone.

In the afternoon the man came upon a trail. It was of another man, who did not walk, but who dragged himself on all fours. The man thought it might be Bill, but he thought in a dull, uninterested way. He had no curiosity. In fact, sensation and emotion had left him. He was no longer susceptible to pain. Stomach and nerves had gone to sleep. Yet the life that was in him drove him on. He was very weary, but it refused to die. It was because it refused to die that he still ate muskeg berries and minnows, drank his hot water, and kept a wary eye on the sick wolf.

He followed the trail of the other man who dragged himself along, and soon came to the end of it—a few fresh-picked bones where the soggy moss was marked by the foot pads of many wolves. He saw a squat moose-hide sack, mate to his own, which had been torn by sharp teeth. He picked it up, though its weight was almost too much for his feeble fingers. Bill had carried it to the last. Ha! ha! He would have the laugh on Bill. He would survive and carry it to the ship in the shining sea. His mirth was hoarse and ghastly, like a raven's croak, and the sick wolf joined him, howling lugubriously. The man ceased suddenly. How could he have the laugh on Bill if that were Bill; if those bones, so pinky-white and clean, were Bill?

He turned away. Well, Bill had deserted him; but he would not take the gold, nor would he suck Bill's bones. Bill would have, though, had it been the other way around, he mused as he staggered on.

He came to a pool of water. Stooping over in quest of minnows, he jerked his head back as though he had been stung. He had caught sight of his reflected face. So horrible was it that sensibility awoke long enough to be shocked. There were three minnows in the pool, which was too large to drain; and after several ineffectual attempts to catch them in the tin bucket he forbore. He was afraid, because of his great weakness, that he might fall in and drown. It was for this reason that he did not trust himself to the river astride one of the many drift-logs which lined its sandspits.

That day he decreased the distance between him and the ship by three miles; the next day by two—for he was crawling now as Bill had crawled; and the end of the fifth day found the ship still seven miles away and him unable to make even a mile a day. Still the Indian Summer held on, and he continued to crawl and faint, turn and turn about; and ever the sick wolf coughed and wheezed at his heels. His knees had become raw meat like his feet, and though he padded them with the shirt from his back it was a red track he left behind him on the moss and stones. Once, glancing back, he saw the wolf licking hungrily his bleeding trail, and he saw sharply what his own end might be—unless—unless he could get the wolf. Then began as grim a tragedy of existence as was ever played—a sick man that crawled, a sick wolf that limped, two creatures dragging their dying carcasses across the desolation and hunting each other's lives.

Had it been a well wolf, it would not have mattered so much to the man; but the thought of going to feed the maw of that loathsome and all but dead thing was repugnant to him. He was finicky. His mind had begun to wander again, and to be perplexed by hallucinations, while his lucid intervals grew rarer and shorter.

He was awakened once from a faint by a wheeze close in his ear. The wolf leaped lamely back, losing its footing and falling in its weakness. It was ludicrous, but he was not amused. Nor was he even afraid. He was too far gone for that. But his mind was for the moment clear, and he lay and considered. The ship was no more than four miles away. He could see it quite distinctly when he rubbed the mists out of his eyes, and he could see the white sail of a small boat cutting the water of the shining sea. But he could never crawl those four miles. He knew that, and was very calm in the knowledge. He knew that he could not crawl half a mile. And yet he wanted to live. It was unreasonable that he should die after all he had undergone. Fate asked too much of him. And, dying, he declined to die. It was stark madness, perhaps, but in the very grip of Death he defied Death and refused to die.

He closed his eyes and composed himself with infinite precaution. He steeled himself to keep above the suffocating languor that lapped like a rising tide through all the wells of his being. It was very like a sea, this deadly languor, that rose and rose and drowned his consciousness bit by bit. Sometimes he was all but submerged, swimming through oblivion with a faltering stroke; and again, by some strange alchemy of soul, he would find another shred of will and strike out more strongly.

Without movement he lay on his back, and he could hear, slowly drawing near and nearer, the wheezing intake and output of the sick wolf's breath. It drew closer, ever closer, through an infinitude of time, and he did not move. It was at his ear. The harsh dry tongue grated like sandpaper against his cheek. His hands shot out—or at least he willed them to shoot out. The fingers were curved like talons, but they closed on empty air. Swiftness and certitude require strength, and the man had not this strength.

The patience of the wolf was terrible. The man's patience was no less terrible. For half a day he lay motionless, fighting off unconsciousness and waiting for the thing that was to feed upon him and upon which he wished to feed. Sometimes the languid sea rose over him and he dreamed long dreams; but ever through it all, waking and dreaming, he waited for the wheezing breath and the harsh caress of the tongue.

He did not hear the breath, and he slipped slowly from some dream to the feel of the tongue along his hand. He waited. The fangs pressed softly; the pressure increased; the wolf was exerting its last strength in an effort to sink teeth in the food for which it had waited so long. But the man had waited long, and the lacerated hand closed on the jaw. Slowly, while the wolf struggled feebly and the hand clutched feebly, the other hand crept across to a grip. Five minutes later the whole weight of the man's body was on top of the wolf. The hands had not sufficient strength to choke the wolf, but the face of the man was pressed close to the throat of the wolf and the mouth of the man was full of hair. At the end of half an hour the man was aware of a warm trickle in his throat. It was not pleasant. It was like molten lead being forced into his stomach, and it was forced by his will alone. Later the man rolled over on his back and slept.

* * *

There were some members of a scientific expedition on the whaleship *Bedford*. From the deck they remarked a strange object on the shore. It was moving down the beach toward the water. They were unable to classify it, and, being scientific men, they climbed into the whaleboat alongside and went ashore to see. And they saw something that was alive but which could hardly be called a man. It was blind, unconscious. It squirmed along the ground like some monstrous worm. Most of its efforts were ineffectual, but it was persistent, and it writhed and twisted and went ahead perhaps a score of feet an hour.

* * *

Three weeks afterward the man lay in a bunk on the whaleship *Bedford,* and with tears streaming down his wasted cheeks told who he was and what he had undergone. He also babbled incoherently of his mother, of sunny Southern California, and a home among the orange groves and flowers.

The days were not many after that when he sat at table with the scientific men and ship's officers. He gloated over the spectacle of so much food, watching it anxiously as it went into the mouths of others. With the disappearance of each mouthful an expression of deep regret came into his eyes. He was quite sane, yet he hated those men at mealtime. He was haunted by a fear that the food would not last. He inquired of the cook, the cabin boy, the captain, concerning the food stores. They reassured him countless times; but he could not believe them, and pried cunningly about the lazarette to see with his own eyes.

It was noticed that the man was getting fat. He grew stouter with each day. The scientific men shook their heads and theorized. They limited the man at his meals, but still his girth increased and he swelled prodigiously under his shirt.

The sailors grinned. They knew. And when the scientific men set a watch on the man, they knew too. They saw him slouch for'ard after breakfast, and, like a mendicant, with outstretched palm, accost a sailor. The sailor grinned and passed him a fragment of sea biscuit. He clutched it avariciously, looked at it as a miser looks at gold, and thrust it into his shirt bosom. Similar were the donations from other grinning sailors.

The scientific men were discreet. They let him alone. But they privily examined his bunk. It was lined with hardtack; the mattress was stuffed with hardtack; every nook and cranny was filled with hardtack. Yet he was sane. He was taking precautions against another possible famine—that was all. He would recover from it, the scientific men said; and he did, ere the *Bedford's* anchor rumbled down in San Francisco Bay.

BROWN WOLF

She had delayed, because of the dew-wet grass, in order to put on her overshoes, and when she emerged from the house found her waiting husband absorbed in the wonder of a bursting almond-bud. She sent a questing glance across the tall grass and in and out among the orchard trees.

"Where's Wolf?" she asked.

"He was here a moment ago." Walt Irvine drew himself away with a jerk from the metaphysics and poetry of the organic miracle of blossom, and surveyed the landscape. "He was running a rabbit the last I saw of him."

"Wolf! Wolf! Here Wolf!" she called, as they left the clearing and took the trail that led down through the waxen-belled manzanita jungle to the county road.

Irvine thrust between his lips the little finger of each hand and lent to her efforts a shrill whistling.

She covered her ears hastily and made a wry grimace.

"My! for a poet, delicately attuned and all the rest of it, you can make unlovely noises. My eardrums are pierced. You outwhistle—"

"Orpheus."

"I was about to say a street-arab," she concluded severely.

"Poesy does not prevent one from being practical—at least it doesn't prevent *me*. Mine is no futility of genius that can't sell gems to the magazines."

He assumed a mock extravagance, and went on:

"I am no attic singer, no ballroom warbler. And why? Because I am practical. Mine is no squalor of song that cannot transmute itself, with proper exchange value, into a flower-crowned cottage, a sweet mountain-meadow, a grove of redwoods, an orchard of thirty-seven trees, one long row of blackberries and two short rows of strawberries, to say nothing of a quarter of a mile of gurgling brook. I am a beauty-merchant, a trader in song, and I pursue utility, dear Madge. I sing a song, and thanks to the magazine editors I transmute my song into a waft of the west wind sighing through our redwoods, into a murmur of waters over mossy stones that sings back to me another song than the one I sang and yet the same song wonderfully—er—transmuted."

"O that all your song-transmutations were as successful!" she laughed.

"Name one that wasn't."

"Those two beautiful sonnets that you transmuted into the cow that was accounted the worst milker in the township."

"She was beautiful—" he began.

"But she didn't give milk," Madge interrupted.

"But she *was* beautiful, now, wasn't she?" he insisted.

"And here's where beauty and utility fall out," was her reply. "And there's the Wolf!"

From the thicket-covered hillside came a crashing of underbrush, and then, forty feet above them, on the edge of the sheer wall of rock, appeared a wolf's head and shoulders. His braced fore paws dislodged a pebble, and with sharp-pricked ears and peering eyes he watched the fall of the pebble till it struck at their feet. Then he transferred his gaze and with open mouth laughed down at them.

"You Wolf, you!" and "You blessed Wolf!" the man and woman called out to him.

The ears flattened back and down at the sound, and the head seemed to snuggle under the caress of an invisible hand.

They watched him scramble backward into the thicket, then proceeded on their way. Several minutes later, rounding a turn in the trail where the descent was less precipitous, he joined them in the midst of a miniature avalanche of pebbles and loose soil. He was not demonstrative. A pat and a rub around the ears from the man, and a more prolonged caressing from the woman, and he was away down the trail in front of them, gliding effortlessly over the ground in true wolf fashion.

In build and coat and brush he was a huge timber-wolf; but the lie was given to his wolfhood by his color and marking. There the dog unmistakably advertised itself. No wolf was ever colored like him. He was brown, deep brown, red-brown, an orgy of browns. Back and shoulders were a warm brown that paled on the sides and underneath to a yellow that was dingy because of the brown that lingered in it. The white of the throat and paws and the spots over the eyes was dirty because of the persistent and in-eradicable brown, while the eyes themselves were twin topazes, golden and brown.

The man and woman loved the dog very much; perhaps this was because it had been such a task to win his love. It had been no easy matter when he first drifted in mysteriously out of nowhere to their little mountain cottage. Footsore and famished, he had killed a rabbit under their very noses and under their very windows, and then crawled away and slept by the spring at the foot of the blackberry bushes. When Walt Irvine went down to inspect the intruder, he was snarled at for his pains, and Madge likewise was snarled at when she went down to present, as a peace-offering, a large pan of bread and milk.

A most unsociable dog he proved to be, resenting all their advances, refusing to let them lay hands on him, menacing them with bared fangs and bristling hair. Nevertheless he remained, sleeping and resting by the spring, and eating the food they gave him after they set it down at a safe distance and retreated. His wretched physical condition explained why he lingered; and when he had recuperated, after several days' sojourn, he disappeared.

And this would have been the end of him, so far as Irvine and his wife were concerned, had not Irvine at that particular time been called away into the northern part of the state. Riding along on the train, near to the line between California and Oregon, he chanced to look out of the window and saw his unsociable guest sliding along the wagon road, brown and wolfish, tired yet tireless, dust-covered and soiled with two hundred miles of travel.

Now Irvine was a man of impulse, a poet. He got off the train at the next station, bought a piece of meat at a butcher shop, and captured the vagrant on the outskirts of the town. The return trip was made in the baggage car, and so Wolf came a second time to the mountain cottage. Here he was tied up for a week and made love to by the man and woman. But it was very circumspect love-making. Remote and alien as a traveler from another planet, he snarled down their soft-spoken love-words. He never barked. In all the time they had him he was never known to bark.

To win him became a problem. Irvine liked problems. He had a metal plate made, on which was stamped: RETURN TO WALT IRVINE, GLEN ELLEN, SONOMA COUNTY, CALIFORNIA. This was riveted to a collar and strapped about the dog's neck. Then he was turned loose, and promptly he disappeared. A day later came a telegram from Mendocino County. In twenty hours he had made over a hundred miles to the north, and was still going when captured.

He came back by Wells Fargo Express, was tied up three days, and was loosed on the fourth and lost. This time he gained southern Oregon before he was caught and returned. Always, as soon as he received his liberty, he fled away, and always he fled north. He was possessed of an obsession that drove him north. The homing instinct, Irvine called it, after he had expended the selling price of a sonnet in getting the animal back from northern Oregon.

Another time the brown wanderer succeeded in traversing half the length of California, all of Oregon, and most of Washington, before he was picked up and returned "Collect." A remarkable thing was the speed with which he traveled. Fed up and rested, as soon as he was loosed he devoted all his energy to getting over the ground. On the first day's run he was known to cover as high as a hundred and fifty miles, and after that he would average a hundred miles a day until caught. He always arrived back lean and hungry and savage, and always departed fresh and vigorous, cleaving his way northward in response to some prompting of his being that no one could understand.

But at last, after a futile year of flight, he accepted the inevitable and elected to remain at the cottage where first he had killed the rabbit and slept by the spring. Even after that, a long time elapsed before the man and woman succeeded in patting him. It was a great victory, for they alone were allowed to put hands on him. He was fastidiously exclusive, and no guest at the cottage ever succeeded in making up to him. A low growl greeted such approach; if any one had the hardihood to come nearer, the lips lifted, the naked fangs appeared, and the growl became a snarl—a snarl so terrible and malignant that it awed the stoutest of them, as it likewise awed the farmers' dogs that knew ordinary dog-snarling, but had never seen wolf-snarling before.

He was without antecedents. His history began with Walt and Madge. He had come up from the south, but never a clue did they get of the owner from whom he had evidently fled. Mrs. Johnson, their nearest neighbor and the one who supplied them with milk, proclaimed him a Klondike dog. Her brother was burrowing for frozen pay-streaks in that far country, and so she constituted herself an authority on the subject.

But they did not dispute her. There were the tips of Wolf's ears, obviously so severely frozen at some time that they would never quite heal again. Besides, he looked like the photographs of the Alaskan dogs they saw published in magazines and newspapers. They often speculated over his past, and tried to conjure up (from what they had read and heard) what his northland life had been. That the northland still drew him, they knew; for at night they sometimes heard him crying softly; and when the north wind blew and the bite of frost was in the air, a great restlessness would come upon him and he would lift a mournful lament which they knew to be the long wolf-howl. Yet he never barked. No provocation was great enough to draw from him that canine cry.

Long discussion they had, during the time of winning him, as to whose dog he was. Each claimed him, and each proclaimed loudly any expression of affection made by him. But the man had the better of it at first, chiefly because he was a man. It was patent that Wolf had had no experience with women. He did not understand women. Madge's skirts were something he never quite accepted. The swish of them was enough to set him a-bristle with suspicion, and on a windy day she could not approach him at all.

On the other hand, it was Madge who fed him; also it was she who ruled the kitchen, and it was by her favor, and her favor alone, that he was permitted to come within that sacred precinct. It was because of these things that she bade fair to overcome the handicap of her garments. Then it was that Walt put forth special effort, making it a practice to have Wolf lie at his feet while he wrote, and, between petting and talking, losing much time from his work. Walt won in the end, and his victory was most probably due to the fact that he was a man, though Madge averred that they would have had another quarter of a mile of gurgling brook, and at least two west winds sighing through their redwoods, had Walt properly devoted his energies to song-transmutation and left Wolf alone to exercise a natural taste and an unbiassed judgment.

"It's about time I heard from those triolets," Walt said, after a silence of five minutes, during which they had swung steadily down the trail. "There'll be a check at the post office, I know, and we'll transmute it into beautiful buckwheat flour, a gallon of maple syrup, and a new pair of overshoes for you."

"And into beautiful milk from Mrs. Johnson's beautiful cow," Madge added. "To-morrow's the first of the month, you know."

Walt scowled unconsciously; then his face brightened, and he clapped his hand to his breast pocket.

"Never mind. I have here a nice beautiful new cow, the best milker in California."

"When did you write it?" she demanded eagerly. Then, reproachfully, "And you never showed it to me."

"I saved it to read to you on the way to the post office, in a spot remarkably like this one," he answered, indicating, with a wave of his hand, a dry log on which to sit.

A tiny stream flowed out of a dense fern-brake, slipped down a mossy-lipped stone, and ran across the path at their feet. From the valley arose the mellow song of meadow-larks, while about them, in and out, through sunshine and shadow, fluttered great yellow butterflies.

Up from below came another sound that broke in upon Walt reading softly from his manuscript. It was a crunching of heavy feet, punctuated now and again by the clattering of a displaced stone. As Walt finished and looked to his wife for approval, a man came into view around the turn of the trail. He was bareheaded and sweaty. With a handkerchief in one hand he mopped his face, while in the other hand he carried a new hat and a wilted starched collar which he had removed from his neck. He was a well-built man, and his muscles seemed on the point of bursting out of the painfully new and ready-made black clothes he wore.

"Warm day," Walt greeted him. Walt believed in country democracy, and never missed an opportunity to practice it.

The man paused and nodded.

"I guess I ain't used much to the warm," he vouch-safed half apologetically. "I'm more accustomed to zero weather."

"You don't find any of that in this country," Walt laughed.

"Should say not," the man answered. "An' I ain't here a-lookin' for it neither. I'm tryin' to find my sister. Mebbe you know where she lives. Her name's Johnson, Mrs. William Johnson."

"You're not her Klondike brother!" Madge cried, her eyes bright with interest, "about whom we've heard so much?"

"Yes'm, that's me," he answered modestly. "My name's Miller, Skiff Miller. I just thought I'd s'prise her."

"You are on the right track then. Only you've come by the foot-path." Madge stood up to direct him, pointing up the canyon a quarter of a mile. "You see that blasted redwood? Take the little trail turning off to the right. It's the short cut to her house. You can't miss it."

"Yes'm, thank you, ma'am," he said. He made tentative efforts to go, but seemed awkwardly rooted to the spot. He was gazing at her with an open admiration of which he was quite unconscious, and which was drowning, along with him, in the rising sea of embarrassment in which he floundered.

"We'd like to hear you tell about the Klondike," Madge said. "Mayn't we come over some day while you are at your sister's? Or, better yet, won't you come over and have dinner with us?"

"Yes'm, thank you, ma'am," he mumbled mechanically. Then he caught himself up and added: "I ain't stoppin' long. I got to be pullin' north again. I go out on tonight's train. You see, I've got a mail contract with the government."

When Madge had said that it was too bad, he made another futile effort to go. But he could not take his eyes from her face. He forgot his embarrassment in his admiration, and it was her turn to flush and feel uncomfortable.

It was at this juncture, when Walt had just decided it was time for him to be saying something to relieve the strain, that Wolf, who had been away nosing through the brush, trotted wolflike into view.

Skiff Miller's abstraction disappeared. The pretty woman before him passed out of his field of vision. He had eyes only for the dog, and a great wonder came into his face.

"Well, I'll be damned!" he enunciated slowly and solemnly.

He sat down ponderingly on the log, leaving Madge standing. At the sound of his voice, Wolf's ears had flattened down, then his mouth had opened in a laugh. He trotted slowly up to the stranger and first smelled his hands, then licked them with his tongue.

Skiff Miller patted the dog's head, and slowly and solemnly repeated, "Well, I'll be damned!"

"Excuse me, ma'am," he said the next moment "I was just s'prised some, that was all."

"We're surprised, too," she answered lightly. "We never saw Wolf make up to a stranger before."

"Is that what you call him—Wolf?" the man asked.

Madge nodded. "But I can't understand his friendliness toward you unless it's because you're from the Klondike. He's a Klondike dog, you know."

"Yes'm," Miller said absently. He lifted one of Wolf's fore legs and examined the foot-pads, pressing them and denting them with his thumb. "Kind of *soft,*" he remarked. "He ain't been on trail for a long time."

"I say," Walt broke in, "it is remarkable the way he lets you handle him."

Skiff Miller arose, no longer awkward with admiration of Madge, and in a sharp, businesslike manner asked, "How long have you had him?"

But just then the dog, squirming and rubbing against the newcomer's legs, opened his mouth and barked. It was an explosive bark, brief and joyous, but a bark.

"That's a new one on me," Skiff Miller remarked.

Walt and Madge stared at each other. The miracle had happened. Wolf had barked.

"It's the first time he ever barked," Madge said.

"First time I ever heard him, too," Miller volunteered.

Madge smiled at him. The man was evidently a humorist.

"Of course," she said, "since you have only seen him for five minutes."

Skiff Miller looked at her sharply, seeking in her face the guile her words had led him to suspect.

"I thought you understood," he said slowly. "I thought you'd tumbled to it from his makin' up to me. He's my dog. His name ain't Wolf. It's Brown."

"Oh, Walt!" was Madge's instinctive cry to her husband.

Walt was on the defensive at once.

"How do you know he's your dog?" he demanded.

"Because he is," was the reply.

"Mere assertion," Walt said sharply.

In his slow and pondering way, Skiff Miller looked at him, then asked, with a nod of his head toward Madge:

"How d'you know she's your wife? You just say, 'Because she is,' and I'll say it's mere assertion. The dog's mine. I bred 'm an' raised 'm, an' I guess I ought to know. Look here. I'll prove it to you."

Skiff Miller turned to the dog. "Brown!" His voice rang out sharply, and at the sound the dog's ears flattened down as to a caress. "Gee!" The dog made a swinging turn to the right. "Now mush-on!" And the dog ceased his swing abruptly and started straight ahead, halting obediently at command.

"I can do it with whistles," Skiff Miller said proudly. "He was my lead dog."

"But you are not going to take him away with you?" Madge asked tremulously.

The man nodded.

"Back into that awful Klondike world of suffering?"

He nodded and added: "Oh, it ain't so bad as all that. Look at me. Pretty healthy specimen, ain't I?"

"But the dogs! The terrible hardship, the heart-breaking toil, the starvation, the frost! Oh, I've read about it and I know."

"I nearly ate him once, over on Little Fish River," Miller volunteered grimly. "If I hadn't got a moose that day was all that saved 'm."

"I'd have died first!" Madge cried.

"Things is different down here," Miller explained. "You don't have to eat dogs. You think different just about the time you're all in. You've never ben all in, so you don't know anything about it."

"That's the very point," she argued warmly. "Dogs are not eaten in California. Why not leave him here? He is happy. He'll never want for food—you know that. He'll never suffer from cold and hardship. Here all is softness and gentleness. Neither the human nor nature is savage. He will never know a whiplash again. And as for the weather—why, it never snows here."

"But it's all-fired hot in summer, beggin' your pardon," Skiff Miller laughed.

"But you do not answer," Madge continued passionately. "What have you to offer him in that northland life?"

"Grub, when I've got it, and that's most of the time," came the answer.

"And the rest of the time?"

"No grub."

"And the work?"

"Yes, plenty of work," Miller blurted out impatiently. "Work without end, an' famine, an' frost, an all the rest of the miseries—that's what he'll get when he comes with me. But he likes it. He is used to it. He knows that life. He was born to it an' brought up to it. An' you don't know anything about it. You don't know what you're talking about. That's where the dog belongs, and that's where he'll be happiest."

"The dog doesn't go," Walt announced in a determined voice. "So there is no need of further discussion."

"What's that?" Skiff Miller demanded, his brows lowering and an obstinate flush of blood reddening his forehead.

"I said the dog doesn't go, and that settles it. I don't believe he's your dog. You may have seen him sometime. You may even sometime have driven him for his owner. But his obeying the ordinary driving commands of the Alaskan trail is no demonstration that he is yours. Any dog in Alaska would obey you as he obeyed. Besides, he is undoubtedly a valuable dog, as dogs go in Alaska, and that is sufficient explanation of your desire to get possession of him. Anyway, you've got to prove property."

Skiff Miller, cool and collected, the obstinate flush a trifle deeper on his forehead, his huge muscles bulging under the black cloth of his coat, carefully looked the poet up and down as though measuring the strength of his slenderness.

The Klondiker's face took on a contemptuous expression as he said finally, "I reckon there's nothin' in sight to prevent me takin' the dog right here an' now."

Walt's face reddened, and the striking-muscles of his arms and shoulders seemed to stiffen and grow tense. His wife fluttered apprehensively into the breach.

"Maybe Mr. Miller is right," she said. "I am afraid that he is. Wolf does seem to know him, and certainly he answers to the name of 'Brown.' He made friends with him instantly, and you know that's something he never did with anybody before. Besides, look at the way he barked. He was just bursting with joy. Joy over what? Without doubt at finding Mr. Miller."

Walt's striking-muscles relaxed, and his shoulders seemed to droop with hopelessness.

"I guess you're right, Madge," he said. "Wolf isn't Wolf, but Brown, and he must belong to Mr. Miller."

"Perhaps Mr. Miller will sell him," she suggested. "We can buy him."

Skiff Miller shook his head, no longer belligerent, but kindly, quick to be generous in response to generousness.

"I had five dogs," he said, casting about for the easiest way to temper his refusal. "He was the leader. They was the crack team of Alaska. Nothin' could touch 'em. In 1898 I refused five thousand dollars for the bunch. Dogs was high, then, anyway; but that wasn't what made the fancy price. It was the team itself. Brown was the best in the team. That winter I refused twelve hundred for 'm. I didn't sell 'm then, an' I ain't a-sellin' 'm now. Besides, I think a mighty lot of that dog. I've ben lookin' for 'm for three years. It made me fair sick when I found he'd ben stole— not the value of him, but the—well, I liked 'm like hell, that's all, beggin' your pardon. I couldn't believe my eyes when I seen 'm just now. I thought I was dreamin'. It was too good to be true. Why, I was his wet-nurse. I put 'm to bed, snug every night. His mother died, and I brought 'm up on condensed milk at two dollars a can when I couldn't afford it in my own coffee. He never knew any mother but me. He used to suck my finger regular, the darn little cuss— that finger right there!"

And Skiff Miller, too overwrought for speech, held up a fore finger for them to see.

"That very finger," he managed to articulate, as though it somehow clinched the proof of ownership and the bond of affection.

He was still gazing at his extended finger when Madge began to speak.

"But the dog," she said. "You haven't considered the dog."

Skiff Miller looked puzzled.

"Have you thought about him?" she asked.

"Don't know what you're drivin' at," was the response.

"Maybe the dog has some choice in the matter," Madge went on. "Maybe he has his likes and desires. You have not considered him. You give him no choice. It has never entered your mind that possibly he might prefer California to Alaska. You consider only what you like. You do with him as you would with a sack of potatoes or a bale of hay."

This was a new way of looking at it, and Miller was visibly impressed as he debated it in his mind. Madge took advantage of his indecision.

"If you really love him, what would be happiness to him would be your happiness also," she urged.

Skiff Miller continued to debate with himself, and Madge stole a glance of exultation to her husband, who looked back warm approval.

"What do you think?" the Klondiker suddenly demanded.

It was her turn to be puzzled. "What do you mean?" she asked.

"D'ye think he'd sooner stay in California?"

She nodded her head with positiveness. "I am sure of it."

Skiff Miller again debated with himself, though

this time aloud, at the same time running his gaze in a judicial way over the mooted animal.

"He was a good worker. He's done a heap of work for me. He never loafed on me, an' he was a joe-dandy at hammerin' a raw team into shape. He's got a head on him. He can do everything but talk. He knows what you say to him. Look at 'm now. He knows we're talkin' about him."

The dog was lying at Skiff Miller's feet, head close down on paws, ears erect and listening, and eyes that were quick and eager to follow the sound of speech as it fell from the lips of first one and then the other.

"An' there's a lot of work in 'm yet. He's good for years to come. An' I do like him. I like him like hell."

Once or twice after that Skiff Miller opened his mouth and closed it again without speaking. Finally he said:

"I'll tell you what I'll do. Your remarks, ma'am, has some weight in them. The dog's worked hard, and maybe he's earned a soft berth an' has got a right to choose. Anyway, we'll leave it up to him. Whatever he says, goes. You people stay right here settin' down. I'll say good-by and walk off casual-like. If he wants to stay, he can stay. If he wants to come with me, let 'm come. I won't call 'm to come an' don't you call 'm to come back."

He looked with sudden suspicion at Madge, and added, "Only you must play fair. No persuadin' after my back is turned."

"We'll play fair," Madge began, but Skiff Miller broke in on her assurances.

"I know the ways of women," he announced. "Their hearts is soft. When their hearts is touched they're likely to stack the cards, look at the bottom of the deck, an' lie like the devil—beggin' your pardon, ma'am. I'm only discoursin' about women in general."

"I don't know how to thank you," Madge quavered.

"I don't see as you've got any call to thank me," he replied. "Brown ain't decided yet. Now you won't mind if I go away slow? It's no more'n fair, seein' I'll be out of sight inside a hundred yards."

Madge agreed, and added, "And I promise you faithfully that we won't do anything to influence him."

"Well, then, I might as well be gettin' along," Skiff Miller said in the ordinary tones of one departing.

At this change in his voice, Wolf lifted his head quickly, and still more quickly got to his feet when the man and woman shook hands. He sprang up on his hind legs, resting his fore paws on her hip and at the same time licking Skiff Miller's hand. When the latter shook hands with Walt, Wolf repeated his act, resting his weight on Walt and licking both men's hands.

"It ain't no picnic, I can tell you that," were the Klondiker's last words, as he turned and went slowly up the trail.

For the distance of twenty feet Wolf watched him

go, himself all eagerness and expectancy, as though waiting for the man to turn and retrace his steps. Then, with a quick low whine, Wolf sprang after him, overtook him, caught his hand between his teeth with reluctant tenderness, and strove gently to make him pause.

Failing in this, Wolf raced back to where Walt Irvine sat, catching his coat-sleeve in his teeth and trying vainly to drag him after the retreating man.

Wolf's perturbation began to wax. He desired ubiquity. He wanted to be in two places at the same time, with the old master and the new, and steadily the distance between them was increasing. He sprang about excitedly, making short nervous leaps and twists, now toward one, now toward the other, in painful indecision, not knowing his own mind, desiring both and unable to choose, uttering quick sharp whines and beginning to pant.

He sat down abruptly on his haunches, thrusting his nose upward, the mouth opening and closing with jerking movements, each time opening wider. These jerking movements were in unison with the recurrent spasms that attacked the throat, each spasm severer and more intense than the preceding one. And in accord with jerks and spasms the larynx began to vibrate, at first silently, accompanied by the rush of air expelled from the lungs, then sounding a low, deep note, the lowest in the register of the human ear. All this was the nervous and muscular preliminary to howling.

But just as the howl was on the verge of bursting from the full throat, the wide-opened mouth was closed, the paroxysms ceased, and he looked long and steadily at the retreating man. Suddenly Wolf turned his head, and over his shoulder just as steadily regarded Walt. The appeal was unanswered. Not a word nor a sign did the dog receive, no suggestion and no clue as to what his conduct should be.

A glance ahead to where the old master was nearing the curve of the trail excited him again. He sprang to his feet with a whine, and then, struck by a new idea, turned his attention to Madge. Hitherto he had ignored her, but now, both masters failing him, she alone was left. He went over to her and snuggled his head in her lap, nudging her arm with his nose— an old trick of his when begging for favors. He backed away from her and began writhing and twisting playfully, curvetting and prancing, half rearing and striking his fore paws to the earth, struggling with all his body, from the wheedling eyes and flattening ears to the wagging tail, to express the thought that was in him and that was denied him utterance.

This, too, he soon abandoned. He was depressed by the coldness of these humans who had never been cold before. No response could he draw from them, no help could he get. They did not consider him. They were as dead.

He turned and silently gazed after the old master. Skiff Miller was rounding the curve. In a moment he would be gone from view. Yet he never turned his head, plodding straight onward, slowly and methodically, as though possessed of no interest in what was occurring behind his back.

And in this fashion he went out of view. Wolf waited for him to reappear. He waited a long minute, silently, quietly, without movement, as though turned to stone—withal stone quick with eagerness and desire. He barked once, and waited. Then he turned and trotted back to Walt Irvine. He sniffed his hand and dropped down heavily at his feet, watching the trail where it curved emptily from view.

The tiny stream slipping down the mossy-lipped stone seemed suddenly to increase the volume of its gurgling noise. Save for the meadow-larks, there was no other sound. The great yellow butterflies drifted silently through the sunshine and lost themselves in the drowsy shadows. Madge gazed triumphantly at her husband.

A few minutes later Wolf got upon his feet. Decision and deliberation marked his movements. He did not glance at the man and woman. His eyes were fixed up the trail. He had made up his mind. They knew it. And they knew, so far as they were concerned, that the ordeal had just begun.

He broke into a trot, and Madge's lips pursed, forming an avenue for the caressing sound that it was the will of her to send forth. But the caressing sound was not made. She was impelled to look at her husband, and she saw the sternness with which he watched her. The pursed lips relaxed, and she sighed inaudibly.

Wolf's trot broke into a run. Wider and wider were the leaps he made. Not once did he turn his head, his wolf's brush standing out straight behind him. He cut sharply across the curve of the trail and was gone.

A RELIC OF THE PLIOCENE

I wash my hands of him at the start. I cannot father his tales, nor will I be responsible for them. I make these preliminary reservations, observe, as a guard upon my own integrity. I possess a certain definite position in a small way, also a wife; and for the good name of the community that honors my existence with its approval, and for the sake of her posterity and mine, I cannot take the chances I once did, nor foster probabilities with the careless improvidence of youth. So, I repeat, I wash my hands of him, this Nimrod, this mighty hunter, this homely, blue-eyed, freckle-faced Thomas Stevens.

Having been honest to myself, and to whatever prospective olive branches my wife may be pleased to tender me, I can now afford to be generous. I shall not criticize the tales told me by Thomas Stevens, and, further, I shall withhold my judgment. If it be asked why, I can only add that judgment I have none. Long have I pondered, weighed, and balanced, but never have my conclusions been twice the same—forsooth! because Thomas Stevens is a greater man than I. If he have told truths, well and good; if untruths, still well and good. For who can prove? or who disprove? I eliminate myself from the proposition, while those of little faith may do as I have done—go find the same Thomas Stevens, and discuss to his face the various matters which, if fortune serve, I shall relate. As to where he may be found? The directions are simple: anywhere between 53 north latitude and the Pole, on the one hand; and, on the other, the likeliest hunting grounds that lie between the east coast of Siberia and farthermost Labrador. That he is there, somewhere, within that clearly defined territory, I pledge the word of an honorable man whose expectations entail straight speaking and right living.

Thomas Stevens may have toyed prodigiously with truth, but when we first met (it were well to mark this point), he wandered into my camp when I thought myself a thousand miles beyond the outermost post of civilization. At the sight of his human face, the first in weary months, I could have sprung forward and folded him in my arms (and I am not by any means a demonstrative man); but to him his visit seemed the most casual thing under the sun. He just strolled into the light of my camp, passed the time of day after the custom of men on beaten trails, threw my snowshoes the one way and a couple of dogs the other, and so made room for himself by the fire. Said he'd just dropped in to borrow a pinch of soda and to see if I had any decent tobacco. He plucked forth an ancient pipe, loaded it with painstaking care, and, without as much as by your leave, whacked half the tobacco of my pouch into his. Yes, the stuff was fairly good. He sighed with the contentment of the just, and literally absorbed the smoke from the crisping yellow flakes, and it did my smoker's heart good to behold him.

Hunter? Trapper? Prospector? He shrugged his shoulders No; just sort of knocking round a bit. Had come up from the Great Slave some time since, and was thinking of traipsing over into the Yukon country. The factor of Koshim had spoken about the discoveries on the Klondike, and he was of a mind to run over for a peep. I noticed that he spoke of the Klondike in the archaic vernacular, calling it the Reindeer River—a conceited custom that the Old Timers employ against the *che-cha-quas* and all tenderfeet in general. But he did it so naively and as such a matter of course, that there was no sting, and I forgave him. He also had it in view, he said, before he crossed the divide into the Yukon, to make a little run up Fort o' Good Hope way.

Now Fort o' Good Hope is a far journey to the north, over and beyond the Circle, in a place where the feet of few men have trod; and when a nondescript ragamuffin comes in out of the night, from nowhere in particular, to sit by one's fire and discourse on such in terms of "traipsing" and "a little run," it is fair time to rouse up and shake off the dream. Wherefore I looked about me; saw the fly and, underneath, the pine boughs spread for the sleeping furs; saw the grub sacks, the camera, the frosty breaths of the dogs circling on the edge of the light; and, above, a great streamer of the aurora, bridging the zenith from southeast to northwest. I shivered. There is a magic in the Northland night, that steals in on one like fevers from malarial marshes. You are clutched and downed before you are aware. Then I looked to the snowshoes, lying prone and crossed where he had flung them. Also I had an eye to my tobacco pouch. Half, at least, of its goodly store had vamosed. That settled it. Fancy had not tricked me after all.

Crazed with suffering, I thought, looking steadfastly at the man—one of those wild stampeders, strayed far from his bearings and wandering like a lost soul through great vastnesses and unknown deeps. Oh, well, let his moods slip on, until, mayhap, he gathers his tangled wits together. Who knows?—the mere sound of a fellow-creature's voice may bring all straight again.

So I led him on in talk, and soon I marvelled, for he talked of game and the ways thereof. He had killed the Siberian wolf of westernmost Alaska, and the chamois in the secret Rockies. He averred he knew the haunts where the last buffalo still roamed; that he had hung on the flanks of the caribou when they ran by the hundred thousand, and slept in the Great Barrens on the musk-ox's winter trail.

And I shifted my judgment accordingly (the first revision, but by no account the last), and deemed him a monumental effigy of truth. Why it was I know not, but the spirit moved me to repeat a tale told to me by a man who had dwelt in the land too long to know better. It was of the great bear that hugs the steep slopes of St. Elias, never descending to the levels of the gentler inclines. Now God so constituted this creature for its hillside habitat that the legs of one side are all of a foot longer than those of the other. This is mighty convenient, as will be readily admitted. So I hunted this rare beast in my own name, told it in the first person, present tense, painted the requisite locale, gave it the necessary garnishings and touches of verisimilitude, and looked to see the man stunned by the recital.

Not he. Had he doubted, I could have forgiven him. Had he objected, denying the dangers of such a hunt by virtue of the animal's inability to turn about and go the other way—had he done this, I say, I could have taken him by the hand for the true sportsman that he was. Not he. He sniffed, looked on me, and sniffed again; then gave my tobacco due praise, thrust one foot into my lap, and bade me examine the gear. It was a *mucluc* of the Innuit pattern, sewed together with sinew threads, and devoid of beads or furbelows. But it was the skin itself that was remarkable. In that it was all of half an inch thick, it reminded me of walrus-hide; but there the resemblance ceased, for no walrus ever bore so marvellous a growth of hair. On the side and ankles this hair was well-nigh worn away, what of friction with underbrush and snow; but around the top and down the more sheltered back it was coarse, dirty black, and very thick. I parted it with difficulty and looked beneath for the fine fur that is common with northern animals, but found it in this case to be absent. This, however, was compensated for by the length. Indeed, the tufts that had survived wear and tear measured all of seven or eight inches.

I looked up into the man's face, and he pulled his foot down and asked, "Find hide like that on your St. Elias bear?"

I shook my head. "Nor on any other creature of land or sea," I answered candidly. The thickness of it, and the length of the hair, puzzled me.

"That," he said, and said without the slightest hint of impressiveness, "that came from a mammoth."

"Nonsense!" I exclaimed, for I could not forbear the protest of my unbelief. "The mammoth, my dear sir, long ago vanished from the earth. We know it once existed by the fossil remains that we have unearthed, and by a frozen carcass that the Siberian sun saw fit to melt from out the bosom of a glacier; but we also know that no living specimen exists. Our explorers—"

At this word he broke in impatiently. "Your explorers? Pish! A weakly breed. Let us hear no more of them. But tell me, O man, what you may know of the mammoth and his ways."

Beyond contradiction, this was leading to a yarn; so I baited my hook by ransacking my memory for whatever data I possessed on the subject in hand. To begin with, I emphasized that the animal was prehistoric, and marshalled all my facts in support of this. I mentioned the Siberian sand bars that abounded with ancient mammoth bones; spoke of the large quantities of fossil ivory purchased from the Innuits by the Alaska Commercial Company; and acknowledged having myself mined six- and eight-foot tusks from the pay gravel of the Klondike creeks. "All fossils," I concluded, "found in the midst of debris deposited through countless ages."

"I remember when I was a kid," Thomas Stevens sniffed (he had a most confounded way of sniffing), "that I saw a petrified watermelon. Hence, though mistaken persons sometimes delude themselves into thinking that they are really raising or eating them, there are no such things as extant watermelons?"

"But the question of food," I objected, ignoring his point, which was puerile and without bearing. "The soil must bring forth vegetable life in lavish abundance to support so monstrous creations. Nowhere in the North is the soil so prolific. Ergo, the mammoth cannot exist."

"I pardon your ignorance concerning many matters of this Northland, for you are a young man and have traveled little; but, at the same time, I am inclined to agree with you on one thing. The mammoth no longer exists. How do I know? I killed the last one with my own right arm."

Thus spake Nimrod, the mighty Hunter. I threw a stick of firewood at the dogs and bade them quit their unholy howling, and waited. Undoubtedly this liar of singular felicity would open his mouth and requite me for my St. Elias bear.

"It was this way," he at last began, after the appropriate silence had intervened. "I was in camp one day—"

"Where?" I interrupted.

He waved his hand vaguely in the direction of the northeast, where stretched a terra incognita into which vastness few men have strayed and fewer emerged. "I was in camp one day with Klooch. Klooch was as handsome a little *kamooks* as ever whined betwixt the traces or shoved nose into a camp kettle. Her father was a full-blood Malemute from Russian Pastilik on Bering Sea, and I bred her, and with understanding, out of a clean-legged bitch of the Hudson Bay stock. I tell you, O man, she was a corker combination. And now, on this day I have in mind, she was brought to pup through a pure wild wolf of the woods—grey, and long of limb, with big lungs and no end of staying powers. Say! Was there ever the like? It was a new breed of dog I had started, and I could look forward to big things.

"As I have said, she was brought neatly to pup, and safely delivered. I was squatting on my hams over the litter—seven sturdy, blind little beggars—when from behind came a bray of trumpets and crash of brass. There was a rush, like the wind-squall that kicks the heels of the rain, and I was midway to my feet when knocked flat on my face. At the same instant I heard Klooch sigh, very much as a man does when you've planted your fist in his belly. You can stake your sack I lay quiet, but I twisted my head around and saw a huge bulk swaying above me. Then the blue sky flashed into view and I got to my feet. A hairy mountain of flesh was just disappearing in the underbrush on the edge of the open. I caught a rear-end glimpse, with a stiff tail, as big in girth as my body, standing out straight behind. The next second only a tremendous hole remained in the thicket, though I could still hear the sounds as of a tornado dying quickly away, underbrush ripping and tearing, and trees snapping and crashing.

"I cast about for my rifle. It had been lying on the ground with the muzzle against a log; but now the stock was smashed, the barrel out of line, and the working-gear in a thousand bits. Then I looked for the slut, and—and what do you suppose?"

I shook my head.

"May my soul burn in a thousand hells if there was anything left of her! Klooch, the seven sturdy, blind little beggars—gone, all gone. Where she had stretched was a slimy, bloody depression in the soft earth, all of a yard in diameter, and around the edges a few scattered hairs."

I measured three feet on the snow, threw about it a circle, and glanced at Nimrod.

"The beast was thirty long and twenty high," he answered, "and its tusks scaled over six times three feet. I couldn't believe, myself, at the time, for all that it had just happened. But if my senses had played me, there was the broken gun and the hole in the brush. And there was—or, rather, there was not—Klooch and the pups. O man, it makes me hot all over now when I think of it Klooch! Another Eve! The mother of a new race! And a rampaging, ranting, old bull mammoth, like a second flood, wiping them, root and branch, off the face of the earth! Do you wonder that the blood-soaked earth cried out to high God? Or that I grabbed the hand-axe and took the trail?"

"The hand-axe?" I exclaimed, startled out of myself by the picture. "The hand-axe, and a big bull mammoth, thirty feet long, twenty feet—"

Nimrod joined me in my merriment, chuckling gleefully. "Wouldn't it kill you?" he cried. "Wasn't it a beaver's dream? Many's the time I've laughed about it since, but at the time it was no laughing matter, I was that danged mad, what of the gun and Klooch. Think of it, O man! A brand-new, unclassified, uncopyrighted breed, and wiped out before ever it opened its eyes or took out its intention papers! Well, so be it. Life's full of disappointments, and rightly so. Meat is best after a famine, and a bed soft after a hard trail.

"As I was saying, I took out after the beast with the hand-axe, and hung to its heels down the valley; but when he circled back toward the head, I was left winded at the lower end. Speaking of grub, I might as well stop long enough to explain a couple of points. Up thereabouts, in the midst of the mountains, is an almighty curious formation. There is no end of little valleys, each like the other much as peas in a pod, and all neatly tucked away with straight, rocky walls rising on all sides. And at the lower ends are always small openings where the drainage or glaciers must have broken out. The only way in is through these mouths, and they are all small, and some smaller than others. As to grub—you've slushed around on the rain-soaked islands of the Alaskan coast down Sitka way, most likely, seeing as you're a traveler. And you know how stuff grows there—big, and juicy, and jungly. Well, that's the way it was with those valleys. Thick, rich soil, with ferns and grasses and such things in patches higher than your head. Rain three days out of four during the summer months; and food in them for a thousand mammoths, to say nothing of small game for man.

"But to get back. Down at the lower end of the valley I got winded and gave over. I began to speculate, for when my wind left me my dander got hotter and hotter, and I knew I'd never know peace of mind till I dined on roasted mammoth-foot. And I knew, also, that that stood for *skookum mamook pukapuk*—excuse Chinook, I mean there was a big fight coming. Now the mouth of my valley was very narrow, and the walls steep. High up on one side was one of those big pivot rocks, or balancing rocks, as some call them, weighing all of a couple of hundred tons. Just the thing. I hit back for camp, keeping an eye open so the bull couldn't slip past, and got my ammunition. It wasn't worth anything with the rifle smashed; so I opened the shells, planted the powder under the rock, and touched it off with slow fuse. Wasn't much of a charge, but the old boulder tilted up lazily and dropped down into place, with just space enough to let the creek drain nicely. Now I had him."

"But how did you have him?" I queried. "Who ever heard of a man killing a mammoth with a hand-axe? And, for that matter, with anything else?"

"O man, have I not told you I was mad?" Nimrod replied, with a slight manifestation of sensitiveness. "Mad clean through, what of Klooch and the gun. Also, was I not a hunter? And was this not new and most unusual game? A hand-axe? Pish! I did not need it. Listen, and you shall hear of a hunt, such as might have happened in the youth of the world when cave-men rounded up the kill with hand-axe of stone. Such would have served me as well. Now is it not a fact that man can outwalk the dog or horse? That he can wear them out with the intelligence of his endurance?"

I nodded.

"Well?"

The light broke in on me, and I bade him continue.

"My valley was perhaps five miles around. The mouth was closed. There was no way to get out. A timid beast was that bull mammoth, and I had him at my mercy. I got on his heels again hollered like a fiend, pelted him with cobbles, and raced him around the valley three times before I knocked off for supper. Don't you see? A race-course! A man and a mammoth! A hippodrome, with sun, moon, and stars to referee!

"It took me two months to do it, but I did it. And that's no beaver dream. Round and round I ran him, me traveling on the inner circle, eating jerked meat and salmon berries on the run, and snatching winks of sleep between. Of course, he'd get desperate at times and turn. Then I'd head for soft ground where the creek spread out, and lay anathema upon him and his ancestry, and dare him to come on. But he was too wise to bog in a mud puddle. Once he pinned me in against the walls, and I crawled back into a deep crevice and waited. Whenever he felt for me with his trunk, I'd belt him with the hand-axe till he pulled out, shrieking fit to split my ear drums, he was that mad. He knew he had me and didn't have me, and it near drove him wild. But he was no man's fool. He knew he was safe as long as I stayed in the crevice, and he made up his mind to keep me there. And he was dead right, only he hadn't figured on the commissary. There was neither grub nor water around that spot, so on the face of it he couldn't keep up the siege. He'd stand before the opening for hours, keeping an eye on me and flapping mosquitoes away with his big blanket ears. Then the thirst would come on him and he'd ramp round and roar till the earth shook, calling me every name he could lay tongue to. This was to frighten me, of course; and when he thought I was sufficiently impressed, he'd back away softly and try to make a sneak for the creek. Sometimes I'd let him get almost there—only a couple of hundred yards away it was—when out I'd pop and back he'd come, lumbering along like the old land-slide he was. After I'd done this a few times, and he'd figured it out, he changed his tactics. Grasped the time element, you see. Without a word of warning, away he'd go, tearing for the water like mad, scheming to get there and back before I ran away. Finally, after cursing me most horribly, he raised the siege and deliberately stalked off to the water hole.

"That was the only time he penned me,—three days of it,—but after that the hippodrome never stopped. Round, and round, and round, like a six days' go-as-I-please, for he never pleased. My clothes went to rags and tatters, but I never stopped to mend, till at last I ran naked as a son of earth, with nothing but the old hand-axe in one hand and a cobble in the other. In fact, I never stopped, save for peeps of sleep in the crannies and ledges of the cliffs. As for the bull, he got perceptibly thinner and thinner—must have lost several tons at least—and as nervous as a school-marm on the wrong side of matrimony. When I'd come up with him and yell, or lain him with a rock at long range, he'd jump like a skittish colt and tremble all over. Then he'd pull out on the run, tail and trunk waving stiff, head over one shoulder and wicked eyes blazing, and the way he'd swear at me was something dreadful. A most immoral beast he was, a murderer, and a blasphemer.

"But towards the end he quit all this, and fell to whimpering and crying like a baby. His spirit broke and he became a quivering jelly-mountain of misery.

He'd get attacks of palpitation of the heart, and stagger around like a drunken man, and fall down and bark his shins. And then he'd cry, but always on the run. O man, the gods themselves would have wept with him, and you yourself or any other man. It was pitiful, and there was so I much of it, but I only hardened my heart and hit up the pace. At last I wore him clean out, and he lay down, broken-winded, brokenhearted, hungry, and thirsty. When I found he wouldn't budge, I hamstrung him, and spent the better part of the day wading into him with the handaxe, he a sniffing and sobbing till I worked in far enough to shut him off. Thirty feet long he was, and twenty high, and a man could sling a hammock between his tusks and sleep comfortably. Barring the fact that I had run most of the juices out of him, he was fair eating, and his four feet, alone, roasted whole, would have lasted a man a twelvemonth. I spent the winter there myself."

"And where is this valley?" I asked

He waved his hand in the direction of the northeast, and said: "Your tobacco is very good. I carry a fair share of it in my pouch, but I shall carry the recollection of it until I die. In token of my appreciation, and in return for the moccasins on your own feet, I will present to you these *muclucs*. They commemorate Klooch and the seven blind little beggars. They are also souvenirs of an unparalleled event in history, namely, the destruction of the oldest breed of animal on earth, and the youngest. And their chief virtue lies in that they will never wear out."

Having effected the exchange, he knocked the ashes from his pipe, gripped my hand good-night, and wandered off through the snow. Concerning this tale, for which I have already disclaimed responsibility, I would recommend those of little faith to make a visit to the Smithsonian Institute. If they bring the requisite credentials and do not come in vacation time, they will undoubtedly gain an audience with Professor Dolvidson. The *muclucs* are in his possession, and he will verify, not the manner in which they were obtained, but the material of which they are composed. When he states that they are made from the skin of the mammoth, the scientific world accepts his verdict. What more would you have?

THE PEARLS OF PARLAY

The Kanaka helmsman put the wheel down and the *Malahini* slipped into the eye of the wind and righted to an even keel. Her headsails emptied; there was a rat-tat of reef points and quick shifting of boom tackles, and she heeled over and filled away on the other tack. Though it was early morning and the wind brisk the five white men who lounged on the poop deck were scantily clad. David Grief and his guest, Gregory Mulhall, an Englishman, were still in pajamas, their naked feet thrust into Chinese slippers. The captain and mate were in thin undershirts and unstarched duck trousers, while the supercargo still held in his hands the undershirt he was reluctant to put on. The sweat stood out on his forehead and he seemed to thrust his bare chest thirstily into the wind that did not cool.

"Pretty muggy for a breeze like this," he complained.

"And what's it doing around in the west? That's what I want to know," was Grief's contribution to the general plaint.

"It won't last and it ain't been there long," said Hermann, the Holland mate. "She is been chop round all night—five minutes here, ten minutes there, one hour somewhere other quarter."

"Something makin', something makin'," Captain

Warfield croaked, spreading his bushy beard with the fingers of both hands and shoving the thatch of his chin into the breeze in a vain search for coolness. "Weather's been crazy for a fortnight. Haven't had the proper trades in three weeks. Everything's mixed up. Barometer was pumping at sunset last night and it's pumping now, though the weather sharps say it don't mean anything. All the same, I've got a prejudice against seeing it pump. Gets on my nerves, sort of, you know. She was pumping that way the time we lost the *Lancaster*. I was only an apprentice, but I can remember that well enough. Brand-new four-masted steel ship; first voyage—broke the old man's heart. He'd been forty years in the company. Just faded away and died the next year."

Despite the wind and the early hour, the heat was suffocating. The wind whispered coolness but did not deliver coolness. It might have blown off the Sahara, save for the extreme humidity with which it was laden. There was no fog or mist, nor hint of fog or mist; yet the dimness of distance produced the impression.

There were no defined clouds; yet so thickly were the heavens covered by a messy cloud pall that the sun failed to shine through.

"Ready about!" Captain Warfield ordered with slow sharpness.

The brown, breechclouted Kanaka sailors moved languidly but quickly to head sheets and boom tackles.

"Hard alee!"

The helmsman ran the spokes over with no hint of gentling and the *Malahini* darted prettily into the wind and about.

"Jove! She's a witch!" was Mulhall's appreciation. "I didn't know you South Sea traders sailed yachts."

"She was a Gloucester fisherman originally," Grief explained, "and the Gloucester boats are all yachts when it comes to build, rig, and sailing."

"But you're heading right in—why don't you make it?" came the Englishman's criticism.

"Try it, Captain Warfield," Grief suggested. "Show him what a lagoon entrance is on a strong ebb."

"Close and by!" the captain ordered.

"Close and by!" the Kanaka repeated, easing half a spoke. The *Malahini* laid squarely into the narrow passage, which was the lagoon entrance of a large, long, and narrow oval of an atoll. The atoll was shaped as if three atolls, in the course of building, had collided and coalesced and failed to rear the partition walls. Coconut palms grew in spots on the circle of sand and there were many gaps where the sand was too low to the sea for coconuts, through which could be seen the protected lagoon where the water lay flat like the ruffled surface of a mirror. Many square miles of water were in the irregular lagoon, all of which surged out on the ebb through the one narrow channel. So narrow was the channel, so large the outflow of water, that the passage was more like the rapids of a river than the mere tidal entrance to an atoll. The

water boiled and whirled and swirled and drove out-
ward in a white foam of stiff, serrated waves. Each
heave and blow on her bows of the upstanding waves
of the current swung the *Malahini* off the straight
lead and wedged her as with wedges of steel toward
the side of the passage. Part way in she was when her
closeness to the coral edge compelled her to go about.
On the opposite tack, broadside to the current, she
swept seaward with the current's speed

"Now's the time for that new and expensive engine of yours," Grief leered good-naturedly.

That the engine was a sore point with Captain
Warfield was patent. He had begged and badgered
for it until, in the end, Grief had given his consent.

"It will pay for itself yet," the captain retorted. "You
wait and see. It beats insurance; and you know the underwriters won't stand for insurance in the Paumotus."

Grief pointed to a small cutter beating up astern
of them on the same course.

"I'll wager five francs the little *Nuhiva* beats us in.

"Sure!" Captain Warfield agreed. "She's overpow-
ered. We're like a liner alongside of her and we've
only got forty horsepower. She's got ten horse, and
she's a little skimming dish. She could skate across
the froth of hell; but just the same she can't buck this
current. It's running ten knots right now."

And at the rate of ten knots, buffeted and jerkily
rolled, the *Malahini* went out to sea with the tide.

"She'll slacken in half an hour—then we'll make
headway," Captain Warfield said with an irritation

explained by his next words. "He has no right to call it Parlay. It's down on the Admiralty charts, and the French charts too, as Hikihoho. Bougainville discovered it and named it from the natives."

"What's the name matter?" the supercargo demanded, taking advantage of speech to pause with arms shoved into the sleeves of the undershirt. "There it is, right under our nose; and old Parlay is there with the pearls."

"Who see them pearls?" Hermann queried, looking from one to another.

"It's well known," was the supercargo's reply. He turned to the steersman. "Tell them, Tai-Hotauri."

The Kanaka, pleased and self-conscious, took and gave a spoke. "My brother dive for Parlay three-four month and he make much talk about pearl. Hikihoho very good place for pearl."

"And the pearl buyers have never got him to part with a pearl," the captain broke in.

"And they say the old man had a hatful for Armande when he sailed for Tahiti," the supercargo carried on the tale.

"That's fifteen years ago and he's been adding to it ever since—stored the shell as well. Everybody's seen that—hundreds of tons of it. They say the lagoon's fished clean now. Maybe that's why he's announced the auction."

"If he really sells what he has, this will be the biggest year's output of pearls in the Paumotus," Grief said.

"I say, now, look here!" Mulhall burst forth, harried by the humid heat as much as the rest of them. "What's it all about? Who's the old beachcomber anyway? What are all these pearls? Why so secretive about it?"

"Hikihoho belongs to old Parlay," the supercargo answered. "He's got a fortune in pearls, saved up for years and years; and he sent the word out weeks ago that he'd auction them off to the buyers tomorrow. See those schooners' masts sticking up inside the lagoon?"

"Eight—so I see," said Hermann.

"What are they doing in a dinky atoll like this?" the supercargo went on. "There isn't a schoonerload of copra a year in the place. They've come for the auction. That's why we're here. That's why the little *Nuhiva's* bumping along astern there—though what she can buy is beyond me. Narii Herring—he's an English Jew half-caste—owns and runs her, and his only assets are his nerve, his debts, and his whisky bills. He's a genius in such things. He owes so much there isn't a merchant in Papeete who isn't interested in his welfare. They go out of their way to throw work in his way. They've got to—and a dandy stunt it is for Narii. Now I owe nobody. What's the result? If I fell down in a fit on the beach they'd let me lie there and die. They wouldn't lose anything. But Narii Herring! What wouldn't they do if he fell in a fit? Their best wouldn't be too good for him. They've got too much money tied up in him to let him lie.

They'd take him into their homes and hand-nurse him like a brother. Let me tell you, honesty in paying bills ain't what it's cracked up to be."

"What's this Narii chap got to do with it?" was the Englishman's short-tempered demand. And, turning to Grief, he said: "What's all this pearl nonsense? Begin at the beginning"

"You'll have to help me out," Grief warned the others as he began. "Old Parlay is a character. From what I've seen of him, I believe he's partly and mildly insane. Anyway, here's the story. Parlay's a full-blooded Frenchman. He told me once that he came from Paris. His accent is the true Parisian. He arrived down here in the old days. Went to trading and all the rest. That's how he got in on Hikihoho. Came in trading when trading was the real thing. About a hundred miserable Paumotans lived on the island. He married the Queen—native fashion. When she died everything was his. Measles came through and there weren't more than a dozen survivors. He fed them and worked them, and was King. Now before the Queen died she gave birth to a girl. That's Armande. When she was three he sent her to the convent at Papeete. When she was seven or eight he sent her to France. You begin to glimpse the situation. The best and most aristocratic convent in France was none too good for the only daughter of a Paumotan island king and capitalist—and you know the old-country French draw no color line. She was educated like a princess and she accepted herself in much the same way. Also she thought she was all white and never dreamed of a bar sinister.

"Now comes the tragedy. The old man had always been cranky and erratic, and he'd played the despot on Hikihoho so long that he'd got the idea in his head that there was nothing wrong with the King—or the princess either. When Armande was eighteen he sent for her. He had slews and slathers of money, as Yankee Bill would say. He'd built the big house on Hikihoho and a whacking fine bungalow in Papeete. She was to arrive on the mail boat from New Zealand and he sailed in his schooner to meet her at Papeete. And he might have carried the situation off, despite the hens and bull beasts of Papeete, if it hadn't been for the hurricane. That was the year, wasn't it, when Mann-Huni was swept and eleven hundred drowned?"

The others nodded and Captain Warfield said: "I was in the *Magpie* that blow and we went ashore, all hands and the cook—*Magpie* and all—a quarter of a mile into the coconuts at the head of Taiohae Bay—and it a supposedly hurricane-proof harbor."

"Well," Grief continued, "old Parlay got caught in the same blow and arrived in Papeete with his hatful of pearls three weeks too late. He'd had to jack up his schooner and build half a mile of ways before he could get her back into the sea.

"Meantime there was Armande at Papeete. Nobody called on her. She did, French fashion, make the initial calls on the governor and the port doctor. They saw her, but neither of their hen wives was at home to her or returned the call. She was out of caste—without caste—though she had never dreamed it; and that was the gentle way they broke the information to her. There was a gay young lieutenant on the French cruiser. He lost his heart to her, but not his head. You can imagine the shock to this young woman, refined, beautiful, raised like an aristocrat, pampered with the best of old France that money could buy! And you can guess the end." He shrugged his shoulders. "There was a Japanese servant in the bungalow. He saw it—said she did it with the proper spirit of the samurai. Took a stiletto—no thrust, no drive, no wild rush for annihilation—took the stiletto, placed the point carefully against her heart, and with both hands slowly and steadily pressed home.

"Old Parlay arrived after that with his pearls. There was one single one of them, they say, worth sixty thousand francs. Peter Gee saw it and has told me he offered that much for it. The old man went clean off for a while. They had him strait-jacketed in the Colonial Club for two days——"

"His wife's uncle, an old Paumotan, cut him out of the jacket and turned him loose," the supercargo corroborated.

"And then old Parlay proceeded to eat things up," Grief went on. "Pumped three bullets into the scalawag of a lieutenant——"

"Who lay in sick bay for three months," Captain Warfield contributed.

"Flung a glass of wine in the governor's face; fought a duel with the port doctor; beat up his native servants, wrecked the hospital; broke two ribs and the collarbone of a man nurse—and escaped; went down to his schooner, a gun in each hand, daring the chief of police and all the gendarmes to arrest him, and sailed for Hikihoho. And they say he's never left the island since."

The supercargo nodded. "That was fifteen years ago, and he's never budged."

"And added to his pearls," said the captain. "He's a blithering old lunatic. Makes my flesh creep. He's a regular Finn."

"What's that?" Mulhall asked.

"Bosses the weather—that's what the natives believe, at any rate. Ask Tai-Hotauri there. Hey, Tai-Hotauri, what you think old Parlay do along weather?"

"Just the same one big weather devil!" came the Kanaka's answer. "I know. He want big blow, he make big blow. He want no wind, no wind come."

"A regular old warlock," said Mulhall.

"No good luck, them pearl," Tai-Hotauri blurted out, rolling his head ominously. "He say he sell. Plenty schooner come. Then he make big hurricane; everybody finish, you see. All native men say so."

"It's hurricane season now," Captain Warfield laughed morosely. "They're not far wrong. It's making for something right now; and I'd feel better if the *Malahini* was a thousand miles away from here."

"He is a bit mad," Grief concluded. "I've tried to

get his point of view. It's—well, it's mixed. For eighteen years he'd centered everything on Armande. Half the time he believes she's still alive—not yet come back from France. That's one of the reasons he held on to the pearls. And all the time he hates white men. He never forgets they killed her, though a great deal of the time he forgets she's dead."

"Hello! Where's your wind?"

The sails bellied emptily overhead and Captain Warfield grunted his disgust. Intolerable as the heat had been, in the absence of wind it was almost overpowering. The sweat oozed out on all their faces; and now one and then another drew deep breaths, involuntarily questing for more air.

"Here she comes again—an eight-point haul! Boom tackles across! Jump!"

The Kanakas sprang to the captain's orders and for five minutes the schooner laid directly into the passage—and even gained on the current. Again the breeze fell flat, then puffed from the old quarter, compelling a shift back of sheets and tackles.

"Here comes the *Nuhiva*," Grief said. "She's got her engine on. Look at her skim!"

"All ready?" the captain asked the engineer, a Portuguese half-caste, whose head and shoulders protruded from the small hatch just for'ard of the cabin, and who wiped the dripping sweat from his face with a bunch of greasy waste.

"Sure!" he replied.

"Then let her go!"

The engineer disappeared into his den and a moment later the exhaust muffler coughed and sputtered overside; but the schooner could not hold her lead. The little cutter traveled three feet to her two and was quickly alongside and forging ahead.

Only natives were on her deck and the man who was steering waved his hand in derisive greeting and farewell.

"That's Narii Herring," Grief told Mulhall, "the big fellow at the wheel—the nerviest and most conscienceless scoundrel in the Paumotus."

Five minutes later a cry of joy from their own Kanakas centered all eyes on the Nuhiva. Her engine had broken down and they were overtaking her. The *Malahini's* sailors sprang into the rigging and jeered as they went by; the little cutter, heeled over by the wind, was going backward on the tide.

"Some engine, that of ours!" Grief approved as the lagoon opened before them and the course was changed across it to the anchorage.

Captain Warfield was visibly cheered, though he merely grunted: "It'll pay for itself; never fear."

The *Malahini* ran well into the center of the little fleet ere she found swinging room to anchor.

"There's Isaacs on the *Dolly,*" Grief observed with a hand wave of greeting. "And Peter Gee's on the *Roberta*. Couldn't keep him away from a pearl sale like this. And there's Francini on the *Cactus*. They're all here—all the buyers. Old Parlay will surely get a price."

"They haven't repaired the engine yet," Captain Warfield grumbled gleefully. He was looking across the lagoon to where the *Nuhiva's* sails showed through the sparse coconuts.

II

The house of Parlay was a big two-story frame affair, built of California lumber, with a galvanized iron roof. So disproportionate was it to the slender ring of the atoll that it showed out upon the sand strip and above it like some monstrous excrescence. They of the *Malahini* paid the courtesy visit ashore immediately after anchoring. Other captains and buyers were in the big room examining the pearls that were to be auctioned next day. Paumotan servants, natives of Hikihoho and relatives of the owner, moved about, dispensing whisky and absinthe. And through the curious company moved Parlay himself, cackling and sneering, the withered wreck of what had once been a tall and powerful man. His eyes were deep-sunken and feverish, his cheeks fallen in and cavernous. The hair of his head seemed to have come out in patches and his mustache and imperial had been shed in the same lopsided way.

"Jove!" Mulhall muttered under his breath. "A long-legged Napoleon III—but burnt out, baked, and fire-crackled. And mangy! No wonder he crooks his head to one side. He's got to keep the balance."

"Goin' to have a blow," was the old man's greeting to Grief. "You must think a lot of pearls to come a day like this."

"They're worth going to inferno for," Grief

laughed genially back, running his eyes over the surface of the table covered by the display.

"Other men have already made that journey for them," old Parlay cackled. "See this one!" He pointed to a large, perfect pearl, the size of a small walnut, that lay apart on a piece of chamois. "They offered me sixty thousand francs for it in Tahiti. They'll bid as much and more for it tomorrow if they aren't blown away. Well, that pearl was found by my cousin—my cousin by marriage. He was a native, you see. Also he was a thief. He hid it. It was mine. His cousin, who was also my cousin—we're all related here—killed him for it and fled away in a cutter to Noo-Nau. I pursued; but the chief of Noo-Nau had killed him for it before I got there. Oh yes, there are many dead men represented on the table there. Have a drink, Captain? Your face is not familiar. You are new in the islands?"

"It's Captain Robinson, of the *Roberta*," Grief said, introducing them.

Meantime Mulhall had shaken hands with Peter Gee.

"I never fancied there were so many pearls in the world," Mulhall said.

"Nor have I ever seen so many together at one time," Peter Gee admitted.

"What ought they to be worth?" asked Mulhall.

"Fifty or sixty thousand pounds—and that's to us buyers. In Paris . . ." He shrugged his shoulders.

Mulhall wiped the sweat from his eyes. All were

sweating profusely and breathing hard. There was no ice, and the whisky and absinthe went down lukewarm.

"Yes, yes!" Parlay was cackling. "Many dead men lie on the table there. I know those pearls, all of them. You see those three—perfectly matched, aren't they? A diver from Easter Island got them for me inside a week. Next week a shark got him—took his arm off and blood poison did the business. And that big baroque there—nothing much; if I'm offered twenty francs for it tomorrow I'll be in luck—it came out of twenty-two fathoms of water. The man was from Rarotonga. He broke all diving records. He got it out of twenty-two fathoms. I saw him. And he burst his lungs at the same time, or got the bends; for he died in two hours. He died screaming. They could hear him for miles. He was the most powerful native I ever saw. Half a dozen of my divers have died of the bends. And more men will die—more men will die!"

"Oh, hush your croaking, Parlay!" chided one of the captains. "It ain't going to blow."

"If I was a strong young man I couldn't get up hook and get out fast enough," the old man retorted in the falsetto of age. "Not if I was a strong young man with the taste for wine yet in my mouth. But not you. You'll all stay. I wouldn't advise you if I thought you'd go. You can't drive buzzards away from the carrion. Have another drink, my brave sailormen. Well, well! What men will dare for a few little oyster drops! There they are, the beauties! Auction tomorrow at ten sharp. Old Parlay's selling out and the buzzards are gathering—old Parlay, who was a stronger man in his day than any of them and who will see most of them dead yet!"

"If he isn't a vile old beast!" the supercargo of the *Malahini* whispered to Peter Gee.

"What if she does blow?" said the captain of the *Dolly*. "Hikihoho's never been swept."

"The more reason she will be, then," Captain Warfield answered back. "I wouldn't trust her."

"Who's croaking now?" Grief reproved.

"I'd hate to lose that new engine before it paid for itself," Captain Warfield replied gloomily.

Parlay skipped with astonishing nimbleness across the crowded room to where a ship's barometer hung on the wall.

"Take a look, my brave sailormen!" he cried exultantly.

The man nearest read the glass. The sobering effect showed plainly on his face.

"It's dropped ten," was all he said, yet every face went anxious and there was a restlessness as if every man desired immediately to start for the door.

"Listen!" Parlay commanded.

In the silence the outer surf seemed to have become unusually loud. There was a great, rumbling roar.

"A big sea is beginning to set," someone said; and there was a movement to the windows, where all gathered.

Through the sparse coconuts they gazed seaward.

An orderly succession of huge, smooth seas was rolling down upon the coral shore. For some minutes they gazed on the strange sight and talked in low voices, and in those few minutes it was manifest to all that the waves were increasing in size. It was uncanny, this rising sea in a dead calm, and their voices unconsciously sank lower. Old Parlay shocked them with his abrupt cackle.

"There is yet time to get away to sea, brave gentlemen. You can tow across the lagoon with your whaleboats."

"It's all right, old man," said Darling, the mate of the *Cactus*, a stalwart youngster of twenty-five. "The blow's to the south'ard and passing on. We'll not get a whiff of it."

An air of relief went through the room. Conversations were started, and the voices became louder. Several of the buyers even went back to the table to continue the examination of the pearls. Parley's cackle rose higher.

"That's right," he encouraged. "If the world was coming to an end you'd go on buying."

"We'll buy these tomorrow," Isaacs assured him.

"Then you'll be doing your buying in hell!"

The chorus of incredulous laughter incensed the old man. He turned fiercely on Darling.

"Since when have children like you come to the knowledge of storms? And who is the man who has plotted the hurricane courses of the Paumotus? What books will you find it in? I sailed the Paumotus before

the oldest of you drew breath. I know! To the eastward
the paths of the hurricanes are on so wide a circle they
make a straight line. To the westward here they make
a sharp curve. Remember your chart. How did it happen the hurricane of '91 swept Auri and Hiolau? The
curve, my brave boy, the curve! In an hour, or two or
three at most, will come the wind. Listen to that!"

A vast, rumbling crash shook the coral founda-
tions of the atoll. The house quivered to it. The native servants, with bottles of whisky and absinthe in
their hands, shrank together as if for protection and
stared with fear through the windows at the mighty
wash of the wave lapping far up the beach to the corner of a copra shed.

Parlay looked at the barometer, giggled, and
leered around at his guests. Captain Warfield strode
across to see.

"Twenty-nine seventy-five!" he read. "She's gone
down five more. The old devil's right. She's
a-coming—and it's me, for one, for aboard!"

"It's growing dark," Isaacs half whimpered.

"Jove! It's like a stage," Mulhall said to Grief,
looking at his watch. "Ten o'clock in the morning
and it's like twilight. Down go the lights for the
tragedy. Where's the slow music?"

In answer another rumbling crash shook the atoll
and the house. Almost in a panic the company started
for the door. In the dim light their sweaty faces appeared ghastly. Isaacs panted asthmatically in the suffocating heat.

"What's your haste?" Parlay chuckled and girded at his departing guests. "A last drink, brave gentlemen!" No one noticed him. As they took the shell-bordered path to the beach he stuck his head out at the door and called: "Don't forget, gentlemen—at ten tomorrow old Parlay sells his pearls!"

III

On the beach a curious scene took place. Whaleboat after whaleboat was being hurriedly manned and shoved off. It had grown still darker. The stagnant calm continued and the sand shook under their feet with each buffet of the sea on the outer shore. Narii Herring walked leisurely along the sand. He grinned at the very evident haste of the captains and buyers. With him were three of his Kanakas and also Tai-Hotauri.

"Get into the boat and take an oar," Captain Warfield ordered the latter.

Tai-Hotauri came over jauntily, while Narii Herring and his Kanakas paused and looked on from forty feet away.

"I work no more for you, skipper," Tai-Hotauri said insolently and loudly; but his face belied his words, for he was guilty of a prodigious wink. "Fire me, skipper," he huskily whispered with a second significant wink.

Captain Warfield took the cue and proceeded to do some acting himself. He raised his fist and his voice.

"Get into that boat, you swine," he thundered, "or I'll knock seven bells out of you!"

The Kanaka drew back truculently and Grief stepped between to placate his captain.

"I go to work on the *Nuhiva*," Tai-Hotauri said, rejoining the other group.

"Come back here!" the captain threatened.

"He's a free man, skipper," Narii Herring spoke up. "He's sailed with me in the past and he's sailing with me again—that's all."

"Come on; we must get on board," Grief urged. "Look how dark it's getting!"

Captain Warfield gave in, but as the boat shoved off he stood up in the stem sheets and shook his fist ashore.

"I'll settle with you yet, Narii!" he cried. "You're the only skipper in the group who steals other men's sailors." He sat down and in a lowered voice queried: "Now what's Tai-Hotauri up to? He's on to something; but what is it?"

IV

As the boat came alongside the *Malahini*, Hermann's anxious face greeted them over the rail.

"Bottom fall out from barometer," he announced. "She's goin' to blow. I got starboard anchor overhaul."

"Overhaul the big one too," Captain Warfield ordered, taking charge. "And here, some of you, hoist in this boat. Lower her down to the deck and lash her, bottom up."

Men were busy at work on the decks of all the schooners. There was a great clanking of chains being overhauled; and now one craft and now another hove in, veered, and dropped a second anchor.

Like the *Malahini,* those that had third anchors were preparing to drop them when the wind showed what quarter it was to blow from.

The roar of the big surf continually grew, though the lagoon lay in mirrorlike calm. There was no sign of life where Parlay's big house perched on the sand. Boat and copra sheds and the sheds where the shell was stored were deserted.

"For two cents I'd up anchors and get out," Grief said. "I'd do it anyway if it were open sea; but those chains of atolls to the north and east have us pocketed. We've a better chance right there. What do you think, Captain Warfield?"

"I agree with you, though a lagoon is no millpond for riding it out. I wonder where she's going to start from? Hello! There goes one of Parlay's copra sheds!"

They could see the grass-thatched shed lift and collapse, while a froth of foam cleared the crest of the sand and ran down to the lagoon.

"Breached across!" Mulhall exclaimed. "That's something for a starter. There she comes again!"

The wreck of the shed was now flung up and left on the sand crest. A third wave buffeted it into fragments, which washed down the slope toward the lagoon.

"If she blow I would as be cooler yet," Hermann grunted. "No longer can I breathe. It is damn hot. I am dry like a stove."

He chopped open a drinking coconut with his heavy sheath knife and drained the contents. The rest of them followed his example, pausing once to watch one of Parlay's shell sheds go down in ruin. The barometer now registered 29.50.

"Must be pretty close to the center of the area of low pressure," Grief remarked cheerfully. "I was never through the eye of a hurricane before. It will be an experience for you too, Mulhall. From the speed the barometer's dropped it's going to be a big one."

Captain Warfield groaned, and all eyes were drawn to him. He was looking through the glasses down the length of the lagoon to the southeast.

"There she comes," he said quietly.

They did not need glasses to see. A flying film, strangely marked, seemed drawing over the surface of the lagoon. Abreast of it, along the atoll, traveling with equal speed, was a stiff bending of the coconut palms and a blur of flying leaves. The front of the wind on the water was a solid, sharply defined strip of dark-colored, wind-vexed water. In advance of this strip, like skirmishers, were flashes of windflaws. Behind this strip, a quarter of a mile in width, was a strip of what seemed glassy calm. Next came another dark strip of wind—and behind that the lagoon was all crisping, boiling whiteness.

"What is that calm streak?" Mulhall asked.

"Calm," Warfield answered.

"But it travels as fast as the wind," was the other's objection.

"It has to, or it would be overtaken and there wouldn't be any calm. It's a double-header. I saw a big squall like that off Savaii once. A regular double-header. Smash! It hit us; then it lulled to nothing and smashed us a second time. Stand by and hold on. Here she is on top of us. Look at the *Roberta*!"

The *Roberta,* lying nearest to the wind at slack chains, was swept off broadside like a straw. Then her chains brought her up, bow on to the wind, with an astonishing jerk. Schooner after schooner—the *Malahini* with them—was now sweeping away with the first gust and fetching up on taut chains.

Mulhall and several of the Kanakas were taken off their feet when the *Malahini* jerked to her anchor.

And then there was no wind. The flying calm streak had reached them. Grief lighted a match and the unshielded flame burned without flickering in the still air. A very dim twilight prevailed. The cloud-sky, lowering as it had been for hours, seemed now to have descended quite down upon the sea.

The *Roberta* tightened to her chains when the second head of the hurricane hit, as did schooner after schooner in swift succession. The sea, white with fury, boiled in tiny, spitting wavelets. The deck of the *Malahini* vibrated under their feet. The taut-stretched halyards beat a tattoo against the masts, and all the rigging, as if smitten by some mighty hand, set up a wild thrumming. It was impossible to face the wind and breathe. Mulhall, crouching with the others behind the shelter of the cabin, discovered

this; and his lungs were filled in an instant with so
great a volume of driven air which he could not expel
that he nearly strangled ere he could turn his head
away.

"It's incredible!" he gasped; but no one heard him.

Hermann and several Kanakas were crawling
for'ard on hands and knees to let go the third anchor.
Grief touched Captain Warfield and pointed to the
Roberta. She was dragging down upon them. Warfield
put his mouth to Grief's ear and shouted:

"We're dragging too!"

Grief sprang to the wheel and put it hard over,
veering the *Malahini* to port. The third anchor took
hold and the *Roberta* went by, stern first, a dozen
yards away. They waved their hands to Peter Gee and
Captain Robinson, who, with a number of sailors,
were at work on the bow.

"He's knocking out the shackles!" Grief shouted.
"Going to chance the passage! Got to! Anchors skat-
ing!"

"We're holding now!" came the answering shout.
"There goes the *Cactus* down on the *Misi*. That settles
them!"

The *Misi* had been holding, but the added
windage of the *Cactus* was too much and the entan-
gled schooners slid away across the boiling white.
Their men could be seen chopping and fighting to
get them apart. The *Roberta*, cleared of her anchors,
with a patch of tarpaulin set for'ard, was heading for
the passage at the northwestern end of the lagoon.

They saw her make it and drive out to sea. The *Misi* and the *Cactus*, however, unable to get clear of each other, went ashore on the atoll half a mile from the passage.

The wind merely increased on itself and continued to increase. To face the full blast of it required all one's strength, and several minutes of crawling on deck against it tired a man to exhaustion. Hermann, with his Kanakas, plodded steadily, lashing and making secure, putting ever more gaskets on the sails. The wind ripped and tore their thin undershirts from their backs. They moved slowly, as if their bodies weighed tons, never releasing a handhold until another had been secured. Loose ends of rope stood out stiffly horizontal, and after whipping the loose ends frazzled and blew away.

Mulhall touched one and then another and pointed to the shore. The grass sheds had disappeared and Parlay's house rocked drunkenly. Because the wind blew lengthwise along the atoll the house had been sheltered by the miles of coconut trees; but the big seas, breaking across from outside, were undermining it and hammering it to pieces. Already tilted down the slope of sand, its end was imminent. Here and there in the coconut trees people had lashed themselves. The trees did not sway or thresh about. Bent over rigidly by the wind, they remained in that position and vibrated monstrously. Underneath, across the sand, surged the white spume of the breakers.

A big sea was likewise making down the length of the lagoon. It had plenty of room to kick up in the ten-mile stretch from the windward rim of the atoll, and all the schooners were bucking and plunging into it. The *Malahini* had begun shoving her bow and fo'c'sle head under the bigger ones, and at times her waist was filled rail-high with water.

"Now's the time for your engine!" Grief bellowed; and Captain Warfield, crawling over to where the engineer lay, shouted emphatic commands.

Under the engine, going full speed ahead, the *Malahini* behaved better. Though she continued to ship seas over her bow, she was not jerked down so fiercely by her anchors. On the other hand, she was unable to get any slack in the chains. The best her forty horsepower could do was to ease the strain.

Still the wind increased. The little *Nuhiva,* lying abreast of the *Malahini* and closer in to the beach, her engine still unrepaired and her captain ashore, was having a bad time of it. She buried herself so frequently and so deeply that they wondered each time if she could clear herself of the water.

At three in the afternoon, buried by a second sea before she could free herself of the preceding one, she did not come up.

Mulhall looked at Grief.

"Burst in her hatches!" was the bellowed answer.

Captain Warfield pointed to the *Winifred,* a little schooner plunging and burying outside of them, and shouted in Grief's ear. His voice came in patches of dim words, with intervals of silence when whisked away by the roaring wind.

"Rotten little tub! . . . Anchors hold. . . . But how she holds together! . . . Old as the ark."

An hour later Hermann pointed to her. Her for'ard bitts, foremast, and most of her bow were gone, having been jerked out of her by her anchors. She swung broadside, rolling in the trough and settling by the head; and in this plight she was swept away to leeward.

Five vessels now remained, and of them the *Malahini* was the only one with an engine. Fearing either the *Nuhiva's* or the *Mildred's* fate, two of them followed the *Roberta's* example, knocking out the chain shackles and running for the passage. The *Dolly* was the first, but her tarpaulin was carried away and she went to destruction on the lee rim of the atoll, near the *Misi* and the *Cactus*. Undeterred by this, the *Moana* let go and followed with the same result.

"Pretty good engine that, eh?" Captain Warfield yelled to his owner.

Grief put out his hand and shook. "She's paying for herself!" he yelled back. "The wind's shifting round to the south'ard and we ought to lie easier!"

Slowly and steadily, but with ever-increasing velocity, the wind veered round to the south and the southwest, till the three schooners that were left pointed directly in toward the beach. The wreck of Parlay's house was picked up, hurled into the lagoon, and blown out upon them. Passing the

Malahini, it crashed into the *Papara,* lying a quarter of a mile astern. There was wild work for'ard on her and in a quarter of an hour the house went clear, but it had taken the *Papara's* foremast and bowsprit with it.

Inshore, on their port bow, lay the *Tahaa,* slim and yacht-like, but excessively oversparred. Her anchors still held, but her captain, finding no abatement in the wind, proceeded to reduce windage by chopping down his masts.

"Pretty good engine that!" Grief congratulated his skipper. "It will save our sticks for us yet."

Captain Warfield shook his head dubiously.

The sea on the lagoon went swiftly down with the change of wind, but they were beginning to feel the heave and lift of the outer sea breaking across the atoll. There were not so many trees remaining. Some had been broke short off, others uprooted. One tree they saw snapped off halfway up, three persons clinging to it, and whirled away by the wind into the lagoon. Two detached themselves from it and swam to the *Tahaa.* Not long after, just before darkness, they saw a man jump overboard from that schooner's stern and strike out strongly for the *Malahini* through the white, spitting wavelets.

"It's Tai-Hotauri," was Grief's judgment. "Now we'll have the news."

The Kanaka caught the bobstay, climbed over the bow, and crawled aft. Time was given him to breathe and then, behind the part shelter of the cabin, in broken snatches and largely by signs he told his story:

"Narii ... Damn robber! ... He want steal ... pearls. Kill Parlay.... One man kill Parlay.... No man know what man.... Three Kanakas, Narii, me ... five beans ... hat.... Narii say one bean black.... Nobody know.... Kill Parlay.... Narii damn liar.... All beans black.... Five black.... Copra shed dark.... Every man get black bean.... Big wind come ... no chance.... Everybody get up tree.... No good luck, them pearls, I tell you before ... no good luck."

"Where's Parlay?" Grief shouted.

"Up tree.... Three of his Kanakas same tree; Narii and one Kanaka 'nother tree... My tree blow to hell; then I come on board."

"Where are the pearls?"

"Up tree along Parlay. Mebbe Narii get them pearl yet." In the ear of one after another Grief shouted Tai-Hotauri's story. Captain Warfield was particularly incensed and they could see him grinding his teeth.

Hermann went below and returned with a riding light, but the moment it was lifted above the level of the cabin wall the wind blew it out. He had better success with the binnacle lamp, which was lighted only after many collective attempts.

"A fine night of wind," Grief yelled in Mulhall's ear, "and blowing harder all the time!"

"How hard?"

"A hundred miles an hour—two hundred! I don't know. Harder than I've ever seen it."

The lagoon grew more and more troubled by the sea that swept across the atoll. Hundreds of leagues of ocean were being backed up by the hurricane, which more than overcame the lowering effect of the ebb tide. Immediately the tide began to rise, the increase in the size of the seas was noticeable. Moon and wind were heaping the South Pacific on Hikihoho atoll.

Captain Warfield returned from one of his periodical trips to the engine room with the word that the engineer lay in a faint.

"Can't let that engine stop!" he concluded helplessly.

"All right!" Grief shouted. "Bring him on deck. I'll spell him."

The hatch to the engine room was battened down, access being gained through a narrow passage from the cabin. The heat and gas fumes were stifling. Grief made one hasty, comprehensive examination of the engine and the fittings of the tiny room, then blew out the oil lamp. After that he worked in darkness, save for the glow from endless cigars that he went into the cabin to light. Even-tempered as he was, he soon began to give evidences of the strain of being pent in with a mechanical monster that toiled and sobbed and slubbered in the shouting dark. Naked to the waist, covered with grease and oil, bruised and skinned from being knocked about by the plunging, jumping vessel, his head swimming from the mixture of gas and air he was compelled to breathe, he labored on hour after hour, by turns petting, blessing, nursing, and cursing the engine and all its parts. The ignition began to go bad. The feed grew worse and, worst of all, the cylinders began to heat. In a consultation held in the cabin the half-caste engineer begged and pleaded to stop the engine for half an hour in order to cool it and to attend to the water circulation.

Captain Warfield was against any stopping. The half-caste swore that the engine would ruin itself and stop anyway, and for good. Grief, with glaring eyes, greasy and battered, yelled and cursed them both down and issued commands. Mulhall, the supercargo, and Hermann were set to work in the cabin at double-straining and triple-straining the gasoline.

A hole was chopped through the engine-room floor and a Kanaka heaved bilge water over the cylinders, while Grief continued to souse the running parts in oil.

"Didn't know you were a gasoline expert," Captain Warfield admired when Grief came into the cabin to catch a breath of little less impure air.

"I bathe in gasoline," he grated savagely through his teeth. "I eat it."

What other uses he might have found for it were never given, for at that moment all the men in the cabin, as well as the gasoline that was being strained, were smashed for'ard against the bulkhead as the *Malahini* took an abrupt, deep dive. For the space of several minutes, unable to gain their feet, they rolled back and forth and pounded and hammered from wall to wall. The schooner, swept by three big seas, creaked and groaned and quivered and, from the weight of water on her decks, behaved loggily. Grief crept to the engine, while Captain Warfield awaited his chance to get through the companionway and out on deck.

It was half an hour before he came back.

"Whaleboat's gone!" he reported. "Galley's gone! Everything gone except the deck and hatches! And if that engine hadn't been going we'd be gone! Keep up the good work!"

By midnight the engineer's lungs and head had been sufficiently cleared of gas fumes to let him relieve Grief, who went on deck to get his own head and lungs clear. He joined the others, who crouched behind the cabin, holding on with their hands and made doubly secure by rope lashings. It was a complicated huddle, for it was the only place of refuge for the Kanakas. Some of them had accepted the skipper's invitation into the cabin, but had been driven out by the fumes. The *Malahini* was being plunged down and swept frequently, and what they breathed was air and spray and water commingled.

"Making heavy weather of it, Mulhall!" Grief yelled to his guest between immersions.

Mulhall, strangling and choking, could only nod. The scuppers could not carry off the burden of water on the schooner's deck. She rolled it out and took it in over one rail and the other; and at times, nose thrown skyward, sitting down on her heel, she avalanched it aft. It surged along the poop gangways, poured over the top of the cabin, submerging and bruising those who clung on, and went out over the stem rail.

Mulhall saw him first and drew Grief's attention. It was Narii Herring, crouching and holding on where the dim binnacle light shone upon him. He was quite naked, save for a belt and a bare-bladed knife thrust between it and the skin.

Captain Warfield untied his lashings and made his way over the bodies of the others. When his face became visible in the light from the binnacle it was working with anger. They could see him shout, but the wind tore the sound away. He would not put his lips to Narii's ear. Instead he pointed over the side. Narii Herring understood. His white teeth showed in an amused and sneering smile, and he stood up—a magnificent figure of a man.

"It's murder!" Mulhall yelled to Grief.

"He'd have murdered old Parlay!" Grief yelled back.

For the moment the poop was clear of water and the *Malahini* on an even keel. Narii made a bravado attempt to walk to the rail, but was flung down by the wind. Thereafter he crawled, disappearing in the darkness, though there was certitude in all of them that he had gone over the side. The *Malahini* dived deep; and when they emerged from the flood that swept aft Grief got Mulhall's ear.

"Can't lose him! He's the Fish Man of Tahiti! He'll cross the lagoon and land on the other rim of the atoll—if there's any atoll left."

Five minutes afterward, in another submergence, a mess of bodies poured down on them over the top of the cabin. These they seized and held till the water cleared, when they carried them below and learned their identity. Old Parlay lay on his back on the floor with closed eyes and without movement. The other two were his Kanaka cousins. All three were naked and bloody. The arm of one Kanaka hung helpless and broken at his side. The other Kanaka bled freely from a hideous scalp wound.

"Narii did that?" Mulhall demanded. Grief shook his head. "No; it's from being smashed along the deck and over the house!"

Something suddenly ceased, leaving them all in dizzying uncertainty. For a moment it was hard to realize there was no wind. With the absolute abruptness of a sword slash the wind had been chopped off. The schooner rolled and plunged, fetching up on her anchors with a crash that for the first time they could hear. Also, for the first time, they could hear the water washing about on deck. The engineer threw off the propeller and eased the engine down.

"We're in the dead center," Grief said. "Now for the shift. It will come as hard as ever." He looked at the barometer.

"Twenty-nine thirty-two," he read.

Not in a moment could he tone down the voice which for hours had shouted against the wind, and so loudly did he speak that, in the quiet, it hurt the others' ears.

"All his ribs are smashed," the supercargo said, feeling along Parlay's side. "He's still breathing; but he's a goner."

Old Parlay groaned, moved one arm impotently, and opened his eyes. In them was the light of recognition.

"My brave gentlemen," he whispered haltingly, "don't forget . . . the auction . . . at ten o'clock . . . in hell!"

His eyes drooped shut and the lower jaw threatened to drop, but he mastered the qualms of dissolution long enough to emit one final, loud, derisive cackle.

Above and below pandemonium broke out. The old familiar roar of the wind was with them. The *Malahini,* caught broadside, was pressed down almost on her beam-ends as she swung the arc compelled by her anchors. They rounded her into the wind, where she jerked to an even keel. The propeller was thrown on and the engine took up its work again.

"Northwest!" Captain Warfield shouted to Grief when he came on deck. "Hauled eight points like a shot!"

"Narii'll never get across the lagoon now!" Grief observed.

"Then he'll blow back to our side—worse luck!"

V

After the passing of the center the barometer began to rise. Equally rapid was the fall of the wind. When it was no more than a howling gale the engine lifted up in the air, parted its bedplates with a last convulsive effort of its forty horsepower, and lay down on its side. A wash of water from the bilge sizzled over it and the steam rose in clouds.

The engineer wailed his dismay, but Grief glanced over the wreck affectionately and went into the cabin to swab the grease off his chest and arms with bunches of cotton waste.

The sun was up and the gentlest of summer breezes blowing when he came on deck, after sewing up the scalp of one Kanaka and setting the other's arm. The *Malahini* lay close to the beach. For'ard, Hermann and the crew were heaving in and straightening out the tangle of anchors.

The *Papara* and the *Tahaa* were gone; and Captain Warfield, through the glasses, was searching the opposite rim of the atoll.

Not a stick left of them," he said. "That's what comes of not having engines. They must have dragged across before the big shift came."

Ashore, where Parlay's house had been, was no vestige of any house. For the space of three hundred yards, where the sea had breached, no tree or even stump was left. Here and there, farther along, stood an occasional palm, and there were numbers which had been snapped off above the ground.

In the crown of one surviving palm Tai-Hotauri asserted he saw something move. There were no boats left to the *Malahini,* and they watched him swim ashore and climb the tree.

When he came back they helped over the rail a young native girl of Parlay's household. But first she passed up to them a battered basket. In it was a litter of blind kittens—all dead save one that feebly mewed and staggered on awkward legs.

"Hello!" said Mulhall. "Who's that?"

Along the beach they saw a man walking. He moved casually, as if out for a morning stroll. Captain Warfield gritted his teeth. It was Narii Herring.

"Hello, Skipper," Narii called when he was abreast of them. "Can I come aboard and get some breakfast?"

Captain Warfield's face and neck began to swell and turn purple. He tried to speak, but choked.

"For two cents . . . ! For two cents . . . !" was all he could manage to articulate.

THE SEA-FARMER

"That wull be the doctor's launch," said Captain MacElrath.

The pilot grunted, while the skipper swept on with his glass from the launch to the strip of beach and to Kingston beyond, and then slowly across the entrance to Howth Head on the northern side.

"The tide's right, and we'll have you docked in two hours," the pilot vouchsafed, with an effort at cheeriness. "Ring's End Basin, is it?"

This time the skipper grunted.

"A dirty Dublin day."

Again the skipper grunted. He was weary with the night of wind in the Irish Channel behind him, the unbroken hours of which he had spent on the bridge. And he was weary with all the voyage behind him—two years and four months between home port and home port, eight hundred and fifty days by his log.

"Proper wunter weather," he answered, after a silence. "The town is undistinct. Ut wull be rainun' guid an' hearty for the day."

Captain MacElrath was a small man, just comfortably able to peep over the canvas dodger of the bridge. The pilot and third officer loomed above him, as did the man at the wheel, a bulky German, deserted from a warship, whom he had signed on in Rangoon. But his lack of inches made Captain

MacElrath a no less able man. At least so the Company reckoned, and so would he have reckoned could he have had access to the carefully and minutely compiled record of him filed away in the office archives. But the Company had never given him a hint of its faith in him. It was not the way of the Company, for the Company went on the principle of never allowing an employee to think himself indispensable or even exceedingly useful; wherefore, while quick to censure, it never praised. What was Captain MacElrath, anyway, save a skipper, one skipper of the eighty-odd skippers that commanded the Company's eighty-odd freighters on all the highways and byways of the sea?

Beneath them, on the main deck, two Chinese stokers were carrying breakfast for'ard across the rusty iron plates that told their own grim story of weight and wash of sea. A sailor was taking down the life-line that stretched from the forecastle, past the hatches and cargo-winches, to the bridge-deck ladder.

"A rough voyage," suggested the pilot.

"Aye, she was fair smokin' ot times, but not thot I minded thot so much as the lossin' of time. I hate like onythun' tull loss time."

So saying, Captain MacElrath turned and glanced aft, aloft and alow, and the pilot, following his gaze, saw the mute but convincing explanation of that loss of time. The smoke-stack, buff-colored underneath, was white with salt, while the whistle-pipe glittered crystalline in the random sunlight that broke for the instant through a cloud-rift. The port lifeboat was missing, its iron davits, twisted and wrenched, testifying to the mightiness of the blow that had been struck the old *Tryapsic*. The starboard davits were also empty. The shattered wreck of the lifeboat they had held lay on the fiddley beside the smashed engine-room skylight, which was covered by a tarpaulin. Below, to star-board, on the bridge deck, the pilot saw the crushed mess-room door, roughly bulkheaded against the pounding seas. Abreast of it, on the smokestack guys, and being taken down by the bos'n and a sailor, hung the huge square of rope netting which had failed to break those seas of their force.

"Twice afore I mentioned thot door tull the owners," said Captain MacElrath. "But they said ut would do. There was bug seas thot time. They was uncreditable bug. And thot buggest one dud the domage. Ut fair carried away the door an' laid ut flat on the mess table an' smashed out the chief's room. He was a but sore about ut."

"It must 'a' been a big un," the pilot remarked sympathetically.

"Aye, ut was thot. Thungs was lively for a but. Ut finished the mate. He was on the brudge wuth me, an' I told hum tull take a look tull the wedges o' number one hatch. She was takin' watter freely an' I was no sure o' number one. I dudna like the look o' ut, an' I was fuggerin' maybe tull heave to tull the marn, when she took ut over abaft the brudge. My word, she was a bug one. We got a but of ut ourselves on the brudge. I dudna miss the mate ot the first, what o' routin' out Chips an' bulkheadun' thot door an' stretchun' the tarpaulin over the sky-light. Then he was nowhere to be found. The mon ot the wheel said as he seen hum goin' down the lodder just afore she hut us. We looked for'ard, we looked tull hus room, we looked tull the engine-room, an' we looked along aft on the lower deck, and there he was, on both sides the cover to the steam-pipe runnun' tull the after-wunches."

The pilot ejaculated an oath of amazement and horror.

"Aye," the skipper went on wearily, "an' on both sides the steam-pipe uz well. I tell ye he was in two pieces, splut clean uz a herrin'. The sea must a-caught hum on the upper brudge deck, carried hum clean across the fiddley, an' banged hum head-on tull the pipe cover. It sheered through hum like so much butter, down atween the eyes, an' along the middle of hum, so that one leg an' arm was fast tull the one piece of hum, an' one leg an' arm fast tull the other piece of hum. I tull ye ut was fair grewsome. We putt hum together an' rolled hum in canvas uz we pulled hum out."

The pilot swore again.

"Oh, ut wasna onythun' tull greet about," Captain MacElrath assured him. "'Twas a guid ruddance. He was no a sailor, thot mate-fellow. He was only fut for a pug-sty, an' a dom puir apology for thot same."

It is said that there are three kinds of Irish—

Catholic, Protestant, and North-of-Ireland—and that the North-of-Ireland Irishman is a transplanted Scotchman. Captain MacElrath was a North-of-Ireland man, and, talking for much of the world like a Scotchman, nothing aroused his ire quicker than being mistaken for a Scotchman. Irish he stoutly was, and Irish he stoutly abided, though it was with a faint lip-lift of scorn that he mentioned mere South-of-Ireland men, or even Orange-men. Himself he was Presbyterian, while in his own community five men were all that ever mustered at a meeting in the Orange Men's Hall. His community was the Island McGill, where seven thousand of his kind lived in such amity and sobriety that in the whole island there was but one policeman and never a public house at all.

Captain MacElrath did not like the sea, and had never liked it. He wrung his livelihood from it, and that was all the sea was, the place where he worked, as the mill, the shop, and the counting-house were the places where other men worked. Romance never sang to him her siren song, and Adventure had never shouted in his sluggish blood. He lacked imagination. The wonders of the deep were without significance to him. Tornadoes, hurricanes, waterspouts, and tidal waves were so many obstacles to the way of a ship on the sea and of a master on the bridge—they were that to him, and nothing more. He had seen, and yet not seen, the many marvels and wonders of far lands. Under his eyelids burned the brazen glories of the tropic seas, or ached the bitter gales of the North Atlantic or far South Pacific; but his memory of them was of mess-room doors stove in, of decks awash and hatches threatened, of undue coal consumption, of long passages, and of fresh paint-work spoiled by unexpected squalls of rain.

"I know my buzz'ness," was the way he often put it, and beyond his business was all that he did not know, all that he had seen with the mortal eyes of him and yet that he never dreamed existed. That he knew his business his owners were convinced, or at forty he would not have held command of the *Tryapsic,* three thousand tons net register, with a cargo capacity of nine thousand tons and valued at fifty thousand pounds.

He had taken up seafaring through no love of it, but because it had been his destiny, because he had been the second son of his father instead of the first. Island McGill was only so large, and the land could support but a certain definite proportion of those that dwelt upon it. The balance, and a large balance it was, was driven to the sea to seek its bread. It had been so for generations. The eldest sons took the farms from their fathers; to the other sons remained the sea and its salt-plowing. So it was that Donald MacElrath, farmer's son and farm-boy himself, had shifted from the soil he loved to the sea he hated and which it was his destiny to farm. And farmed it he had, for twenty years, shrewd, cool-headed, sober, industrious, and thrifty, rising from ship's boy and forecastle hand to mate and master of sailing-ships and thence into steam, second officer, first, and master, from small command to larger, and at last to the bridge of the old *Tryapsic*—old, to be sure, but worth her fifty thousand pounds and still able to bear up in all seas, and weather her nine thousand tons of freight.

From the bridge of the *Tryapsic,* the high place he had gained in the competition of men, he stared at Dublin Harbor opening out, at the town obscured by the dark sky of the dreary wind-driven day, and at the tangled tracery of spars and rigging of the harbor shipping. Back from twice around the world he was, and from interminable junketings up and down on far stretches, home-coming to the wife he had not seen in eight-and-twenty months, and to the child he had never seen and that was already walking and talking. He saw the watch below of stokers and trimmers bobbing out of the forecastle doors like rabbits from a warren and making their way aft over the rusty deck to the mustering of the port doctor. They were Chinese, with expressionless, Sphinxlike faces, and they walked in peculiar shambling fashion, dragging their feet as if the clumsy brogans were too heavy for their lean shanks.

He saw them and he did not see them, as he passed his hand beneath his visored cap and scratched reflectively his mop of sandy hair. For the scene before him was but the background in his brain for the vision of peace that was his—a vision that was his often dur-

ing long nights on the bridge when the old *Tryapsic*
wallowed on the vexed ocean floor, her decks awash,
her rigging thrumming in the gale gusts or snow
squalls or driving tropic rain. And the vision he saw
was of farm and farm-house and straw-thatched out-
buildings, of children playing in the sun, and the
good wife at the door, of lowing kine, and clucking
fowls, and the stamp of horses in the stable, of his father's farm next to his, with beyond the woodless,
rolling land and the hedged fields, neat and orderly,
extending to the crest of the smooth, soft hills. It was
his vision and his dream, his Romance and Adventure, the goal of all his effort, the high reward for the
salt-plowing and the long, long furrows he ran up
and down the whole world around in his farming of
the sea.

In simple taste and homely inclination this much-
traveled man was more simple and homely than the
veriest yokel. Seventy-one years his father was, and
had never slept a night out of his own bed in his own
house on Island McGill. That was the life ideal, so
Captain MacElrath considered, and he was prone to
marvel that any man, not under compulsion, should
leave a farm to go to sea. To this much-traveled man
the whole world was as familiar as the village to the
cobbler sitting in his shop. To Captain MacElrath the
world was a village. In his mind's eye he saw its
streets a thousand leagues long, aye, and longer; turn-
ings that doubled earth's stormiest headlands or were
the way to quiet inland ponds; cross-roads, taken one

way, that led to flower-lands and summer seas, and
that led the other way to bitter, ceaseless gales and
the perilous bergs of the great west wind drift. And
the cities, bright with lights, were as shops on these
long streets—shops where business was transacted,
where bunkers were replenished, cargoes taken or
shifted, and orders received from the owners in Lon-
don town to go elsewhere and beyond, ever along the
long sea-lanes, seeking new cargoes here, carrying
new cargoes there, running freights wherever
shillings and pence beckoned and underwriters did
not forbid. But it was all a weariness to contemplate,
and, save that he wrung from it his bread, it was
without profit under the sun.

The last good-by to his wife had been at Cardiff,
twenty-eight months before, when he sailed for Valparaiso with coals—nine thousand tons and down to
his marks. From Valparaiso he had gone to Australia,
light, a matter of six thousand miles on end with a
stormy passage and running short of bunker coal.
Coals again to Oregon, seven thousand miles, and
nigh as many more with general cargo for Japan and
China. Thence to Java, loading sugar for Marseilles,
and back along the Mediterranean to the Black Sea,
and on to Baltimore, down to her marks with crome
ore, buffeted by hurricanes, short again of bunker coal
and calling at Bermuda to replenish. Then a time
charter, Norfolk, Virginia, loading mysterious contraband coal and sailing for South Africa under orders
of the mysterious German supercargo put on board

by the charterers. On to Madagascar, steaming four knots by the supercargo's orders, and the suspicion forming that the Russian fleet might want the coal. Confusion and delays, long waits at sea, international complications, the whole world excited over the old *Tryapsic* and her cargo of contraband, and then on to Japan and the naval port of Sassebo. Back to Australia, another time charter and general merchandise picked up at Sydney, Melbourne, and Adelaide, and carried on to Mauritius, Lorenzo Marques, Durban, Algoa Bay, and Cape Town. To Ceylon for orders, and from Ceylon to Rangoon to load rice for Rio Janeiro. Thence to Buenos Aires and loading maize for the United Kingdom or the Continent, stopping at St. Vincent, to receive orders to proceed to Dublin. Two years and four months, eight hundred and fifty days by the log, steaming up and down the thousand-league-long sea-lanes and back again to Dublin town. And he was well aweary.

A little tug had laid hold of the *Tryapsic,* and with clang and clatter and shouted command, with engines half-ahead, slow-speed, or half-astern, the battered old sea-tramp was nudged and nosed and shouldered through the dock-gates into Ring's End Basin. Lines were flung ashore, fore and aft, and a 'midship spring got out. Already a small group of the happy shore-staying folk had clustered on the dock.

"Ring off," Captain MacElrath commanded in his slow thick voice; and the third officer worked the lever of the engine-room telegraph.

"Gangway out!" called the second officer; and when this was accomplished, "That will do."

It was the last task of all, gangway out. "That will do" was the dismissal. The voyage was ended, and the crew shambled eagerly forward across the rusty decks to where their sea-bags were packed and ready for the shore. The taste of the land was strong in the men's mouths, and strong it was in the skipper's mouth as he muttered a gruff good day to the departing pilot, and himself went down to his cabin. Up the gangway were trooping the customs officers, the surveyor, the agent's clerk, and the stevedores. Quick work disposed of these and cleared his cabin, the agent waiting to take him to the office.

"Dud ye send word tull the wife?" had been his greeting to the clerk.

"Yes, a telegram, as soon as you were reported."

"She'll likely be comin' down on the marnin' train," the skipper had soliloquized, and gone inside to change his clothes and wash.

He took a last glance about the room and at two photographs on the wall, one of the wife, the other of an infant—the child he had never seen. He stepped out into the cabin, with its paneled walls of cedar and maple, and with its long table that seated ten, and at which he had eaten by himself through all the weary time. No laughter and clatter and wordy argument of the mess-room had been his. He had eaten silently, almost morosely, his silence emulated by the noiseless Asiatic who had served him. It came to him suddenly, the overwhelming realization of the loneliness of

those two years and more. All his vexations and anx-
ieties had been his own. He had shared them with no
one. His two young officers were too young and
flighty, the mate too stupid. There was no consulting
with them. One tenant had shared the cabin with
him, that tenant his responsibility. They had dined
and supped together, walked the bridge together, and
together they had bedded.

"Och!" he muttered to that grim companion, "I'm
quit of you, an' wull quit . . . for a wee."

Ashore he passed the last of the seamen with their
bags, and, at the agent's, with the usual delays, put
through his ship business. When asked out by them
to drink he took milk and soda.

"I am no teetotaler," he explained; "but for the life
o' me I canna bide beer or whusky."

In the early afternoon, when he finished paying off
his crew, he hurried to the private office where he had
been told his wife was waiting.

His eyes were for her first, though the temptation
was great to have more than a hurried glimpse of the
child in the chair beside her. He held her off from
him after the long embrace, and looked into her face
long and steadily, drinking in every feature of it and
wondering that he could mark no changes of time. A
warm man, his wife thought him, though had the
opinion of his officers been asked it would have been:
a harsh man and a bitter one.

"Wull, Annie, how is ut wi' ye?" he queried, and
drew her to him again.

And again he held her away from him, this wife of

ten years and of whom he knew so little. She was almost a stranger—more a stranger than his Chinese
steward, and certainly far more a stranger than his
own officers whom he had seen every day, day and
day, for eight hundred and fifty days. Married ten
years, and in that time he had been with her nine
weeks—scarcely a honeymoon. Each time home had
been a getting acquainted again with her. It was the
fate of the men who went out to the salt-plowing.
Little they knew of their wives and less of their children. There was his chief engineer—old, near-sighted
MacPherson—who told the story of returning home
to be locked out of his house by his four-year kiddie
that never had laid eyes on him before.

"An' thus 'ull be the loddie," the skipper said,
reaching out a hesitant hand to the child's cheek.

But the boy drew away from him, sheltering
against the mother's side.

"Och!" she cried, "and he doesna know his own father."

"Nor I hum. Heaven knows I could no a-picked
hum out of a crowd, though he'll be havin' your nose
I'm thunkun'."

"An' your own eyes, Donald. Look ut them. He's
your own father, laddie. Kiss hum like the little mon
ye are."

But the child drew closer to her, his expression of
fear and distrust growing stronger, and when the father attempted to take him in his arms he threatened
to cry.

The skipper straightened up, and to conceal the pang at his heart he drew out his watch and looked at it.

"Ut's time to go, Annie," he said. "Thot train 'ull be startun'."

He was silent on the train at first, divided between watching the wife with the child going to sleep in her arms and looking out of the window at the tilled fields and green unforested hills vague and indistinct in the driving drizzle that had set in. They had the compartment to themselves. When the boy slept she laid him out on the seat and wrapped him warmly. And when the health of relatives and friends had been inquired after, and the gossip of Island McGill narrated, along with the weather and the price of land and crops, there was little left to talk about save themselves, and Captain MacElrath took up the tale brought home for the good wife from all his world's-end wandering. But it was not a tale of marvels he told, nor of beautiful flower-lands nor mysterious Eastern cities.

"What-like is Java?" she asked once.

"Full o' fever. Half the crew down wuth ut an' luttle work. Ut was quinine an' quinine the whole blessed time. Each marnun' 'twas quinine an' gin for all hands on an empty stomach. An' they who was no sick made ut out to be hovun' ut bad uz the rest."

Another time she asked about Newcastle.

"Coals an' coal-dust—thot's all. No a nice sutty. I lost two Chinks there, stokers the both of them. An' the owners paid a fine tull the Government of a hundred pounds each for them. 'We regret tull note,' they wrut me—I got the letter tull Oregon—'We regret tull note the loss o' two Chinese members o' yer crew ot Newcastle, an' we recommend greater carefulness un the future.' Greater carefulness! And I could no a-been more careful. The Chinks hod forty-five pounds each comun' tull them in wages, an' I was no a-thunkun' they 'ud run.

"But thot's their way—'we regret tull note,' 'we beg tull advise,' 'we recommend,' 'we canna understand'—an' the like o' thot. Domned cargo tank! An' they would thunk I could drive her like a *Lucania,* an' wi'out burnun' coals. There was thot propeller. I was after them a guid while for ut. The old one was iron, thuck on the edges, an' we couldna make our speed. An' the new one was bronze—nine hundred pounds ut cost, an' then wantun' their returns out o' ut, an' me wuth a bod passage an' lossin' time every day. 'We regret tull note your long passage from Voloparaiso tull Sydney wuth an average daily run o' only one hundred an' suxty-seven. We hod expected better results wuth the new propeller. You should a-made an average daily run o' two hundred and suxteen.'

"An' me on a wunter passage, blowin' a luvin' gale half the time, wuth hurricane force in atweenwhiles, an' hove to sux days, wuth engines stopped an' bunker coal runnun' short, an' me wuth a mate thot stupid he could no pass a shup's light ot night wi'out callun' me tull the brudge. I wrut an' told 'em so. An' then: 'Our nautical adviser suggests you kept too far south,' an' 'We are lookun' for better results from thot propeller.' Nautical adviser!—shore pilot! Ut was the regular latitude for a wunter passage from Voloparaiso tull Sydney.

"An' when I come un tull Auckland short o' coal, after lettun' her druft sux days wuth the fires out tull save the coal, an' wuth only twenty tons in my bunkers, I was thunkun' o' the lossin' o' time an' the expense, an' tull save the owners I took her un an' out wi'out pilotage. Pilotage was no compulsory. An' un Yokohama, who should I meet but Captun Robinson o' the *Dyapsic*. We got a-talkun' about ports an' places down Australia-way, an' first thing he says: 'Speakun' o' Auckland—of course, Captun, you was never un Auckland?' 'Yus,' I says, 'I was un there very recent.' 'Oh, ho,' he says, very angry-like, 'so you was the smart Aleck thot fetched me thot letter from the owners: 'We note item of fufteen pounds for pilotage ot Auckland. A shup o' ours was un tull Auckland recently an' uncurred no such charge. We beg tull advise you thot we conseeder thus pilotage an onnecessary expense which should no be uncurred un the future.' "

"But dud they say a word tull me for the fufteen pounds I saved tull them? No a word. They send a letter tull Captun Robinson for no savun' them the fufteen pounds, an' tull me: 'We note item of two guineas doctor's fee at Auckland for crew. Please explain thus onusual expunditure.' Ut was two o' the

Chinks. I was thunkun' they hod beri-beri, an' thot was the why o' sendun' for the doctor. I buried the two of them ot sea not a week after. But ut was: 'Please explain thus onusual expunditure,' an' tull Captun Robinson, 'We beg tull advise you thot we conseeder thus pilotage an onnecessary expense.'

"Dudna I cable them from Newcastle, tellun' them the old tank was thot foul she needed dry-dock? Seven months out o' drydock, an' the West Coast the quickest place for foulun' un the world. But freights was up, an' they hod a charter o' coals for Portland. The *Arrata,* one o' the Woor Line, left port the same day uz us, bound for Portland, an' the old *Tryapsic* makun' sux knots, seven ot the best. An' ut was ot Comox, takun' un bunker coal, I got the letter from the owners. The boss humself hod signed ut, an' ot the bottom he wrut un hus own bond: 'The *Arrata* beat you by four an' a half days. Am dusappointed.' Dusappointed! When I had cabled them from New-castle. When she drydocked ot Portland, there was whuskers on her a foot long, barnacles the size o' me fust, oysters like young sauce plates. Ut took them two days afterward tull clean the dock o' shells an' muck.

"An' there was the motter o' them fire-bars ot Newcastle. The firm ashore made them heavier than the engineer's speecifications, an' then forgot tull charge for the dufference. Ot the last moment, wuth me ashore gettun' me clearance, they come wuth the bill: 'Tull error on fire-bars, sux pounds.' They'd been tull the shup an' MacPherson hod O.K.'d ut. I said ut was strange an' would no pay. 'Then you are dootun' the chief engineer,' says they. 'I'm no dootun',' says I, 'but I canna see my way tull sign. Come wuth me tull the shup. The launch wull cost ye naught an' ut 'ull brung ye back. An' we wull see what MacPherson says.'

"But they would no come. Ot Portland I got the bill un a letter. I took no notice. Ot Hong-Kong I got a letter from the owners. The bill hod been sent tull them. I wrut them from Java explainun'. At Marseilles the owners wrut me: 'Tull extra work un engine-room, sux pounds. The engineer has O.K.'d ut, an' you have no O.K.'d ut. Are you dootun' the engineer's honesty?' I wrut an' told them I was no dootun' his honesty; thot the bill was for extra weight o' fire-bars; an' thot ut was O.K. Dud they pay ut? They no dud. They must unvestigate. An' some clerk un the office took sick, an' the bill was lost. An' there was more letters. I got letters from the owners an' the firm—'Tull error on fire-bars, sux pounds'—ot Baltimore, ot Delagoa Bay, ot Moji, ot Rangoon, ot Rio, an' ot Montevuddio. Ut uz no settled yut. I tell ye, Annie, the owners are hard tull please."

He communed with himself for a moment, and then muttered indignantly: "Tull error on fire-bars, sux pounds."

"Hov ye heard of Jamie?" his wife asked in the pause.

Captain MacElrath shook his head.

"He was washed off the poop wuth three seamen."

"Whereabouts?"

"Off the Horn. 'Twas on the *Thornsby*."

"They would be runnun' homeward bound?"

"Aye," she nodded. "We only got the word three days gone. His wife is greetin' like tull die."

"A good lod, Jamie," he commented, "but a stiff one ot carryun' on. I mind me when we was mates together un the Abion. An' so Jamie's gone."

Again a pause fell, to be broken by the wife.

"An' ye will no a-heard o' the *Bankshire*? Mac-Dougall lost her in Magellan Straits. 'Twas only yesterday ut was in the paper."

"A cruel place, them Magellan Straits," he said. "Dudna thot domned mate-fellow nigh putt me ashore twice on the one passage through? He was a eediot, a lunatuc. I wouldna have hum on the brudge a munut. Comun' tull Narrow Reach, thuck weather, wuth snow squalls, me un the chart-room, dudna I guv hum the changed course? 'Southeast-by-East,' I told hum. 'South-East-by-East, sir,' says he. Fufteen munuts after I comes on tull the brudge. 'Funny,' says thot mate-fellow, 'I'm no rememberun' ony islands un the mouth o' Narrow Reach. I took one look ot the islands an' yells, 'Putt your wheel hard a-starboard,' tull the mon ot the wheel. An' ye should a-seen the old *Tryapsic* turnun' the sharpest circle she ever turned. I waited for the snow tull clear, an' there was Narrow Reach, nice uz ye please, tull the east'ard an' the islands un the mouth o' False Bay tull the south'ard. 'What course was ye steerun'?' I says tull the mon ot the wheel. 'South-by-East, sir,' says he. I looked tull the mate-fellow. What could I say? I was thot wroth I could a-kult hum. Four points dufference. Five munuts more an' the old *Tryapsic* would a-been funushed.

"An' was ut no the same when we cleared the Straits tull the east'ard? Four hours would a-seen us guid an' clear. I was forty hours then on the brudge. I guv the mate his course, an' the bearun' o' the Askthar Light astern. 'Don't let her bear more tull the north'ard than West-by-North,' I said tull hum, 'an' ye wull be all right.' An' I went below an' turned un. But I couldna sleep for worryun'. After forty hours on the brudge, what was four hours more? I thought. An' for them four hours wull ye be lettun' the mate loss her on ye? 'No,' I says to myself. An' wuth thot I got up, hod a wash an' a cup o' coffee, an' went tull the brudge. I took one look ot the bearun' o' Askthar Light. 'Twas Nor'west-by-West, and the old *Tryapsic* down on the shoals. He was a eediot, thot mate-fellow. Ye could look overside an' see the duscoloration of the watter. 'Twas a close call for the old *Tryapsic* I'm tellun' ye. Twice un thirty hours he'd a-hod her ashore uf ut hod no been for me."

Captain MacElrath fell to gazing at the sleeping child with mild wonder in his small blue eyes, and his wife sought to divert him from his woes.

"Ye remember Jummy MacCaul?" she asked. "Ye went tull school wuth hus two boys. Old Jummy

MacCaul thot hoz the farm beyond Doctor Hay-thorn's place."

"Oh, aye, an' what o' hum? Uz he dead?"

"No, but he was after askun' your father, when he sailed last time for Voloparaiso, uf ye'd been there afore. An' when your father says no, then Jummy says, 'An' how wull he be knowun a' tull find hus way?' An' with thot your father says: 'Verry sumple ut uz, Jummy. Supposun' you was goin' tull the mainland tull a mon who luved un Belfast. Belfast uz a bug sutty, Jummy, an' how would ye be findun' your way?' 'By way o' me tongue,' says Jummy; 'I'd be askun' the folk I met.' 'I told ye ut was sumple,' says your father. 'Ut's the very same way my Donald finds the road tull Voloparaiso. He asks every shup he meets upon the sea tull ot last he meets wuth a shup thot's been tull Voloparaiso, an' the captun o' thot shup tells hum the way.' An' Jummy scratches hus head an' says he understands an' thot ut's a very sumple motter after all."

The skipper chuckled at the joke, and his tired blue eyes were merry for the moment.

"He was a thun chap, thot mate-fellow, oz thun oz you an' me putt together," he remarked after a time, a slight twinkle in his eye of appreciation of the bull. But the twinkle quickly disappeared and the blue eyes took on a bleak and wintry look. "What dud he do ot Voloparaiso but land sux hundred fathom o' chain cable an' take never a receipt from the lighter-mon. I was gettun' my clearance ot the time. When we got tull sea, I found he hod no receipt for the cable.

"'An' ye no took a receipt for ut?' says I.

"'No,' says he. 'Wasna ut goin' direct tull the agents?'

"'How long ha' ye been goin' tull sea,' says I, 'not tull be knowin' the mate's duty uz tull deluver no cargo wuthout receipt for same? An' on the West Coast ot thot. What's tull stop the lighter-mon from stealun' a few lengths o' ut?'

"An' ut come out uz I said. Sux hundred fathom went over the side, but four hundred an' ninety-five was all the agents received. The lighter-mon swore ut was all he received from the mate—four hundred an' ninety-five fathom. I got a letter from the owners ot Portland. They no blamed the mate for ut, but me, an' me ashore ot the time on shup's buzz'ness. I could no be in the two places ot the one time. An' the letters from the owners an' the agents uz still comun' tull me.

"Thot mate-fellow was no a proper sailor, an' no a mon tull work for owners. Dudna he want tull break me wuth the Board of Trade for bein' below my marks? He said as much tull the bos'n. An' he told me tull my face homeward bound thot I'd been half an inch under my marks. 'Twas at Portland, loadun' cargo un fresh watter an' goin' tull Comox tull load bunker coal un salt watter. I tell ye, Annie, ut takes close fuggerin', an' I *was* half an inch under the load-line when the bunker coal was un. But I'm no tellun' any other body but you. An' thot mate-fellow unten-dun' tull report me tull the Board o' Trade, only for thot he saw fut tull be sliced un two pieces on the steam-pipe cover.

"He was a fool. After loadun' ot Portland I hod tull take on suxty tons o' coal tull last me tull Comox. The charges for lighterun' was heavy, an' no room ot the coal dock. A French barque was lyin' alongside the dock an' I spoke tull the captun, askun' hum what he would charge when work for the day was done, tull haul clear for a couple o' hours an' let me un. 'Twenty dollars,' said he. Ut was savun' money on lighters tull the owner, an' I gave ut tull hum. An' thot night, after dark, I hauled un an' took on the coal. Then I started tull go out un the stream an' drop anchor—under me own steam, of course.

"We hod tull go out stern first, an' somethun' went wrong wuth the reversun' gear. Old MacPher-son said he could work ut by hond, but very slow ot thot. An' I said 'All right.' We started. The pilot was on board. The tide was ebbun' stuffly, an' right abreast an' a but below was a shup lyin' wuth a lighter on each side. I saw the shup's ridun' lights, but never a light on the lighters. Ut was close quar-ters to shuft a bug vessel onder steam, wuth MacPherson workun' the reversun' gear by hond. We hod to come close down upon the shup afore I could go ahead an' clear o' the shups on the dock-ends. An' we struck the lighter stern-on, just uz I rung tull MacPherson half ahead.

"'What was thot?' says the pilot, when we struck the lighter.

"'I dunna know,' says I, 'an' I'm wonderun'.'

"The pilot was no keen, ye see, tull hus job. I went on tull a guid place an' dropped anchor, an' ut would all a-been well but for thot domned eediot mate.

"'We smashed thot lighter,' says he, comun' up the lodder tull the brudge—an' the pilot stondun' there wuth his ears cocked tull hear.

"'What lighter?' says I.

"'Thot lighter alongside the shup,' says the mate.

"'I dudna see no lighter,' says I, and wuth thot I steps on hus fut guid an' hard.

"After the pilot was gone I says tull the mate: 'Uf you dunna know onythun', old mon, for Heaven's sake keep your mouth shut.'

"'But ye dud smash thot lighter, dudn't ye?' says he.

"'Uf we dud,' says I, 'ut's no your buzz'ness tull be tellun' the pilot—though, mind ye, I'm no admuttun' there was ony lighter.'

"'An' next marnun', just uz I'm after dressun', the steward says, 'A mon tull see ye, sir.' 'Fetch hum un,' says I. An' un he come. 'Sut down,' says I. An' he sot down.

"He was the owner of the lighter, an' when he hod told hus story, I says, 'I dudna see ony lighter.'

"'What, mon?' says he. 'No see a two-hundred-ton lighter, bug oz a house, alongside thot shup?'

"'I was goin' by the shup's lights,' says I, 'an' I dudna touch the shup, thot I know.'

"'But ye dud touch the lighter,' says he. 'Ye smashed her. There's a thousand dollars' domage done, an' I'll see ye pay for ut.'

"'Look here, muster,' says I, 'when I'm shuftun' a shup ot night I follow the law, an' the law dustunctly says I must regulate me actions by the lights o' the shuppun'. Your lighter never hod no ridun' light, nor dud I look for ony lighter wuthout lights tull show ut.'

"'The mate says—' he beguns.

"'Domn the mate,' says I. 'Dud your lighter hov a ridun' light?'

"'No, ut dud not,' says he, 'but ut was a clear night wuth the moon a-showun'.'

"'Ye seem tull know your buzz'ness,' says I. 'But let me tell ye thot I know my buzz'ness uz well, an' thot I'm no a-lookun' for lighters wuthout lights. Uf ye thunk ye hov a case, go ahead. The steward will show ye out. Guid day.'

"An' thot was the end o' ut. But ut wull show ye what a puir fellow thot mate was. I call ut a blessun' for all masters thot he was sliced un two on thot steam-pipe cover. He had a pull un the office an' thot was the why he was kept on."

"The Wekley farm wull soon be for sale, so the agents be tellun' me," his wife remarked, slyly watching what effect her announcement would have upon him.

His eyes flashed eagerly on the instant, and he straightened up as might a man about to engage in some agreeable task. It was the farm of his vision, adjoining his father's, and her own people farmed not a mile away.

"We wull be buyun' ut," he said, "though we wull be no tellun' a soul of ut ontul ut's bought an' the money paid down. I've savun' consuderable these days, though pickun's uz no what they used to be, an' we hov a tidy nest-egg laid by. I wull see the father an' hove the money ready tull hus hond, so uf I'm ot sea he can buy whenever the land offers."

He rubbed the frosted moisture from the inside of the window and peered out at the pouring rain, through which he could discern nothing.

"When I was a young mon I used tull be afeard thot the owners would guv me the sack. Stull afeard I am of the sack. But once thot farm is mine I wull no be afeard ony longer. Ut's a puir job thus sea-farmun'. Me managin' un all seas an' weather an' perils o' the deep a shup worth fufty thousand pounds, wuth cargoes ot times worth fufty thousand more—a hundred thousand pounds, half a million dollars uz the Yankees say, an' me wuth all the responsubility gettun' a screw o' twenty pounds a month. What mon ashore, managin' a buzz'ness worth a hundred thousand pounds wull be gettun' uz small a screw uz twenty pounds? An' wuth such masters uz a captun serves— the owners, the underwriters, an' the Board o' Trade, all pullun' an wantun' dufferent thungs—the owners wantun' quick passages an' domn the rusk, the underwriters wantun' safe passages an' domn the delay, an' the Board o' Trade wantun' cautious passages an' caution always meanun' delay. Three dufferent masters, an' all three able an' wullun' to break ye uf ye don't serve their dufferent wushes."

He felt the train slackening speed, and peered again through the misty window. He stood up, buttoned his overcoat, turned up the collar, and awkwardly gathered the child, still asleep, in his arms.

"I wull see the father," he said, "an' hov the money ready tull hus hond so uf I'm ot sea when the land offers he wull no muss the chance tull buy. An' then the owners can guv me the sack uz soon uz they like. Ut will be all night un, an' I wull be wuth you, Annie, an' the sea can go tull hell."

Happiness was in both their faces at the prospect, and for a moment both saw the same vision of peace. Annie leaned toward him, and as the train stopped they kissed each other across the sleeping child.

SAMUEL

Margaret Henan would have been a striking figure under any circumstances, but never more so than when I first chanced upon her, a sack of grain of fully a hundred-weight on her shoulder, as she walked with sure though tottering stride from the cart-tail to the stable, pausing for an instant to gather strength at the foot of the steep steps that led to the grain-bin. There were four of these steps, and she went up them, a step at a time, slowly, unwaveringly, and with so dogged certitude that it never entered my mind that her strength could fail her and let that hundred-weight sack fall from the lean and withered frame that well-nigh doubled under it. For she was patently an old woman, and it was her age that made me linger by the cart and watch.

Six times she went between the cart and the stable, each time with a full sack on her back, and beyond passing the time of day with me she took no notice of my presence. Then, the cart empty, she fumbled for matches and lighted a short clay pipe, pressing down the burning surface of the tobacco with a calloused and apparently nerveless thumb. The hands were noteworthy. They were large-knuckled, sinewy and malformed by labor, rimed with callouses, the nails blunt and broken, and with here and there cuts and bruises, healed and healing, such as are common to the hands of hard-working men. On the back were huge, upstanding veins, eloquent of age and toil. Looking at them, it was hard to believe that they were the hands of the woman who had once been the belle of Island McGill. This last, of course, I learned later. At the time I knew neither her history nor her identity.

She wore heavy man's brogans. Her legs were stockingless, and I had noticed when she walked that her bare feet were thrust into the crinkly, iron-like shoes that sloshed about her lean ankles at every step. Her figure, shapeless and waistless, was garbed in a rough man's shirt and in a ragged flannel petticoat that had once been red. But it was her face, wrinkled, withered and weather-beaten, surrounded by an aureole of unkempt and straggling wisps of greyish hair, that caught and held me. Neither drifted hair nor serried wrinkles could hide the splendid dome of a forehead, high and broad without verging in the slightest on the abnormal.

The sunken cheeks and pinched nose told little of the quality of the life that flickered behind those clear blue eyes of hers. Despite the minutiae of wrinkle-work that somehow failed to weazen them, her eyes were clear as a girl's—clear, out-looking, and far-seeing, and with an open and unblinking steadfastness of gaze that was disconcerting. The remarkable thing was the distance between them. It is a lucky man or woman who has the width of an eye between, but with Margaret Henan the width between her eyes was fully that of an eye and a half. Yet so symmetrically molded was her face that this remarkable feature produced no uncanny effect, and, for that matter, would have escaped the casual observer's notice. The mouth, shapeless and toothless, with down-turned corners and lips dry and parchment-like, nevertheless lacked the muscular slackness so usual with age. The lips might have been those of a mummy, save for that impression of rigid firmness they gave. Not that they were atrophied. On the contrary, they seemed tense and set with a muscular and spiritual determination. There, and in the eyes, was the secret of the certitude with which she carried the heavy sacks up the steep steps, with never a false step or overbalance, and emptied them in the grain-bin.

"You are an old woman to be working like this," I ventured.

She looked at me with that strange, unblinking gaze, and she thought and spoke with the slow deliberateness that characterized everything about her, as if well aware of an eternity that was hers and in which there was no need for haste. Again I was impressed by the enormous certitude of her. In this eternity that seemed so indubitably hers, there was time and to spare for safe-footing and stable equilibrium—for certitude, in short. No more in her spiritual life than in carrying the hundred-weights of grain was there a possibility of a misstep or an overbalancing. The feeling produced in me was uncanny. Here was a human soul that, save for the most glimmering of contacts, was beyond the humanness of me. And the more I learned of Margaret Henan in the weeks that followed the more mysteriously remote she became. She was as alien as a far-journeyer from some other star, and no hint could she nor all the countryside give me of what forms of living, what heats of feeling, or rules of philosophic contemplation actuated her in all that she had been and was.

"I wull be suvunty-two come Guid Friday a fortnight," she said in reply to my question.

"But you are an old woman to be doing this man's work, and a strong man's work at that," I insisted.

Again she seemed to immerse herself in that atmosphere of contemplative eternity, and so strangely did it affect me that I should not have been surprised to have awaked a century or so later and found her just beginning to enunciate her reply:

"The work hoz tull be done, an' I am beholden tull no one."

"But have you no children, no family, relations?"

"Oh, aye, a-plenty o' them, but they no see fut tull be helpun' me."

She drew out her pipe for a moment, then added, with a nod of her head toward the house, "I luv' wuth meself."

I glanced at the house, straw-thatched and commodious, at the large stable, and at the large array of fields I knew must belong with the place.

"It is a big bit of land for you to farm by yourself."

"Oh, aye, a bug but, suvunty acres. Ut kept me old

mon buzzy, along wuth a son an' a hired mon, tull say naught o' extra honds un the harvest an' a maid-servant un the house."

She clambered into the cart, gathered the reins in her hands, and quizzed me with her keen, shrewd eyes.

"Belike ye hail from over the watter—Ameruky, I'm meanun'?"

"Yes, I'm a Yankee," I answered.

"Ye wull no be findun' mony Island McGill folk stoppun' un Ameruky?"

"No; I don't remember ever meeting one, in the States."

She nodded her head.

"They are home-luvun' bodies, though I wull no be sayin' they are no fair-traveled. Yet they come home ot the last, them oz are no lost ot sea or kult by fevers an' such-like un foreign parts."

"Then your sons will have gone to sea and come home again?" I queried.

"Oh, aye, all savun' Samuel oz was drownded."

At the mention of Samuel I could have sworn to a strange light in her eyes, and it seemed to me, as by some telepathic flash, that I divined in her a tremendous wistfulness, an immense yearning. It seemed to me that here was the key to her inscrutableness, the clue that if followed properly would make all her strangeness plain. It came to me that here was a contact and that for the moment I was glimpsing into the soul of her. The question was tickling on my tongue, but she forestalled me.

She *tchk'd* to the horse, and with a "Guid day tull you, sir," drove off.

* * *

A simple, homely people are the folk of Island McGill, and I doubt if a more sober, thrifty, and industrious folk is to be found in all the world. Meeting them abroad—and to meet them abroad one must meet them on the sea, for a hybrid seafaring and farmer breed are they—one would never take them to be Irish. Irish they claim to be, speaking of the North of Ireland with pride and sneering at their Scottish brothers; yet Scotch they undoubtedly are, transplanted Scotch of long ago, it is true, but none the less Scotch, with a thousand traits, to say nothing of their tricks of speech and woolly utterance, which nothing less than their Scotch clannishness could have preserved to this late day.

A narrow loch, scarcely half a mile wide, separates Island McGill from the mainland of Ireland; and, once across this loch, one finds himself in an entirely different country. The Scotch impression is strong, and the people, to commence with, are Presbyterians. When it is considered that there is no public house in all the island and that seven thousand souls dwell therein, some idea may be gained of the temperateness of the community. Wedded to old ways, public opinion and the ministers are powerful influences, while fathers and mothers are revered and obeyed as in few other places in this modern world. Courting lasts never later than ten at night, and no girl walks out with her young man without her parents' knowledge and consent.

The young men go down to the sea and sow their wild oats in the wicked ports, returning periodically, between voyages, to live the old intensive morality, to court till ten o'clock, to sit under the minister each Sunday, and to listen at home to the same stern precepts that the elders preached to them from the time they were laddies. Much they learned of women in the ends of the earth, these seafaring sons, yet a canny wisdom was theirs and they never brought wives home with them. The one solitary exception to this had been the schoolmaster, who had been guilty of bringing a wife from half a mile the other side of the loch. For this he had never been forgiven, and he rested under a cloud for the remainder of his days. At his death the wife went back across the loch to her own people, and the blot on the escutcheon of Island McGill was erased. In the end the sailor-men married girls of their own homeland and settled down to become exemplars of all the virtues for which the island was noted.

Island McGill was without a history. She boasted none of the events that go to make history. There had never been any wearing of the green, any Fenian conspiracies, any land disturbances. There had been but one eviction, and that purely technical—a test case, and on advice of the tenant's lawyer. So Island McGill was without annals. History had passed her by. She paid her taxes, acknowledged her crowned rulers, and left the world alone; all she asked in return was that the world should leave her alone. The world was composed of two parts—Island McGill and the rest of it. And whatever was not Island McGill was outlandish and barbarian; and well she knew, for did not her seafaring sons bring home report of that world and its ungodly ways?

* * *

It was from the skipper of a Glasgow tramp, as passenger from Colombo to Rangoon, that I had first learned of the existence of Island McGill; and it was from him that I had carried the letter that gave me entrance to the house of Mrs. Ross, widow of a master mariner, with a daughter living with her and with two sons, master mariners themselves and out upon the sea. Mrs. Ross did not take in boarders, and it was Captain Ross's letter alone that had enabled me to get from her bed and board. In the evening, after my encounter with Margaret Henan, I questioned Mrs. Ross, and I knew on the instant that I had in truth stumbled upon mystery.

Like all Island McGill folk, as I was soon to discover, Mrs. Ross was at first averse to discussing Margaret Henan at all. Yet it was from her I learned that evening that Margaret Henan had once been one of the island belles. Herself the daughter of a well-to-do farmer, she had married Thomas Henan, equally well-to-do. Beyond the usual housewife's tasks she had never been accustomed to work. Unlike many of the island women, she had never lent a hand in the fields.

"But what of her children?" I asked.

"Two o' the sons, Jamie an' Timothy uz married an' be goun' tull sea. Thot bug house close tull the post office uz Jamie's. The daughters thot ha' no married be luvun' wuth them as dud marry. An' the rest be dead."

"The Samuels," Clara interpolated, with what I suspected was a giggle.

She was Mrs. Ross's daughter, a strapping young woman with handsome features and remarkably handsome black eyes.

" 'Tuz naught to be smuckerun' ot," her mother reproved her.

"The Samuels?" I intervened. "I don't understand."

"Her four sons thot died."

"And were they all named Samuel?"

"Aye."

"Strange," I commented in the lagging silence.

"Very strange," Mrs. Ross affirmed, proceeding stolidly with the knitting of the woollen singlet on her knees—one of the countless undergarments that she interminably knitted for her skipper sons.

"And it was only the Samuels that died?" I queried, in further attempt.

"The others luved," was the answer. "A fine fomuly—no finer on the island. No better lods ever sailed out of Island McGill. The munuster held them up oz models tull pottern after. Nor was ever a whusper breathed again' the girls."

"But why is she left alone now in her old age?" I persisted. "Why don't her own flesh and blood look after her? Why does she live alone? Don't they ever go to see her or care for her?"

"Never a one un twenty years an' more now. She fetched ut on tull herself. She drove them from the house just oz she drove old Tom Henan, thot was her husband, tull hus death."

"Drink?" I ventured.

Mrs. Ross shook her head scornfully, as if drink was a weakness beneath the weakest of Island McGill.

A long pause followed, during which Mrs. Ross knitted stolidly on, only nodding permission when Clara's young man, mate on one of the Shire Line sailing ships, came to walk out with her. I studied the half-dozen ostrich eggs, hanging in the corner against the wall like a cluster of some monstrous fruit. On each shell were painted precipitous and impossible seas through which full-rigged ships foamed with a lack of perspective only equalled by their sharp technical perfection. On the mantelpiece stood two large pearl shells, obviously a pair, intricately carved by the patient hands of New Caledonian convicts. In the center of the mantel was a stuffed bird of paradise, while about the room were scattered gorgeous shells from the southern seas, delicate sprays of coral sprouting from barnacled *pi-pi* shells and cased in glass, assegais from South Africa, stone axes from New Guinea, huge

Alaskan tobacco-pouches beaded with heraldic totem designs, a boomerang from Australia, divers ships in glass bottles, a cannibal *kai-kai* bowl from the Marquesas, and fragile cabinets from China and the Indies and inlaid with mother-of-pearl and precious woods.

I gazed at this varied trove brought home by sailor sons, and pondered the mystery of Margaret Henan, who had driven her husband to his death and been forsaken by all her kin. It was not the drink. Then what was it?——some shocking cruelty? some amazing infidelity? or some fearful, old-world peasant-crime?

I broached my theories, but to all Mrs. Ross shook her head.

"Ut was no thot," she said. "Margaret was a guid wife an' a guid mother, an' I doubt she would harm a fly. She brought up her fomuly God-fearin' an' decent-minded. Her trouble was thot she took lunatic——turned eediot."

Mrs. Ross tapped significantly on her forehead to indicate a state of addlement.

"But I talked with her this afternoon," I objected, "and I found her a sensible woman——remarkably bright for one of her years."

"Aye, an' I'm grantun' all thot you say," she went on calmly. "But I am no referrun' tull thot. I am referrun' tull her wucked-headed an' vucious stubbornness. No more stubborn woman ever luv'd than Margaret Henan. Ut was all on account o' Samuel, which was the name o' her youngest an' they do say her favourut brother——hum oz died by hus own hond all through the munuster's mustake un no registerun' the new church ot Dublin. Ut was a lesson thot the name was musfortunate, but she would no take ut, an' there was talk when she called her first child Samuel—hum thot died o' the croup. An' wuth thot what does she do but call the next one Samuel, an' hum only three when he fell un tull the tub o' hot watter an' was plain cooked tull death. Ut all come, I tell you, o' her wucked-headed an' foolush stubbornness. For a Samuel she must hov; an' ut was the death of the four of her sons. After the first, dudna her own mother go down un the dirt tull her feet, a-beggun' an' pleadun' wuth her no tull name her next one Samuel? But she was no tull be turned from her purpose. Margaret Henan was always set on her ways, an' never more so thon on thot name Samuel.

"She was fair lunatuc on Samuel. Dudna her neighbors' an' all kuth an' kun savun' them thot luv'd un the house wuth her, get up an' walk out ot the christenun' of the second—hum thot was cooked? Thot they dud, an' ot the very moment the munuster asked what would the bairn's name be. 'Samuel,' says she; an' wuth thot they got up an' walked out an' left the house. An' ot the door dudna her Aunt Fannie, her mother's suster, turn an' say loud for all tull hear: 'What for wull she be wantun' tull murder the wee thing?' The munuster heard fine, an' dudna like ut, but, oz he told my Larry afterward, what could he do? Ut was the woman's wush, an' there was no law again' a mother callun' her child accordun' tull her wush.

"An' then was there no the third Samuel? An' when he was lost ot sea off the Cape, dudna she break all laws o' nature tull hov a fourth? She was forty-seven, I'm tellun' ye, an' she hod a child ot forty-seven. Thunk on ut! Ot forty-seven! Ut was fair scand'lous."

* * *

From Clara, next morning, I got the tale of Margaret Henan's favourite brother; and from here and there, in the week that followed, I pieced together the tragedy of Margaret Henan. Samuel Dundee had been the youngest of Margaret's four brothers, and, as Clara told me, she had well-nigh worshiped him. He was going to sea at the time, skipper of one of the sailing ships of the Bank Line, when he married Agnes Hewitt. She was described as a slender wisp of a girl, delicately featured and with a nervous organization of the supersensitive order. Theirs had been the first marriage in the "new" church, and after a two-weeks' honeymoon Samuel had kissed his bride good-bye and sailed in command of the *Loughbank,* a big four-masted barque.

And it was because of the "new" church that the minister's blunder occurred. Nor was it the blunder of the minister alone, as one of the elders later explained; for it was equally the blunder of the whole Presbytery of Coughleen, which included fifteen churches on Island McGill and the mainland. The old church, beyond repair, had been torn down and the new one built on the original foundation. Looking upon the foundation stones as similar to a ship's keel, it never entered the minister's nor the Presbytery's head that the new church was legally any other than the old church.

"An' three couples was married the first week un the new church," Clara said. "First of all, Samuel Dundee an' Agnes Hewitt; the next day Albert Mahan an' Minnie Duncan; an' by the week-end Eddie Troy and Flo Mackintosh—all sailor-men, an' un sux weeks' time the last of them back tull their ships an' awa', an' no one o' them dreamin' of the wuckedness they'd been ot."

The Imp of the Perverse must have chuckled at the situation. All things favored. The marriages had taken place in the first week of May, and it was not till three months later that the minister, as required by law, made his quarterly report to the civil authorities in Dublin. Promptly came back the announcement that his church had no legal existence, not being registered according to the law's demands. This was overcome by prompt registration; but the marriages were not to be so easily remedied. The three sailor husbands were away, and their wives, in short, were not their wives.

"But the munuster was no for alarmin' the bodies," said Clara. "He kept hus council an' bided hus time, waitun' for the lods tull be back from sea. Oz luck would have ut, he was away across the island tull a christenun' when Albert Mahan arrives home onexpected, hus shup just docked ot Dublin. Ut's nine o'clock ot night when the munuster, un hus sluppers an' dressun' gown, gets the news. Up he jumps an' calls for horse an' saddle, an' awa' he goes like the wund for Albert Mahan's. Albert uz just goun' tull bed an' hoz one shoe off when the munuster arrives.

" 'Come wuth me, the pair o' ye,' says he, breathless-like. 'What for, an' me dead weary an' goun' tull bed?' says Albert. 'Yull be lawful married,' says the munuster. Albert looks black an' says, 'Now, munuster, ye wull be jokun',' but tull humself, oz I've heard hum tell mony a time, he uz wonderun' thot the munuster should a-took tull whusky ot hus time o' life.

" 'We be no married?' says Minnie. He shook his head. 'An' I om no Mussus Mahan?' 'No,' says he, 'ye are no Mussus Mahan. Ye are plain Muss Duncan.' 'But ye married us yoursel',' says she. 'I dud an' I dudna,' says he. An' wuth thot he tells them the whole upshot, an' Albert puts on hus shoe, an' they go wuth the munuster an' are married proper an' law-ful, an' oz Albert Mahan says afterward mony's the time, "Tus no every mon thot hoz two weddun' nights on Island McGill.' "

Six months later Eddie Troy came home and was promptly remarried. But Samuel Dundee was away on a three-years' voyage and his ship fell overdue. Further to complicate the situation, a baby boy, past two years old, was waiting for him in the arms of his wife. The months passed, and the wife grew thin with worrying. "Ut's no meself I'm thunkun' on," she is reported to have said many times, "but ut's the puir fatherless bairn. Uf aught happened tull Samuel where wull the bairn stond?"

Lloyd's posted the *Loughbank* as missing, and the owners ceased the monthly remittance of Samuel's half-pay to his wife. It was the question of the child's legitimacy that preyed on her mind, and, when all hope of Samuel's return was abandoned, she drowned herself and the child in the loch. And here enters the greater tragedy. The *Loughbank* was not lost. By a series of sea disasters and delays too interminable to relate, she had made one of those long, unsighted passages such as occur once or twice in half a century. How the Imp must have held both his sides! Back from the sea came Samuel, and when they broke the news to him something else broke somewhere in his heart or head. Next morning they found him where he had tried to kill himself across the grave of his wife and child. Never in the history of Island McGill was there so fearful a deathbed. He spat in the minister's face and reviled him, and died blaspheming so terribly that those that tended on him did so with averted gaze and trembling hands.

And, in the face of all this, Margaret Henan named her first child Samuel.

* * *

How account for the woman's stubbornness? Or was it a morbid obsession that demanded a child of hers should be named Samuel? Her third child was a girl, named after herself, and the fourth was a boy again. Despite the strokes of fate that had already bereft her, and despite the loss of friends and relatives, she persisted in her resolve to name the child after her brother. She was shunned at church by those who had grown up with her. Her mother, after a final appeal, left her house with the warning that if the child were so named she would never speak to her again. And though the old lady lived thirty-odd years longer she kept her word. The minister agreed to christen the child any name but Samuel, and every other minister on Island McGill refused to christen it by the name she had chosen. There was talk on the part of Margaret Henan of going to law at the time, but in the end she carried the child to Belfast and there had it christened Samuel.

And then nothing happened. The whole island was confuted. The boy grew and prospered. The schoolmaster never ceased averring that it was the brightest lad he had ever seen. Samuel had a splendid constitution, a tremendous grip on life. To everybody's amazement he escaped the usual run of childish afflictions. Measles, whooping-cough and mumps knew him not. He was armor-clad against germs, immune to all disease. Headaches and earaches were things unknown. "Never so much oz a boil or a pumple," as one of the old bodies told me, ever marred his healthy skin. He broke school records in scholarship and athletics, and whipped every boy of his size or years on Island McGill.

It was a triumph for Margaret Henan. This paragon was hers, and it bore the cherished name. With the one exception of her mother, friends and relatives drifted back and acknowledged that they had been mistaken; though there were old crones who still abided by their opinion and who shook their heads ominously over their cups of tea. The boy was too wonderful to last. There was no escaping the curse of the name his mother had wickedly laid upon him. The young generation joined Margaret Henan in laughing at them, but the old crones continued to shake their heads.

Other children followed. Margaret Henan's fifth was a boy, whom she called Jamie, and in rapid succession followed three girls, Alice, Sara, and Nora, the boy Timothy, and two more girls, Florence and Katie. Katie was the last and eleventh, and Margaret Henan, at thirty-five, ceased from her exertions. She had done well by Island McGill and the Queen. Nine healthy children were hers. All prospered. It seemed her ill-luck had shot its bolt with the deaths of her first two. Nine lived, and one of them was named Samuel.

Jamie elected to follow the sea, though it was not so much a matter of election as compulsion, for the eldest sons on Island McGill remained on the land, while all other sons went to the salt plowing. Timothy followed Jamie, and by the time the latter had got his first command, a steamer in the Bay trade out of Cardiff, Timothy was mate of a big sailing ship.

Samuel, however, did not take kindly to the soil. The farmer's life had no attraction for him. His brothers went to sea, not out of desire, but because it was the only way for them to gain their bread; and he, who had no need to go, envied them when, returned from far voyages, they sat by the kitchen fire, and told their bold tales of the wonderlands beyond the sea-rim.

Samuel became a teacher, much to his father's disgust, and even took extra certificates, going to Belfast for his examinations. When the old master retired, Samuel took over his school. Secretly, however, he studied navigation, and it was Margaret's delight when he sat by the kitchen fire, and, despite their master's tickets, tangled up his brothers in the theoretics of their profession. Tom Henan alone was outraged when Samuel, school teacher, gentleman, and heir to the Henan farm, shipped to sea before the mast. Margaret had an abiding faith in her son's star, and whatever he did she was sure was for the best. Like everything else connected with his glorious personality, there had never been known so swift a rise as in the case of Samuel. Barely with two years' sea experience before the mast, he was taken from the forecastle and made a provisional second mate. This occurred in a fever port on the West Coast, and the committee of skippers that examined him agreed that he knew more of the science of navigation than they had remembered or forgotten. Two years later he sailed from Liverpool, mate of the *Starry Grace,* with both master's and extra-master's tickets in his possession. And then it happened—the thing the old crones had been shaking their heads over for years.

It was told me by Gavin McNab, bos'n of the *Starry Grace* at the time, himself an Island McGill man.

"Wull do I remember ut," he said. "We was runnin' our Eastun' down, an' makun' heavy weather of ut. Oz fine a sailor-mon oz ever walked was Samuel Henan. I remember the look of hum wull thot last marnun', a-watch-un' them bug seas curlun' up astern, an' a-watchun' the old girl an' seeun' how she took them—the skupper down below an' drunkun' for days. Ut was ot seven thot Henan brought her up on tull the wund, not darun' tull run longer on thot fearful sea. Ot eight, after havun' breakfast, he turns un, an' a half hour after up comes the skupper, bleary-eyed an' shaky an' holdun' on tull the companion. Ut was fair smokun', I om tellun' ye, an' there he stood, blunkun' an' noddun' an' talkun' tull humsel'. 'Keep off,' says he ot last tull the mon ot the wheel. 'My God!' says the second mate, standun' beside hum. The skupper never looks tull hum ot all, but keeps on mutterun' an' jabberun' tull humsel'. All of a suddent-like he straightens up an' throws hus head back, an' says: 'Put your wheel over, me mon—now domn ye! Are ye deef thot ye'll no be hearun' me?'

"Ut was a drunken mon's luck, for the *Starry Grace* wore off afore thot God-Almighty gale wuthout shuppun' a bucket o' watter, the second mate shoutun' orders an' the crew jumpun' like mod. An' wuth thot the skupper nods contented-like tull humself an' goes below after more whusky. Ut was plain murder o' the lives o' all of us, for ut was no the time for the buggest shup afloat tull be runnun'. Run? Never hov I seen the like! Ut was beyond all thunkun', an' me goun' tull sea, boy an' men, for forty year. I tell you ut was fair awesome.

"The face o' the second mate was white oz death, an' he stood ut alone for half an hour, when ut was too much for hum an' he went below an' called Samuel an' the third. Aye, a fine sailor-mon thot Samuel, but ut was too much for hum. He looked an' studied, and looked an' studied, but he could no see hus way. He durst na heave tull. She would ha' been sweeput o' all honds an' stucks an' everythung afore she could a-fetched up. There was naught tull do but keep on runnun'. An' uf ut worsened we were lost ony way, for soon or late that overtakun' sea was sure tull sweep us clear over poop an' all.

"Dud I say ut was a God-Almighty gale? Ut was worse nor thot. The devil himself must ha' hod a hond un the brewun' o' ut, ut was thot fearsome. I ha' looked on some sights, but I om no carun' tull look on the like o' thot again. No mon dared tull be un hus bunk. No, nor no mon on the decks. All honds of us stood on top the house an' held on an' watched. The three mates was on the poop, with two men ot the wheel, an' the only mon below was thot whusky-blighted captain snorun' drunk.

"An' then I see ut comun', a mile away, risun' above all the waves like an island un the sea—the buggest wave ever I looked upon. The three mates stood tulgether an' watched ut comun', a-prayun' like we thot she would no break un passun' us. But ut was no tull be. Ot the last, when she rose up like a mountain, curlun' above the stern an' blottun' out the sky, the mates scattered, the second an' third runnun' for the mizzen-shrouds an' climbun' up, but the first runnun' tull the wheel tull lend a hond. He was a brave men, thot Samuel Henan. He run straight un tull the face o' thot father o' all waves, no thunkun' on humself but thunkun' only o' the shup. The two men was lashed tull the wheel, but he would be ready tull hond un the case they was kult. An' then she took ut. We on the house could no see the poop for the thousand tons o' watter thot hod hut ut. Thot wave cleaned them out, took everythung along wuth ut— the two mates, climbun' up the mizzen-ruggun', Samuel Henan runnun' tull the wheel, the two men ot the wheel, aye, an' the wheel utself. We never saw aught o' them, for she broached tull what o' the wheel goun', an' two men o' us was drownded off the house, no tull mention the carpenter thot we pucked up ot the break o' the poop wuth every bone o' hus body broke tull he was like so much jelly."

* * *

And here enters the marvel of it, the miraculous wonder of that woman's heroic spirit. Margaret

Henan was forty-seven when the news came home of the loss of Samuel; and it was not long after that the unbelievable rumor went around Island McGill. I say unbelievable. Island McGill would not believe. Doctor Hall pooh-pooh'd it. Everybody laughed at it as a good joke. They traced back the gossip to Sara Dack, servant to the Henans', and who alone lived with Margaret and her husband. But Sara Dack persisted in her assertion and was called a low-mouthed liar. One or two dared question Tom Henan himself, but beyond black looks and curses for their presumption they elicited nothing from him.

The rumor died down, and the island fell to discussing in all its ramifications the loss of the *Grenoble* in the China seas, with all her officers and half her crew born and married on Island McGill. But the rumor would not stay down. Sara Dack was louder in her assertions, the looks Tom Henan cast about him were blacker than ever, and Dr. Hall, after a visit to the Henan house, no longer pooh-pooh'd. Then Island McGill sat up, and there was a tremendous wagging of tongues. It was unnatural and ungodly. The like had never been heard. And when, as time passed, the truth of Sara Dack's utterances was manifest, the island folk decided, like the bos'n of the *Starry Grace,* that only the devil could have had a hand in so untoward a happening. And the infatuated woman, so Sara Dack reported, insisted that it would be a boy. "Eleven bairns ha' I borne," she said; "sux o' them lossies an' five o' them loddies. An' sunce there be balance un all thungs, so wull there be balance wuth me. Sux o' one an' half a dozen o' the other—there uz the balance, an' oz sure oz the sun rises un the mar- nun', thot sure wull ut be a boy."

And boy it was, and a prodigy. Doctor Hall raved about its unblemished perfection and massive strength, and wrote a brochure on it for the Dublin Medical Society as the most interesting case of the sort in his long career. When Sara Dack gave the babe's unbelievable weight, Island McGill refused to believe and once again called her liar. But when Dr. Hall attested that he had himself weighed it and seen it tip that very notch, Island McGill held its breath and accepted whatever report Sara Dack made of the infant's progress or appetite. And once again Mar- garet Henan carried a babe to Belfast and had it chris- tened Samuel.

* * *

"Oz good oz gold ut was," said Sara Dack to me.

Sara, at the time I met her, was a buxom, phleg- matic spinster of sixty, equipped with an experience so tragic and unusual that though her tongue ran on for decades its output would still be of imperishable interest to her cronies.

"Oz good oz gold," said Sara Dack. "Ut never fret- ted. Sut ut down un the sun by the hour an' never a sound ut would make oz long oz ut was no hungered! An' thot strong! The grup o' uts honds was like a mon's. I mind me, when ut was but hours old, ut

grupped me so mighty thot I fetched a scream I was
thot frightened. Ut was the punk o' health. Ut slept
an' ate, an' grew. Ut never bothered. Never a night's
sleep ut lost tull no one, nor ever a munut's, an' thot
wuth cuttin' uts teeth an' all. An' Margaret would
dandle ut on her knee an' ask was there ever so fine a
loddie un the three Kungdoms.

"The way ut grew! Ut was un keepun' wuth the
way ut ate. Ot a year ut was the size o' a bairn of two.
Ut was slow tull walk an' talk. Exceptun' for gurgly
noises un uts throat an' for creepun' on all fours, ut
dudna monage much un the walkun' an' talkun' line.
But thot was tull be expected from the way ut grew.
Ut all went tull growun' strong an' healthy. An' even
old Tom Henan cheered up ot the might of ut an' said
was there ever the like o' ut un the three Kungdoms.
Ut was Doctor Hall thot first suspicioned, I mind me
well, though ut was luttle I dreamt what he was up
tull ot the time. I see hum holdun' thungs' un fronto'
luttle Sammy's eyes, an' a-makun' noises, loud an'
soft, an' far an' near, un luttle Sammy's ears. An' then
I see Doctor Hall go away, wrunklun' hus eyebrows
an' shakun' hus head like the bairn was ailun'. But he
was no ailun', oz I could swear tull, me a-seeun' hum
eat an' grow. But Doctor Hall no said a word tull
Margaret an' I was no for guessun' the why he was
sore puzzled.

"I mind me when luttle Sammy first spoke. He
was two years old an' the size of a child o five, though
he could no monage the walkun' yet but went around

on all fours, happy an' contented-like an' makun' no trouble oz long oz he was fed promptly, which was onusual often. I was hangun' the wash on the line ot the time when out he comes, on all fours, hus bug head waggun' tull an' fro an' blunkun' un the sun. An' then, suddent, he talked. I was thot took a-back I near died o' fright, an' fine I knew ut then, the shakun' o' Doctor Hall's head. Talked? Never a bairn on Island McGill talked so loud an' tull such purpose. There was no mustakun' ut. I stood there all tremblun' an' shakun'. Little Sammy was brayun'. I tell you, sir, he was brayun' like an ass—just like thot, loud an' long an' cheerful tull ut seemed hus lungs ud crack.

"He was a eediot—a great, awful, monster eediot. Ut was after he talked thot Doctor Hall told Margaret, but she would no believe. Ut would all come right, she said. Ut was growun' too fast for aught else. Guv ut time, said she, an' we would see. But old Tom Henan knew, an' he never held up hus head again. He could no abide the thung, an' would no brung humsel' tull touch ut, though I om no denyun' he was fair fascinated by ut. Mony the time, I see hum watchun' of ut around a corner, lookun' ot ut tull hus eyes fair bulged wuth the horror; an' when ut brayed old Tom ud stuck hus fungers tull hus ears an' look thot miserable I could a-puttied hum.

"An' bray ut could! Ut was the only thung ut could do besides eat an' grow. Whenever ut was hungry ut brayed, an' there was no stoppun' ut save wuth food. An' always of a marnun', when first ut crawled tull the kutchen-door an' blunked out ot the sun, ut brayed. An' ut was brayun' that brought about uts end.

"I mind me well. Ut was three years old an' oz bug oz a led o' ten. Old Tom hed been goun' from bed tull worse, plowhun' up an' down the fields an' talkun' an' mutterun' tull humself. On the marnun' o' the day I mind me, he was suttun' on the bench outside the kutchen, a-futtun' the handle tull a puck-axe. Unbeknown, the monster eediot crawled tull the door an' brayed after hus fashion ot the sun. I see old Tom start up an' look. An' there was the monster ee-diot, waggun' uts bug head an' blunkun' an' brayun' like the great bug ass ut was. Ut was too much for Tom. Somethun' went wrong wuth hum suddent-like. He jumped tull hus feet an' fetched the puck-handle down on the monster eediot's head. An' he hut ut again an' again like ut was a mod dog an' hum afeard o' ut. An' he went straight tull the stable an' hung humsel' tull a rafter. An' I was no for stoppun' on after such-like, an' I went tull stay along wuth me suster thot was married tull John Martin an' comfortable-off."

* * *

I sat on the bench by the kitchen door and re-garded Margaret Henan, while with her callous thumb she pressed down the live fire of her pipe and gazed out across the twilight-sombered fields. It was

the very bench Tom Henan had sat upon that last san-
guinary day of life. And Margaret sat in the doorway
where the monster, blinking at the sun, had so often
wagged its head and brayed. We had been talking for
an hour, she with that slow certitude of eternity that
so befitted her; and, for the life of me, I could lay no
finger on the motives that ran through the tangled
warp and woof of her. Was she a martyr to Truth? Did
she have it in her to worship at so abstract a shrine?
Had she conceived Abstract Truth to be the one high
goal of human endeavour on that day of long ago
when she named her first-born Samuel? Or was hers
the stubborn obstinacy of the ox? The fixity of purpose of the balky horse? The stolidity of the self-
willed peasant-mind? Was it whim or fancy?—the
one streak of lunacy in what was otherwise an emi-
nently rational mind? Or, reverting, was hers the
spirit of a Bruno? Was she convinced of the intellec-
tual rightness of the stand she had taken? Was hers a
steady, enlightened opposition to superstition? or—
and a subtler thought—was she mastered by some
vaster, profounder superstition, a fetish-worship of
which the Alpha and the Omega was the cryptic
Samuel?

"Wull ye be tellun' me," she said, "thot uf the second Samuel hod been named Larry thot he would no
hov fell un the hot watter an' drownded? Atween you
an' me, sir, an' ye are untellugent-lookun' tull the
eye, would the name hov made ut onyways dufferent?
Would the washun' no be done thot day uf he hod

been Larry or Michael? Would hot watter no be hot, an' would hot watter no burn uf he hod hod ony other name but Samuel?"

I acknowledged the justice of her contention, and she went on.

"Do a wee but of a name change the plans o' God? Do the world run by hut or muss, an' be God a weak, shully-shallyun' creature thot ud alter the fate an' destiny o' thungs because the worm Margaret Henan seen fut tull name her bairn Samuel? There be my son Jamie. He wull no sign a Rooshan-Funn un hus crew because o' believun' thot Rooshan-Funns do be mon-ajun' the wunds an' hov the makun' o' bod weather. Wull you be thunkun' so? Wull you be thunkun' thot God thot makes the wunds tull blow wull bend Hus head from on high tull lussen tull the word o' a greasy Rooshan-Funn un some dirty shup's fo'c'sle?"

I said no, certainly not; but she was not to be set aside from pressing home the point of her argument.

"Then wull you be thunkun' thot God thot directs the stars un their courses, an' tull whose mighty foot the world uz but a footstool, wull you be thunkun' thot He wull take a spite again' Margaret Henan an' send a bug wave off the Cape tull wash her son un tull eternity, all because she was for namun' hum Samuel?"

"But why Samuel?" I asked.

"An' thot I dinna know. I wantud ut so."

"But *why* did you want it so?"

"An' uz ut me thot would be answerun' a such-like

question? Be there ony mon luvun' or dead thot can answer? Who can tell the *why* o' like? My Jamie was fair daft on buttermilk, he would drunk ut tull, oz he said humself, hus back teeth was awash. But my Tumothy could no abide buttermilk. I like tull lussen tull the thunder growlun' an' roarun', an' rampajun'. My Katie could no abide the noise of ut, but must scream an' flutter an' go runnun' for the mudmost o' a feather-bed. Never yet hov I heard the answer tull the *why* o' like, God alone hoz thot answer. You an' me be mortal an' we canna know. Enough for us tull know what we like an' what we duslike. *I like*—thot uz the first word an' the last. An' behind thot *like* no men can go an' find the *why* o' ut. I *like* Samuel, an' I like ut well. Ut uz a sweet name, an' there be a rollun' wonder un the sound o' ut thot passes onderstandun'."

The twilight deepened, and in the silence I gazed upon that splendid dome of a forehead which time could not mar, at the width between the eyes, and at the eyes themselves—clear, out-looking, and wide-seeing. She rose to her feet with an air of dismissing me, saying:

"Ut wull be a dark walk home, an' there wull be more thon a sprunkle o' wet un the sky."

"Have you any regrets, Margaret Henan?" I asked, suddenly and without forethought.

She studied me a moment.

"Aye, thot I no ha' borne another son."

"And you would . . . ?" I faltered.

"Aye, thot I would," she answered. "Ut would ha' been hus name."

I went down the dark road between the hawthorn hedges puzzling over the why of like, repeating *Samuel* to myself and aloud and listening to the rolling wonder in its sound that had charmed her soul and led her life in tragic places. *Samuel*! There was a rolling wonder in the sound. Aye, there was!